CYBER
ARMAGEDDON
BOOK THREE: REIGN OF THE LOCUSTS

MARK GOODWIN

ACKNOWLEDGMENTS

I would like to thank my Editor in Chief Catherine Goodwin, as well as the rest of my fantastic editing team, Jeff Markland, Frank Shackleford, Stacey Glemboski, Sherrill Hesler, and Claudine Allison.

CHAPTER 1

The waters compassed me about, even to the
soul: the depth closed me round about, the
weeds were wrapped about my head. I went
down to the bottoms of the mountains; the
earth with her bars was about me for ever:
yet hast thou brought up my life from
corruption, O Lord my God. When my soul
fainted within me I remembered the Lord:
and my prayer came in unto thee, into thine
holy temple.   They that observe lying
vanities forsake their own mercy. But I will
sacrifice unto thee with the voice of
thanksgiving; I will pay that that I have
vowed. Salvation is of the Lord.

Jonah 2:5-9

Kate ran her fingers across the smooth joints where the fresh drywall met the original section of wall. "Jack did a really good job. You can't tell that there used to be a door here."

Annie Cobb tied a bandana around her head to shield it from the paint. "Anyone who pays attention will wonder why the master bedroom doesn't have his and her closets."

Amanda McDowell dipped her brush in the paint can and began to cut the bottom edge of the baseboard. "Probably not unless they're looking to buy. And if this place ever goes back on the market, we won't need a false wall to hide our stash of weapons and food."

Kate started on the outside edge of the baseboard, giving it a fresh coat of white paint while Annie worked from the other side with the roller. "I hope we made the right call, moving everyone up to Perry Hine's place."

"We needed a house big enough for all thirteen of us to live in." Annie dipped her roller in the paint and continued applying it with long up and down motions. "I, for one, am happy to be in Laurel Ridge. Apple Blossom Acres feels like a graveyard, full of ghosts."

"Amen." Amanda focused on the fine bead of paint at the tip of her brush and continued to neatly run it along the seam of the baseboard. "I'll always remember Scott, and I know David will never forget his father, but it's really hard to heal when you're living in ground zero. And in our case, everyone in the community has lost someone dear to them, most more than one." She looked up at Annie. "Troy is the youngest. How is he holding up to losing his grandma and grandpa?"

Annie lifted her shoulders and continued working. "I don't know. I think he feels pretty much like I do; too afraid to grieve."

Kate was sorry for her friend and ten-year-old Troy. She felt terrible for everyone in the house. However, she took some solace in hearing that Annie was experiencing the same emotions that were nagging at her own heart. "You're both good moms. Troy and David are blessed to have you."

Annie smiled tenderly. "Vicky is fortunate to have you. I think she's lost more than anyone else. Her brother, her mother, and her dad."

"It's a big void to fill. I could never replace them."

Amanda paused from her work. "You don't have to. Just keep loving her the way you do and she'll pull through. Vicky might be the toughest person here."

"Thanks." Kate made broad horizontal strokes. "I hope Jack made the right call, stashing two rifles and two handguns in the wall. That only leaves us with seven firearms to defend ourselves with." She turned around to see Jack standing in the doorway.

He didn't look offended by the comment but neither did he smile. Of course, like most of the people in the house, he'd not been seen smiling once since the massacre that took the life of his wife three days prior. "It's the right call, Kate. If we get attacked, the people with guns can hold them off long enough for someone to swing a sledgehammer through the wall and get the other four. However, if the military comes back, they'll take all of our guns. We'll need those behind the false wall."

"You're right. I shouldn't have questioned your judgment."

"Actually, you should question my judgment. I'm not in the best state of mind right now. I'm trying to hold it together for Rainey, but I'm having a hard time." His lip quivered and his eyes welled up.

Kate didn't know whether to hug him or let him be. She stood up and stepped toward him. He shook his head and pulled away from her. Kate changed the subject to get through the awkwardness of the moment. "We need to replace the guns we lost. Despite the ammo that we had stashed under the bed, we need more bullets, too."

Annie let the roller rest in the paint tray. "I'm surprised the soldiers didn't think to look there."

Kate bit her lip. "Sam's body was laid out on the bed where the .270, the shotgun, and the AR-15 were stashed. All the ammo was underneath. Out of respect, they didn't search that bed. Even after Sam sacrificed himself by holding off the Reverend's men while we got out of the house, he still performed one last act of service by guarding those guns and ammo."

Jack's eyes had cleared up. He'd obviously pushed his emotions back down inside. "I can't imagine where we'd be able to obtain any more guns. The military searched every house in Apple Blossom Acres."

Kate looked at the false wall. "The man who owned the store where we bought a lot of our supplies told me that many folks around here were getting ready for one catastrophe or another. I've got to believe some of them were stocking up on guns and ammo."

Amanda looked up from her work. "Are you talking about Carolina Readiness over on Montgomery? I'm pretty sure they're closed, like everything else around here."

"Yeah, but he gave me a Ham radio frequency to monitor if things ever got bad."

"We don't have anything to trade with," Annie said. "We need all of our supplies. We might be able to feed everyone until the crops start coming in, but it will be by the skin of our teeth."

Kate swirled the brush in the paint bucket while she thought about her plan. "When I realized that we weren't going to be able to stop the virus in the bank's computers, I converted most of my cash into gold. I doubt most people would be willing to sell their guns, but if someone had bought a horde of weapons, they might consider an exchange."

"It sounds like a big risk for potentially no payoff." Jack crossed his arms tightly.

"I at least have to warn, Bill, the man from Carolina Readiness about the military confiscating firearms. The information he and his wife gave me, along with the supplies I bought from them will be what saves us all from starvation. I owe it to them."

Jack shifted his weight to the other foot. "You said you have a radio frequency for him. Just call him and tell him."

"The military is probably monitoring the airwaves. If I talk about gun confiscation, they'll know to search Bill and Jan's group."

Jack shook his head. "If you leave the neighborhood, you'll have to take protection. I guarantee the soldiers have checkpoints. We'll end up losing even more guns. Heaven forbid they recognize you as being from the shootout. If they realize you held out on them, they might throw you in lockup."

"Then I'll go on foot."

"How many guns and how much ammo do you plan on hiking through the mountains with?" Jack seemed unimpressed by the idea.

Kate shook her head. "I don't know. I'll figure it out when I meet up with them."

"If you meet up with them." Jack frowned. "Who are you planning to take with you? Gavin is still nursing a bullet wound, and I'm not leaving my little girl here while I go tromping off on a wild goose chase."

"I'll go," Annie said.

Amanda nodded. "Me, too."

Kate looked at her sisters in arms and grinned. "I'll dig up that frequency Bill gave me and try to make contact."

An hour later, Kate slung her AK-47 over her shoulder. She held a radio and a business card with a Ham frequency scribbled on the back. "I'll be back in a few."

"I'm coming with you." Gavin holstered his pistol and slipped his boots on.

"You're supposed to be resting."

"I'll rest better knowing you're safe." He draped

his jacket over his injured shoulder.

"I'm only going to the top of the hill. The Martin place is the next property over."

"Then it won't be a major violation of my instructions to take it easy." Gavin followed her down the hall and out the door.

The air was crisp and cool. Kate could see her breath as she hiked through the woods and up the steep incline to the place that had been the home of Ernest Martin before he'd been cut down by Reverend Graves. Gavin drew his pistol when they arrived at the house. Kate turned the knob and opened the door.

Gavin went in first. "Nice of the military to leave the doors unlocked for us."

Kate looked around at the interior of the quaint log cabin. "I wish we could have taken this little place for ourselves. Where we're staying is a huge house, but I'm already starting to feel claustrophobic living around so many other people."

Gavin searched each room before lowering his gun. "Safety in numbers, Kate. We need to all be under one roof. It's our only hope for security."

"I know, but a girl can dream, can't she?"

"Sure." Gavin motioned toward the loft. "I guess we'll get the best reception topside."

"Reception isn't what I'm worried about." Kate began climbing the permanent ladder. "I'm praying this little radio has enough juice to transmit to wherever Bill and Jan are." She cautiously looked around before climbing into the small loft space. "All clear."

"I might just hang out down here rather than make the climb with one hand. I can hear everything just as well."

She looked down the ladder. "Suit yourself." She checked the time on her watch. "3:00. The broadcast should be starting." Kate powered on the radio and entered the frequency.

"Happy Thanksgiving, Western North Carolina."

Kate's stomach sank. She and everyone else had missed the fact that it was Thanksgiving. Having barely survived a brutal attack only days earlier, they had an excuse, but she was determined to rectify the situation upon her return. They had breath in their lungs, so her group had something to be thankful for. She continued listening.

"This is K4CDN AKA Radio Rick with a short update on what we've been able to pick up from the rumor mills, grapevines, and other nefarious information sources. In all honesty, I only report things that I believe to be true, but the vetting process in times like these is more of an art than a science.

"If you've been on a paved road in the past few days, you've undoubtedly seen military vehicles humming by. An Army Battalion is setting up operations in downtown Waynesville and will be securing the area as part of a larger mission to restore order and civility in and around Asheville. It's welcome news as the reports of robberies and burglaries are too numerous for us to report.

"Most of you have heard by now that the computer attacks are worldwide. No single country survived the attacks, which means that it is unlikely that the Locusts were triggered by a nation-state. The most probable scenario is that the original program was developed by a sophisticated agency and then fell into the hands of terrorists wanting to bring about anarchy. If that was their aim, I'd say they did a good job of it.

"That's all I have for today. We'll open it up for the communication nets. I trust that everyone participating will work to keep things orderly. This is K4CDN monitoring."

Kate pressed her talk key. "Hi, sorry. I'm not familiar with proper radio etiquette, but my name is Kate and I'm looking for Bill or Jan from Carolina Readiness."

Kate waited a while. No one responded.

"Nothing?" Gavin called from below.

"No. I don't think we're transmitting far enough."

Just then, another voice came over the radio. "This is N4WSW. Kate, what type of radio are you using?"

She looked at the model and called back. "Um, it says Any Tone."

"A hand-held radio?"

"Yes."

"That explains it. Let me try to repeat your call for you. This is N4WSW. Kate is looking for Bill or Jan from Carolina Readiness. She's on a hand-held unit, and I'm acting as a repeater for her."

Radio Rick's voice came over the air. "This is K4CDN. I can raise Bill if you'll give me about five minutes."

"Thank you," said the other man. "Did you get that, Kate?"

"Yes. Thank you so much."

"No problem. When Bill gets on the air, you'll be able to hear him, but I'll have to repeat everything you say. You're close enough for me to hear you, but too far from K4CDN's radio for him to hear you."

"I really appreciate it," said Kate.

Minutes later, Bill came on. "Go ahead for Bill."

"Bill, hi. It's Kate from Atlanta. I came in your store a couple of times, right before the attacks. You called me lucky if that helps you remember."

The other man repeated her message.

Bill replied, "Oh, yes. The luckiest girl in the world. How could I forget?"

She felt reassured to know that he recalled her visit. "I'd like to meet up if possible. I have some information that I think you'd want to know." Kate waited for the man to relay the statement.

Bill's voice came back directly. "Okay, head on up toward the Cataloochee Ski Resort tomorrow. That's not where I'm at, but we'll be watching. As long as everything looks hunky-dory, we'll make contact with you before you get to the resort. So don't be too jumpy if you know what I mean. What vehicle will you be in, and what time should we expect you?"

Kate replied. "We'll be on foot. Hopefully, we can be there by noon."

After the message was restated by the man acting as a repeater, Bill said, "We'll be looking for you."

Kate powered off the radio. "That's going to be a long hike."

"How long?"

"Probably about ten miles by the time you work in all the detours to stay out of sight." Kate descended the ladder.

"Better give ourselves at least five hours to get through the woods."

"Ourselves? You can't even climb a ladder into the loft. You're not going anywhere."

"I could climb the ladder if I had to. I was just saving myself for something that matters, like this."

She kissed him on the lips. "I appreciate your concern, but I'm a big girl. I'll be alright. Amanda and Annie are coming. They both know how to shoot if we get into a situation. Come on, we need to go convince everyone in the house to have Thanksgiving."

"That's going to be a hard sell. Every one of us has lost family members, we're all still in mourning."

"But we're alive, and we have food when so many don't. We have a place to sleep, and we have each other to watch out for one another. I'm sure no one feels like cooking up a big feast when we're all so grief stricken, but it's important that we tell God that we're grateful for those things." Kate followed Gavin out the door and pulled it closed behind her.

CHAPTER 2

> When thou passest through the waters, I will be with thee; and through the rivers, they shall not overflow thee: when thou walkest through the fire, thou shalt not be burned; neither shall the flame kindle upon thee.
>
> Isaiah 43:2

Sitting on her bed, Kate stuffed a Tupperware bowl filled with rice and an old two-liter soda bottle of water into her pack. She glanced up at Gavin who was sitting beside her. "Tune into Radio Rick's broadcast this afternoon. If we get into any trouble, I'll get a message out to you. If we don't make it at all, I'm sure they'll reach out on that frequency."

"That makes me feel better," he said

sarcastically.

"I'm ready." With a rifle over her shoulder, Annie walked into the master bedroom, which Kate and Gavin shared with Vicky.

Vicky's bed was a full-size mattress sitting directly on the floor next to the window. In their haste to equip the large Laurel Ridge home for thirteen people, the group had scavenged mattresses and bedding but skipped box springs and bed frames. Vicky reclined against a wall of pillows which she'd stacked in the corner to make her bed a plush throne that would make any princess green with envy. "I'm coming with you, Aunt Kate."

"Not this time, Vicky." Kate continued to prepare her gear. "We have to get going by 7:00 AM in order to make it on time."

"That's fine. I'm already packed." Vicky pulled a backpack from under the pile of pillows.

Gavin shook his head. "It's a losing battle, Vicky. I've already tried. Just hang around here with me today. Help me hold down the fort."

"No offense, Gavin, but Aunt Kate is my last living relative. I'm not letting her out of my sight."

Jack came into the room. "You guys heading out?"

"Just waiting on Amanda." Kate zipped up her jacket.

Jack eyeballed the two rifles which Annie and Kate had nearby. "Those will stick out like a sore thumb if you walk by the military. You should take pistols instead."

Amanda and David McDowell walked into the room.

"We can't fend off an attack with pistols," Kate protested.

Jack shook his head. "You can't win a firefight against the military either. You need to leave those rifles here."

Gavin grabbed his AK and folded the stock. "Kate, take my paratrooper and give me your rifle. You can carry mine in a large pack. Let Annie and Amanda carry concealed pistols. If you get in trouble, they can lay down cover while you retrieve the rifle from the pack."

Kate didn't like it, but she had no time to argue. "Okay, that's fine, I guess."

Harold Pritchard came in. "Made y'all a thermos full of coffee. Brought you a canned ham, too. From my private stock."

"Thank you, Mr. Pritchard." Kate took the offering and stowed it in the large pack as she reorganized her gear to accommodate the rifle.

Jack addressed David, "Hey, buddy, can you switch weapons with your mom for the day? She needs your pistol."

"I'm not letting my mom go without me. I'm going with them."

"Okay, but the rifle stays here." Jack turned his attention to Vicky. "Can Annie use your pistol?"

"I'm going also."

"This party was originally three people." Jack's brow showed heavy creases. "Now it's grown to five. You can't all take a weapon. If you're confronted by the military and lose them, we won't be able to defend this place."

Pritchard pointed at Kate. "The girl knows that

Tai Chi. She don't need no gun."

Annoyed at being delayed by the belabored conversation, Kate forced a smile. "Jiu-Jitsu. But basically, the same thing except that instead of trying to become one with the universe, in Jiu-Jitsu, the goal is to choke out your opponent. However, I'm only a lowly white belt. And even if I was a fifth-degree black belt, it wouldn't do me much good in a shootout, so I'm taking a gun."

"Well, the other two pistols are stashed behind the false wall, so regardless of how many of you go, you're only taking three firearms." Jack ran his hand over the smooth wall where the closet door had been two days prior. "But in theory, if your mission is successful, you'll have more when you come back."

Pritchard nodded and lifted his jacket. He pulled out his old 1861Colt Navy. He handed it to Annie. "I reckon you can borrow this'n long as you bring it back. It was my grand pappy's. Been in the family for 150 years. I had it stuck in a hole, down in the cellar."

Annie took the large revolver with the wooden handle. "Thank you."

"Here's some extra caps, balls, and powder pellets. Takes all day to reload it, so best kill 'em all in six shots." Pritchard took a leather pouch from his pocket and walked her through the reloading process while Kate and the others made their final preparations.

Kate's team finally embarked on their mission at 7:30 AM, Friday morning. "Come on, we have to make up for lost time." She set a quick pace to get the others moving. The group followed the ridgeline west toward Maggie Valley, a course that stayed more or less parallel to US-19 and kept them out of populated areas. At 9:30, Kate leaned against a tall slender poplar tree. "Let's take fifteen minutes to rest, hydrate, and find a sccluded tree if you need to."

Most of the group split off into the trees to relieve themselves. Kate pulled the map out of her back pocket and looked out toward the main road searching for landmarks. Vicky returned minutes later and studied the map. "Where are we?"

Kate pointed northwest over the trees toward US-19. "Maggie Valley is that way. The ski slopes are all cleared of trees, so they should come into view after we reach the next peak."

Annie returned to the group. "We have to go all the way down into that valley and back up on the mountain across from us?"

"Afraid so. It keeps us out of sight and out of mind." Kate folded the map.

"Do you mind if I have a look?" Amanda McDowell asked.

Kate passed her the map. "Go ahead."

Amanda spread it out on the ground so she and her son, David, could have a look. "What route are you planning to take up to the resort?"

Kate squatted next to David and pointed to the map. "Fie Top Road, I guess. It's the only road I see. It's off the main road, so we shouldn't run into military vehicles. Even so, we'll stay off the pavement."

Amanda glanced at Kate. "That might be tough to do. Fie Top isn't what you'd call densely populated but the houses up through there are pretty close together, at least at the bottom of the hill."

Agitated by the situation, Kate twisted her mouth to one side. "That's not good. I can imagine how we'd feel if a band of five people came tromping across our neighborhood. Any suggestions?"

David used his finger to trace out an alternate route. "The chair lift to the ghost town amusement park has a trail which leads to the top of the mountain. It zigzags beneath the chair lift."

Kate smiled and tousled his hair. "It's good to have some locals on this mission."

"Thanks for letting me come." David grinned. "It's pretty cool up there, it looks like an old wild west town. They used to have gunfighters, cancan girls in the saloon, a train that ran around the property, that sort of stuff."

"How do you know about a trail under the chair lift and how do you know about the ghost town?" Amanda's eyes narrowed.

David fought to suppress his smile. "Guys from school, you know."

"Yeah, I know." Her gaze was that of a mother who understood all boys had a mischievous streak. "That place never stayed open long enough for us to take you there. The only way you'd be able to describe it so well is if you were trespassing."

"We better take this conversation on the road." Kate motioned for the group to get moving.

Amanda hustled to keep up with her son. "You've got some explaining to do."

"We just went up there to look around. We didn't hurt anything."

"Still, you could have been arrested."

David chuckled. "Yeah, but all the guys were like, so what, your dad's a cop." Before he'd even finished speaking, his voice trailed off, losing its joy, as if the renewed pain of losing his father had just sucked the wind out of him.

Amanda pulled him close and kissed his head. She seemed to be choking back tears herself. "And they were right. Your dad would have gotten you out of it." She forced a smile. "But once you got home, you'd have wished he'd left you in jail."

David appeared to be remembering his father fondly. "Yep, that sounds about right."

Vicky kept pace with David. "So why didn't the amusement park ever stay open?"

David lifted his shoulders. "One time the chair lift broke down and people were stuck in the rain, another time somebody put a real bullet in one of the guns and one of the actors got shot in the leg, they had a mudslide once, just lots of problems. They'd shut down for a year or two, someone else would buy it, sink a ton of cash into it, then reopen for a year or so before shutting it down again."

Annie stayed close behind Kate. "Sounds like a cursed property."

As they began to descend into the valley, Kate noticed a solitary home sitting on the hillside in front of them. She noticed no smoke coming from the chimney nor anything else that suggested recent human activity but she remained cautious. She motioned for everyone to stay low. "Spread out a little. If anyone is in that house up ahead, they'll be able to see us since the trees have no leaves on them. Stay quiet until we're well out of view."

The team moved carefully through the trees, circling wide to keep their distance from the dwelling, then started up toward the next ridge.

A dog barked behind them. Kate turned to see a big black mixed breed standing near the house they'd just passed. "Come on! Let's pick up the pace!" She hurried through the woods, being careful not to trip over any vines or brambles. The rest of her team kept pace up the hill, the nagging big black dog still sounding the alarm of their presence. Fifteen minutes later Kate reached the top of the hill and kept going.

Annie grabbed Kate's jacket sleeve, her lungs heaving as she spoke. "I have to ... catch my breath."

Kate turned to see Amanda bent over, her hands on her knees. Even in the cool late-November mountain air, her forehead was dotted with perspiration. Too winded to talk, Amanda pointed at Annie and nodded in agreement.

Kate looked back toward the house. It was out of sight, and she could no longer hear the dog. "Okay, but just for a minute."

Reaching into her pack, Vicky retrieved a recycled juice container filled with water. She took a long drink and passed the bottle to David. "Do you know where we are, Aunt Kate?"

Kate quickly referenced the map and looked down toward the road. "We'll follow the ridgeline north, then this mountain should dump us right by the old ghost town parking lot."

Kate gave Amanda and Annie another moment to regulate their breathing. "Ready?"

Both nodded.

"Okay, let's get going." Kate didn't push the team as hard but maintained an even pace.

Less than an hour later, Kate and the others arrived at the tree line on the roadside opposite the ghost town parking lot. She heard vehicles coming around the bend. "Everyone, get down!" Kate and the members of her team lay flat on their stomachs.

A motorcade of four OD green Humvees slowly drove eastbound down US-19. Kate watched the faces of the drivers and passengers to see if anyone noticed her team lying on the forest floor so close to the side of the road. With the lack of foliage, the soldiers had an unobstructed view. She held her breath, daring not to breathe as each vehicle passed at glacial speeds.

No one moved or said a word until the last Humvee was well out of view.

"They didn't see us?" Vicky's voice sounded panicked.

Kate remained still, waiting to see if they would come back around or if another vehicle might pass by. "I suppose not."

"We're wearing the right colors." David slowly rose to his feet but kept behind a tree. "Muted grays, browns, and dark greens. Plus, they weren't looking for us." Warily, he peered out from behind the tree. "The coast is clear. We should cross the road while we can."

Kate came up to one knee and looked back at the

rest of her team. "Let's go! Don't stop running until you're behind the chair lift building." Kate led the way, sprinting across the highway, over a narrow footbridge, which crossed a shallow stream on the roadside, then through the parking lot, alongside the towering A-frame welcome building, and around back to the cover of the chair lift building.

Annie and Amanda were the last to arrive.

Kate caught her breath. "Anybody see you?"

Both were huffing and puffing to breathe. They shook their heads but did not speak.

"We'll take five, then start heading up the mountain." Kate took out the thermos of coffee Pritchard had given her. She took a sip. "Still warm. Want some?" She offered it to Vicky who nodded and took the thermos. The coffee was passed around to each person in the group and the thermos soon ran dry.

"Anyone hungry?" Kate pulled the Tupperware of rice out of her pack and took a few bites.

David looked sheepishly at her. "Are you thinking of opening that canned ham?"

"David!" Amanda scolded. "That's not polite."

Kate giggled and tossed the ham to David. "Mr. Pritchard gave it to all of us."

"Make sure everyone gets a couple of bites." Amanda watched him closely as he popped off the metal lid and cut into the artificially ham-shaped substance with his pocket knife.

David covered his mouth as he chewed. He cut another slice and offered it to Vicky. "Want some?"

"Sure." Vicky blushed.

Kate figured that Vicky would accept a bag of

bear scat if David offered it to her.

"I have some leftover pancakes if anybody wants one." Annie scratched through her pack and passed around the treats.

Kate washed down her food with a long drink of water from her old soda bottle and rested while the others finished eating and drinking. "If you guys are finished, we should get moving."

The team nodded and readied their gear to move out.

The incline was steep and Kate moved at a moderate pace knowing that she should save her team's energy in case they had to make a hasty retreat.

Eventually, the group made it to the top of the mountain. Kate paused and looked around. She saw an old rollercoaster with a loop which once took riders upside down. Weeds and bushes were grown up all around the tarnished lengths of track which looked like the skeleton of some ancient mechanical dragon. A swing carousel sat abandoned to the left, and several dilapidated structures which appeared to have once been games or concession stands. "I don't really see anything that makes me think about an old wild west town. I guess I expect too much out of abandoned amusement parks."

"No, you're right." Annie gazed from left to right. "It's kinda anticlimactic."

"We're not there yet. This is just the old coaster. The town is on up ahead." David hurried ahead with Vicky following close behind. "Come on, you'll love it!"

"You seem to know this place like the back of

your hand." Amanda's forehead wrinkled, as with lingering disappointment over her son's former trespassing crimes.

"Slow it down, cowboy. You, too, Vicky. We need to stay together." Kate called out to the teens.

Kate, Amanda, and Annie hustled up the paved path to keep pace with the youngsters. Kate came around the corner of the first building and was amazed at what she saw. An old west town had been recreated complete with a train station for the kids' train, which ran around the outside of the town, a saloon, a bank, a general store, an old country church, a boarding house, a restaurant, and a hotel. The tiny train, old west photo shop, and a few broken glass display cases were the only evidence that it was, in fact, not an actual wild west town. "Wow! I bet this place was really cool back in the day."

"It's really cool now!" Vicky exclaimed.

"And kinda spooky," Amanda added. "If I see a tumbleweed roll through, I'm heading back."

Just then, the wind blew and a squeaky hinge echoed in the canyon of dilapidated buildings.

Annie giggled. "This would make a good Scooby Doo episode."

Kate signaled for them to be quiet and listened closely.

"It was just the wind, Aunt Kate." Vicky smiled as if amused by her aunt's caution.

"Maybe, but let's not forget we're in the apocalypse. The stakes are high, and we have to be sure 100 percent of the time." Kate scanned the windows of the shops and those behind the second story balconies. An odd feeling of being watched came over her. "We need to keep moving."

"This would have made a good compound for our group!" Vicky sounded excited by the thought.

David took her hand and walked beside her. "Not really, every kid in town has been up here. Everybody knows about it."

"For what?" she asked.

"Some kids would sneak guns up here to shoot." David pointed out the bullet holes in several of the windows. "Others came up here to make out, and the druggie kids liked to come up here to drink beer and get high."

"Did you ever bring a girl up here?" Vicky asked.

He blushed. "No!"

"The answer better be *no*," Amanda chided. "It better be *no* for all that other stuff too."

PING! A rifle shot rang out and the bullet struck the lamp post two feet away from Kate's arm.

"Take cover!" Kate yelled and dashed under the overhang in front of the general store.

The others followed but more gunfire peppered the ground around them.

David pointed across the street. "We need to get to that alley. A stairway behind the boarding house takes you to the second floor. We can get to that balcony and see where the people shooting at us are."

"Won't it be locked?" Annie asked.

David looked sheepishly at his mother. "Probably not."

Kate pulled the AK out of her pack, loaded a

magazine, and racked a round into the chamber. "Okay. I'll put down cover fire so you can all get across the street. Once you're across, Vicky, pop off a couple rounds so I can cross."

Everyone nodded that they understood the plan.

"Go!" Kate came out from under the porch and began shooting at the windows on the second floor, figuring that was the most likely origin of the attack.

The rest of the group hurried across.

"Come on, Aunt Kate!" Vicky fired five rounds while Kate charged toward the rear of the alleyway.

Amanda handed the .357 revolver to her son who was intent on being the first one up the stairs. "Be careful!"

Kate climbed up behind him. "Vicky, you come last. Watch our backs!"

"Okay." She kept vigilant guard for a rear attack.

David stormed in the upper room with his pistol drawn. Kate rushed in right behind him. They scanned the area which was filled with boxes.

"All clear." Kate waved for the others to come in.

Annie held the old Civil War pistol with both hands. "Looks like a storage room."

"Yeah. When they did the cowboy shows, they would go out on this balcony to shoot at the bandits coming out of the bank across the street." David looked out the corner of the window.

"Not too close, David," Amanda warned.

Kate looked out the other side. "See anything?"

"No, do you?" David inquired.

"We're sitting ducks up here." Vicky topped off

the magazine of her small 9mm with more bullets. "We need to get out of here while we can."

Kate instantly understood the reason for her concern. The situation was all too familiar. Caught in an upstairs room with no way out. She attempted to quell her fears. "These guys aren't like the Reverend or even James Dean. They had us set up for a perfect ambush, we were in the middle of the street, and we didn't even know they were there. Still, they didn't manage to hit one of us. This is amateur hour."

Vicky slapped the magazine back in the butt of her pistol. "I hope you're right, because we're not even armed well enough for amateur hour."

CHAPTER 3

No weapon that is formed against thee shall prosper; and every tongue that shall rise against thee in judgment thou shalt condemn. This is the heritage of the servants of the Lord, and their righteousness is of me, saith the Lord.

Isaiah 54:17

Kate stepped out the back door onto the wooden landing of the stairs. She looked in both directions down the street which ran behind the old west town.

POW! A shot rang out from the woods surrounding the town. Kate ducked back inside and slammed the door. "They're in the forest also."

"So we're surrounded," Vicky huffed. "Doesn't

sound much like amateurs to me."

"Kate's right." Annie peeked out the front window. "These aren't seasoned fighters and there can't be very many of them. We just need to identify where their weakest link is and punch a hole through it."

"Then what? Pray we can outrun them?" Vicky pressed her lips tight. "Because we certainly can't outshoot them."

Kate looked back toward the saloon. She saw a flash of sunlight reflecting off metal inside the downstairs window. She took aim and waited to see if the light would present itself again. She saw a dark figure inside and pulled the trigger. CRACK! The sound of the AK-47 firing inside the small room was deafening. "Sorry about that."

Amanda put her fingers in her ears. "No need to apologize. Better deaf than dead. Do what you have to do."

Kate watched the window below through the shattered glass she'd just shot.

David fired his pistol. Once again, the sound of the gun being fired inside was piercing.

Kate looked across the street to see a man with a rifle fall backward on the roof of the saloon. "You got him! Good shot."

David lowered the pistol. "I never understood why my dad made me target practice with a pistol. I always figured I'd have a rifle."

"You only have six rounds." Kate gave him an affirming pat on the shoulder. "You should take every opportunity to reload."

David nodded and replaced the spent shell.

Annie held her pistol with the hammer back. "Do you have a plan?"

Kate glanced at the old pistol, which looked right at home in the old west town. "For starters, save your ammo until you absolutely have to shoot. Let us do the heavy lifting. If you see a target, let me know. We'll need every weapon we have if we decide to shoot our way out.

"Beyond that, we'll keep doing what we're doing, looking for opportunities to weaken their numbers."

POW, POW, POW! Shots crashed through the front window.

"Get down!" Kate grabbed Vicky and pulled her to the floor.

The gunfire kept going for several seconds, then finally subsided.

Kate looked at her team members. "Anybody hit?"

They all shook their heads.

David pointed toward the front. "Those shots came from the direction of the bank. Either they have people posted up all over the place or they are moving around a lot."

"I wish we knew which." Kate lifted her head to peek out at the roof of the bank. She saw no one.

"What if they're just trying to scare us off? If someone came on our property, we'd do the same thing," Amanda said. "Maybe we should offer to go in peace. Admit our mistake at stumbling upon their camp and tell them we'll go."

Kate considered the option. "Annie, what do you think?"

"What do we have to lose by asking?" she replied.

David immediately objected. "We'll look weak, that's what we have to lose."

Kate turned to Vicky. "What do you think?"

"I'm with David on this." Vicky stared at her aunt with serious eyes. "And not just because it's David. If you're wrong, if these guys *are* like the Reverend or Dean, they'll smell fear and they'll close in on us like sharks in a feeding frenzy."

Kate felt perplexed.

"We're evenly split. You have the deciding vote, Kate." David held his pistol close to his chest. "But I'll support whatever call you make."

"Thanks." Kate swapped her magazine for a fresh one. "But just to be clear, I'm calling the shots on this operation. Even if it was four to one, I'm the tactical commander. When I ask for input, it's because I value the counsel of everyone here, but I'm still going to do what I think is best for all of us. It has to be that way."

David lowered his eyes. "Yes, ma'am."

Kate thought another few seconds then crawled close to the window. "Hold your fire!" she yelled. "We want to propose a truce."

"Okay. Let's hear it," a man called back.

Kate held her hand by her mouth to project her voice toward the window. "We were just passing through. We didn't mean to trespass on your compound. We had no idea anyone was here."

"Then why did you kill two of our men?"

David whispered. "They *are* amateurs. We didn't know for sure that we'd shot two of them. They just tipped their hand."

"Because you shot at us first," yelled Kate.

"Those were warning shots. If we'd been trying to kill you, you'd all be dead."

"Maybe, maybe not," Kate replied. "But either way, when someone shoots at me, I take it personally."

"Whatever, let's hear about your truce."

"Let us walk away. We'll leave and never come through here again."

"How do I know that you're telling the truth?"

"You'll have to trust me."

The man was silent for a long while, as if he were discussing the matter with his group. Minutes later he called out. "Okay, lady, you get your wish."

Amanda and Annie gave each other hugs accompanied by smiles of elation. "Yes!" said Annie.

The man continued, "Leave your weapons and your packs in the room where you are and exit out the back door. Don't look back, and don't return to this area."

Kate's stomach sank. She yelled, "That's not going to happen."

Amanda and Annie both lost their smiles.

"So, what's the plan?" David inquired grimly.

Kate gave an elongated exhale. "We don't know how many of them are out there and we don't know where they're at. Any plan we come up with is going to be little more than a Hail Mary."

"We can't just sit here. We have to move." Vicky paced the floor, looking out the window.

Kate tore the top flap off one of the cardboard

boxes stacked beside her. She tore the flap into smaller pieces and arranged them on the floor in the same pattern as the buildings in the wild west town. "We're here. They've got shooters in front of us at the saloon and the bank, here and here." She pointed to the bits of cardboard. "They also have people watching us from the back, right here."

Kate looked up at her team. "Unless they have a lot more fighters than we think, I doubt they'd have anyone around back of the town on the saloon side. David, do you know of anything that would give us cover on that side? We need to leapfrog from here to another place of relative security. From there, we can put down cover fire and retreat into the woods. I can't guarantee that they won't pursue us, but it gives us an out."

David put his finger on one of the cardboard swatches. "That side goes straight down the mountain. It's pretty steep. However, from the back landing, we can climb onto the roof of the ice cream shop and break into the second floor of the hotel. From there, we can take the stairs down to the first floor and exit out the side. That will put us at the edge of the town and heading in the direction we need to get to the ski resort. Up that road is the old arcade, shooting gallery, and where they used to have all the kiddie rides. We would have several options for short-term cover."

Kate nodded. "Then that's what we'll do. Once we head out the back door, I'll put down a few rounds to keep their heads low while we climb over onto the roof. Any questions?"

"It doesn't sound like we have any better

options." Annie looked out the window once more.

Kate adjusted the straps on her pack and readied her rifle. "Okay, David, you take the lead. Annie, you're behind him. If you see a target, now is the time to use that thing. Amanda, you're in the middle. If someone drops a hostile and you think you can get to his weapon, do it. It would be nice if we were all armed. Vicky, you're in front of me. Once we get inside the hotel, we'll flip positions. I'll take point, Vicky behind me and so on."

Amanda nodded. "Sounds good. Let's go."

Kate stepped out onto the landing and began peppering the woods with rifle fire while her team climbed over the railing onto the roof of the one-story ice cream shop. Vicky let off a couple of rounds toward the trees once she was over. "Come on, Aunt Kate!"

Kate jumped the handrail and tucked low as she sprinted to the window. David had already broken the glass and had the window open.

"Careful, watch out for the shards on the floor," David warned his mother as he helped her inside.

Once Kate was in, she looked around. She took a quick peek over the banister to the ground level. "I don't see anyone in here, but let's stay alert." She kept her rifle ready and hurried down the stairs. Kate ran across the room and raised the sash of the window. One by one, her team crawled out the window.

POW! POW! Bullets broke through the front window and door of the hotel. Kate was the last one inside. She dropped low to the floor and returned fire. The front door flew open and a young man with long straight hair and a pistol charged into the room. Behind him another young man, who couldn't have been older than twenty, barreled through the door with a semi-automatic .22 rifle. Both shot in Kate's direction. She unleashed a barrage of bullets from the AK-47 and cut them both down. She jumped to her feet and attempted to climb out the window. Before she could get out, another hostile, this one an early-twenties girl, came through the door wielding a shotgun.

Amanda grabbed Kate's backpack and pulled her out the window. Kate crashed to the ground on the other side just as the shotgun went off.

"Are you okay?" Amanda asked.

"Thanks to you." Kate looked up to see Vicky and David both shooting into the window.

"Got her!" Vicky exclaimed.

"We need to move. David, lead the way!" Kate got up from the ground.

David bolted toward the train tracks and down the paved path to the arcade. Kate and Vicky kept pace with him while Amanda and Annie struggled to keep up.

Kate slid around the corner of the arcade building and took several shots at the vandals chasing after them. "David, keep moving. I'll hold them back until you can get the rest of the team to safety."

"No, Aunt Kate!" Vicky protested. "We're staying together."

"Don't worry, I'll be right behind you."

Vicky changed magazines. "I'm not leaving you." She fired three rounds and dropped another of the attackers.

Kate shot two more. "I don't see any others. Let's go!"

Vicky and Kate ran as fast as they could and soon caught up with David, Annie, and Amanda.

"Anyone hit?" Kate asked.

"No, we're fine," Amanda replied.

"Good, let's get out of here before they catch us!" Kate switched magazines and pushed her team into the woods.

An older man's voice yelled out from ahead. "Stop where you are. Hands up! You're surrounded."

Kate paused long enough to look around. She spotted no less than eight gunmen, all heavily armed and in positions behind trees. These men had tactical vests, battle rifles, and looked like a paramilitary group. She slowed her sprint until she came to a full stop.

"Put down your weapons," the man called.

"Don't do it!" David whispered.

"We grossly underestimated this group." Kate slowly lowered her AK. "These aren't amateurs. Everyone, put your weapons down."

"And then what?" Vicky asked. "I don't want to be somebody's slave...or worse."

"I understand," Kate said softly. "We wandered into their territory, maybe they'll still just let us leave."

"Put the weapons down, or we will kill you! This is your final warning!" the man yelled.

"Vicky, put it down," Kate pleaded.

"You, too, David," Amanda said.

The teenagers eventually capitulated and placed their pistols on the ground.

The men closed in on them. One commanded, "Face down! On the ground!"

Kate hated this situation but did as she'd been ordered. She wished she'd never left the house in Laurel Ridge. She felt a plastic zip tie being tightened around her wrists and heard the first man issue an order to his men. "Search the ghost town. See if there are any more. We'll take this group back to camp."

Someone put a black bag over Kate's head, and she could see nothing when they picked her up and set her on her feet. "Start walking," said the first man.

"Please, we were just trying to find some friends. We didn't see any warning signs that let us know we were trespassing," Annie cried.

"We'll discuss it when we get back to camp," replied the man.

Vicky's voice sounded distressed. "What are you going to do with us?"

"That all depends. But like I said, we'll discuss it when we get to camp."

"If you hurt any of them, I swear, I'll kill you," David scolded the man.

The man sniggered. "You ain't in much of a position to be killin' nobody. But I like your spunk. I reckon that's how you've lasted as long as you have in this world. Don't fret, boy. Ain't nobody getting' hurt if you all cooperate and do as you're told."

Kate had a horrible feeling about this. Perhaps

Vicky was right. Maybe they should have just fought to the death. She had no illusions about the fact that there were far worse things than death.

CHAPTER 4

My God, my God, why hast thou forsaken me? why art thou so far from helping me, and from the words of my roaring? O my God, I cry in the day time, but thou hearest not; and in the night season, and am not silent. But thou art holy, O thou that inhabitest the praises of Israel.

Psalm 22:1-3

Kate had lost all concept of time and distance while having the black bag over her head. Her best estimate was that they'd walked five miles and roughly two hours had passed since being captured. She heard a large door open, like that of a barn. She felt someone push her down onto a chair, and then place new zip ties over her arms, securing her to the chair. Finally, someone removed the bag over her head. Amanda, David, Vicky, and Annie were all in chairs placed in a semicircle. Light slipped between the planks in the barn, illuminating small particles of dust, which danced in the narrow rays.

Two women came in and gave them water. The men who'd escorted them to the barn sat on hay bales along the barn wall and rested from the long walk.

"Are you going to let us go?" Vicky demanded.

"We'll see. I ain't the one who decides that." It was the man who'd given Kate's team the orders to drop their weapons. He was in his early sixties but in good shape. He had an evenly-cut flat top, which was gray but seemed to be heading in the direction of white.

"Then who is it up to?" Vicky asked harshly.

"Dennis, he's our security administrator."

Kate tried to take a more pleasant tone than Vicky had. "The first group of people we encountered at the ghost town didn't strike me as the type who were operating under a security administrator. No offense."

The man laughed. "Those little punks back there? They don't have anything to do with us."

"Then why did you join up with them? Why did you take us hostage?" Annie inquired.

"We weren't sticking up for them. That ghost town has been a thorn in our side ever since things fell apart. We go over there and clear it out every once in a while, but it's like a magnet for trouble. We keep getting new groups of squatters, and they're almost always delinquents."

"What do you care who lives there?" David asked.

"Too close for comfort. This is our neighborhood and we're sorta like the community association board. We decide who lives in our neighborhood and who doesn't. Might sound a little harsh, but it's how it's gotta be, at least for now."

Another man walked into the barn. His attire looked like clothing for farm work, but new and clean. He was very well manicured and obviously hadn't gotten around to his farm work for the day. Like the other man, he was older, early sixties, Kate thought. Rugged looking, not thin, but certainly not fat either.

"Who have we got here, Sarge?"

The first man stood up from the bale of hay. "The blonde had an AK-47. The others just had pistols. We also found five ounces of gold in the blonde's pack."

The man Kate figured to be Dennis walked over toward her. "AK-47, huh? Where did you get that?"

"A girl has the right to defend herself, doesn't she? I see you folks are fairly well set in the firearms department."

"Yeah, but I'm not the one on trial here."

"So we're on trial?"

He nodded. "Yes, ma'am. I need to know who I'm dealing with here. So you'd best enlighten me as to how you came to have an AK-47 and five ounces of gold."

"I bought the gold right before things went bad."

"That was lucky."

"Yeah, I keep hearing that, but it hasn't done me much good yet."

"What about the AK?"

"My boyfriend bought it, right before the first wave of locusts."

"What brings you folks our way?"

"Looking for some friends."

"In the ghost town?"

Kate didn't want to give away too much information. "No. Some people I know who live up this way."

"What's your friend's name?"

She sighed and didn't say anything.

"You know what I think?" Dennis squatted down to look into her eyes.

She glanced up at him, then looked back at the dirt floor of the barn. "What?"

"I think you're scouts, looking for places to raid."

"You think I'd be packing around five ounces of gold on a scouting mission?"

Dennis stood and inspected the other members of Kate's team. "Maybe you happened upon some poor defenseless soul and took what you could get. You decided not to report the plunder to your boss and have to carry it around on your person. That can be a dangerous move, especially if you're linked up with a rough crew.

"Which gang are you working with? Any association with Reverend Graves' outfit?"

"What? No!"

"But you've heard of him."

"Yeah, I've heard of him."

"She killed his brother, that filthy puke!" Vicky shouted.

"Vicky! Be quiet!" Kate scolded.

Dennis looked at Sarge. "You caught a wild one, here." He turned back to Kate. "You killed Jason Graves? And Lloyd hasn't taken you out yet?"

"He's tried, and killing Jason was in self-defense. They raided our house over in Apple Blossom Acres. I had no choice."

"How did you get entangled with the Badger Creek Gang?" Dennis seemed to be growing more fascinated with Kate's story by the minute.

"It's a long story."

"I've got all day. Enlighten me."

"My alcoholic brother set up a trade with Jason—supplies for booze. I walked in on the deal and shut it down. Jason didn't like the fact that I forced my brother to back out and came back to take our stuff in the middle of the night. He killed my other brother, Terry."

Vicky's jaw was tight. "Then the Reverend's men came back six weeks later to finish us off. They killed my brother, Sam."

"You two are related?" Dennis asked.

"She's my niece," Kate answered. "Terry was her dad."

"Sorry to hear that. Sounds like you folks have had a tough time of it. Still, that doesn't mean that you're not here to do us harm. Good people get desperate and do bad things. I have a community to look after. If you can't convince me of why you're up here, things may not end well for you."

Kate glanced at Annie.

"You have to tell him, Kate." Annie's eyes were pleading.

"Kate? Your name is Kate?" Dennis asked.

"Yeah." She figured that small bit of information couldn't make her circumstances any more dire.

Dennis looked at one of the other guards who'd brought them in. "Vince, go ask Rick what that girl's name is who is supposed to be coming up here."

"Rick?" Kate asked. "As in Radio Rick?" She watched the other guard, Vince, walk out of the barn. He had long straight, layered hair, like that of a rock star from the 80s.

Dennis seemed hesitant to answer. "We'll have this figured out in a second, but I have a feeling we could have skipped all this if you'd have just told me who you were coming to see."

Minutes later, Bill, the man from Carolina Readiness walked into the barn. "Kate, we were looking for you to be coming up the road. I got worried when you didn't make it."

"Cut 'em loose," Dennis ordered. "Give them back their guns and their gear."

Kate rubbed her wrists and stretched her back. "Yeah, we got hung up at the old ghost town."

Bill patted her on the back. "Yeah, I heard. I guess you had them about all cleared out by the time our team arrived to see what the commotion was about. Sorry about the misunderstanding, but I'm sure you can appreciate our position."

Vicky put no effort into hiding her annoyance as she holstered her pistol and slipped the straps of her pack over her shoulders. "You knew we were coming. Seems like your team could have been a little more hospitable."

"Vicky, I'll handle this. These are our hosts. Let's try to be gracious guests." Kate knew that her entire group's survival might depend on what the members of Bill's compound thought of them.

Bill tightened his lips. "She's right. We should have made a better effort to find out how many of you were coming and what direction you'd be coming from. It's just that when you're talking on open channels like that you never know who's listening. It's a fine line between getting enough information and maintaining operational security.

"But let me make it up to you. Jan and some of the girls made a nice meal for all of you. It was piping hot two hours ago, but I'm sure it will still be good."

"I could eat." David took Vicky's hand and walked beside her.

"Pardon me for being so direct, but my imagination has been eating at me ever since we spoke over the radio yesterday." Bill grinned. "You said you had some information I might be interested in."

"Yeah, on Monday, our group was attacked by a man who calls himself the Reverend. His real name is Lloyd Graves. He ran the Badger Creek Gang, but a bunch of lowlifes they used to sell meth to in Charlotte and Atlanta have moved up here and the gang has leveled up."

"We're familiar with the Reverend. I'm sorry to hear that. I'm glad you survived. Most people don't live to tell about a skirmish with that bunch." Bill's expression was heavy.

Kate looked at the ground and continued following Bill. "The majority of our group didn't survive. The only reason we made it is because the military showed up."

"Colonel Forrestal's outfit." Bill seemed well aware of the military's presence. "We've been trying to figure him out. We can't exactly tell whether to label him as friend or foe. For the time being, we've been trying to stay out of his path."

Kate twisted her mouth to one side. "I wish I could offer you some clarity about his role, but I'm afraid I may make matters more opaque by what I'm about to tell you."

"Let's hear it." Bill motioned toward a row of picnic tables in a large open dining area covered by a roof.

Kate took a seat. "The military showed up and took out several of the Reverend's men, the rest retreated into the woods. But, after the threat had been eliminated, they confiscated all of our guns."

Bill glanced at her AK-47 as she took it off of her shoulder. "Not all of them, obviously."

She took off her cap and pulled her long blonde hair back out of her face. "We had a few stashed, but not many. Obviously, we wouldn't be so far from home with only one long gun and a few pistols if we had more choices."

Bill's wife, Jan, and another lady came out of a small chinked log cabin carrying two large casserole dishes. "Kate, it's so good to see you. I'm sure you must be hungry. We heard you had a tough trip getting up here. You folks eat, and we'll chat more after your bellies are full."

"Thank you." Annie took some paper plates from another woman and passed them around.

Bill said a quick prayer over the food and remained seated at the picnic table. "How many are left in your group?"

"Thirteen," Kate replied.

Bill looked her team over once more. "Most of the men were killed?"

"Yeah, three men are back at our house, but one is injured, one is elderly, and the other is in charge of security for the remainder of the group."

"I see."

"I took your advice about converting some cash into gold."

"Good."

Kate took a drink of water from a red plastic cup that had been served to her by another member of Bill's group. "I was wondering if you might know of anyone who'd be willing to sell a battle rifle or two. I brought five ounces of gold."

Bill's brow creased deeply. "That's a tall order."

"I know, but I was hoping that perhaps we might have earned some goodwill, by risking our lives to tell you about the gun confiscations."

Bill crossed his hands on the wooden tabletop. "We certainly appreciate the effort. It's actionable intelligence, and we'll act on it right away. Why don't you folks finish eating, and I'll go talk to some people."

"Thank you. I know I'm asking a lot, but we'll have trouble getting by if we can't defend ourselves." Kate watched the man get up and walk away.

CHAPTER 5

The lips of the righteous feed many: but fools die for want of wisdom. The blessing of the Lord, it maketh rich, and he addeth no sorrow with it.

Proverbs 10:21-22

Jan and a few of the other woman came out and cleared the table. Afterward, Jan took a seat with Kate and the others. "It's so good to see that you've made it this long."

Kate's smile was shallow. "I doubt we'd still be here if it hadn't been for the information you and Bill gave us."

Jan took Kate's hand. "Thank you for telling me that. It's why we kept that place open for so long.

Don't get me wrong, we had some good years, but we had some years where it was tough to stay open. It was a sense of mission, of wanting to get folks informed and prepared that kept us going in the slow times."

"The meal was fantastic!" Amanda said. "We didn't really have a proper Thanksgiving, so turkey and stuffing casserole was very nice."

"From what I remember, you stocked up pretty well." Jan turned her attention back to Kate. "You should've had plenty to celebrate Thanksgiving."

"We still have food," Kate replied. "But we lost most of the people in our neighborhood from an attack on Monday. We all went around the table last night and said what we were thankful for, but it wasn't a very joyous Thanksgiving."

"I'm so sorry." Jan took her hand once more. "What about the young man you came in the store with the first time?"

"Gavin, oh he's back at the house. He was shot but is healing well," Kate replied.

"Then there was that younger boy who came in with you, right after the first round of attacks." Jan looked somber, as if she already knew the answer.

Kate looked at Vicky then back to Jan. "Sam, he was my nephew. He was killed in the raid."

"We're very sorry for your loss." Jan gripped her hand tighter.

Bill returned with Dennis, the security administrator, and Vince, the guard with the 80s rock star hair. "Kate, why don't you take a walk with us?"

"Can I come?" Vicky asked.

"She'll be right back." Bill smiled. "We have some business to discuss."

"It's fine, Vicky." Kate stood up to follow Bill. "I won't be long."

Dennis talked while they walked toward another of the small chinked log cabins. "Kate, I can't thank you enough for sharing that information with us. We had our suspicions about Colonel Forrestal, but what you told us solidifies our concerns. As you know, the people who attacked you had a few weapons. We collected those when we cleared the ghost town, so they're yours to take with you when you go. I'm afraid none of those weapons are what you're looking for. We picked up a couple .22 rifles, a .22 revolver, a .25 auto pistol, a .380 auto pistol, a pump action 12 gauge, and a .30-30. That .30-30 and the shotgun should help out if you have bullets for them. We didn't find much ammo on the deceased."

"We have some 12-gauge shells, but that's it."

Dennis opened the door of the cabin. "I'll ask around. Still, you've got a few rounds for each weapon. I suppose they'll serve you better than a fly swatter."

She followed Bill into the house. "Any luck with the battle rifles?"

Bill took a seat on an old couch. "I'll let Vince answer that."

Vince whipped his head to the side and slung his hair out of his face. "Like most of the people here, I figured something bad was coming. Instead of stocking up on gold and silver, I invested in some AR-15s. I can sell you two rifles, and four 30-round magazines for five ounces of gold. That might sound high, but I can assure you that it's a fair deal. Might even be a little below the going rate."

"Will those magazines be loaded?" Kate asked.

"I can do that, but I don't have any more wiggle room. Sorry, it's a take-it-or-leave-it deal."

"Do the rifles have any optics?"

"Simple iron sights. No bells and whistles," Vince replied.

"Okay, I'll take them." She retrieved the five coins from her pack and gave them to the rocker.

Vince inspected the gold bullion. "Canadian Maple Leaves. Nice. I'll be right back."

When Vince walked out the door, the man with the flattop walked in. "Dennis, we've got a problem. That thing Rick has been monitoring just went south."

"Okay, let's hear it."

Sarge looked at Kate. "In front of her?"

Bill said, "She's good people. This is Kate, by the way. Kate, meet US Army Sergeant Major Bobby Donovan. Most folks just call him Sarge."

"We met, but not formally." Kate stood and offered him her hand. "Pleasure to meet you, Sergeant Major."

"I hope you'll forgive me if I was a little abrasive. I was just doing my job." He embraced her hand firmly. "Sergeant Major Retired; the pleasure is mine, ma'am."

"So, what do you have for us?" Dennis asked.

Sarge looked at Kate once more before speaking. "Rick picked up the latest about the bugs in the reactors. The Army Corp of Engineers has given up on trying to remove the malware or replace the software. They've decided to SCRAM the reactors."

Kate took a seat next to Bill on the couch, "I assume you're talking about nuclear power reactors. Which ones?"

Sarge tightened his jaw. "All of them."

"That's not good." Kate thought about the problem.

Bill said, "Kate worked at the bank where they found the first locust. She won't talk much about it, but I suspect she had something to do with identifying it."

Dennis reclined on the loveseat. "What's your opinion, Kate? What do you think they should have done with the infected reactors?"

"They never would have been able to deactivate the virus, so yes, they had to take them offline. I don't think they had a better solution. From what I understand, they all rely on diesel generators to keep the cooling pools filled. Given the current state of affairs, fuel may get harder and harder to come by. But I'm no expert on the subject of nuclear reactors."

Bill added, "All rely on diesel generators except one. Oconee, which is about sixty miles south of us, gets its backup power from the Keowee Hydroelectric Plant at the Jocassee Dam. Having a preparedness store, I read up on all the nearby hazards. All the other nuclear power plants in the country are well over a hundred miles from us and represent a minimal threat to our area."

"What good is a hydroelectric plant going to do us when the entire US grid is down?" Dennis asked.

"Oconee has its own power lines that come straight from the dam's generators. It's completely independent of the Keowee switchyard and the US grid.

"As for the rest of the reactors, I think once they initiate a SCRAM and insert the control rods, the decay heat starts to drop exponentially. I can't remember all the numbers, but after ten days I think decay heat drops to .2% of what it was when the reactors were active. By then, a handful of volunteers could literally bring water in buckets and keep the cooling pools filled. Of course, I think it takes about twenty years for the rods to be completely cooled to the point that they aren't a danger at all."

Kate looked at Bill. "Under our present circumstances, would you volunteer to keep the pools filled for twenty years?"

"Nope."

Sarge took a seat in the lounge chair. "The Army will take care of that. They won't let those plants go into meltdown."

"I hope you're right." Dennis' face looked grim. "Did Rick have anything else to say?"

"Yep. Since DC has so many nuclear plants in the immediate vicinity, they've decided to relocate the federal government to Asheville."

"There goes the neighborhood." Bill shook his head in disgust.

Sarge laughed. "Oh, come on, Bill. Asheville was already full of pinkos. A few more won't hurt nothing."

Bill crossed his arms tightly. "We'll see about

that. If this Colonel Forrestal is running around grabbing guns now, just wait until he gets his expanded authority because of the capital's relocation."

"I don't understand why they are going to relocate the federal government. Seems like a big undertaking." Kate scratched her head.

Sarge took a map of the United States out of his back pocket and spread it out on the coffee table. With a red pen, he made three circles to the north, south, and southwest of Washington DC. "Washington has three plants within 100 miles including Calver Cliffs, which is about 45 miles out. If they were to all go into meltdown, DC would be getting some level of radioactive fallout regardless of which way the wind blows.

"If they relocate, they only have one plant to worry about. It's more than fifty miles away and lots of mountains in between. Asheville is almost due north of the Oconee plant, so that puts them well out of the way of the prevailing winds. But I'm sure the federal government will do everything they can to keep the cooling pools at Oconee filled."

"Wow. You've done your homework." Kate studied the map.

Bill grinned. "Like I told you back at the store when we first met, I know folks who have run about every doomsday scenario there is."

Kate traced the line from the Calvert Cliffs Power Plant to DC. "Seems like any radiation they'd get would be minimal from that distance."

"Probably so," Sarge said. "But the combined effects of all three stations around them would act as a constant bombardment on the soil, water, animal life, and people for decades to come. Asheville offers a much more pristine environment, not to mention a lower population density. It will be easier to control. And like I said before, the pinkos from Asheville and DC will get along like peas in a pod."

"It might be time to consider linking up with Morgan Meyer's team." Bill looked at the other members of his group.

"Who's that?" Kate asked.

Sarge answered, "A fellow who used to live around here. Made his money in real estate; buying, selling, managing rental cabins. He felt like it was getting too crowded around here and bought 400 acres up by Bryson City. Built a big survival compound up there. He gave us an open invitation if we wanted to come up. Of course, it's his property and his rules."

"Morgan is a fair man. I wouldn't have any problems going along with anything he's likely to ask of me." Bill sat back on the couch.

Dennis rubbed his chin. "My worry is that they'll widen the perimeter. If the military is currently tasked with controlling a 50-mile radius from Asheville, it wouldn't take much of an expansion to include Bryson City. It's what, sixty-five miles from Asheville?"

Kate leaned on the arm of the comfortable old couch. "A 50-mile radius equates to a 100-mile diameter, and that's a 314-mile circumference to enforce. With the strain on resources, they'll be doing good to hold that down, at least for now."

"It's good to have a math nerd around." Sarge laughed.

"Oh, no." Kate waved her hand. "The only reason I know it's 314 miles is because Pi Day is on March 14th. Everyone who works in the tech sector celebrates Pi Day by ordering out pizza and pie."

Sarge grinned. "Like I said, good to have a math nerd around."

Vince returned, carrying two AR-15s and two extra magazines. "They're loaded, but nothing in the chamber. Keep 'em clean."

Kate stood to take the guns. "Thank you so much. These will make a big difference for my group."

"It was a pleasure doing business with you." Vince swept the hair back out of his face and shook Kate's hand.

"Likewise." She looked at Bill. "I suppose I should be going. We'll be traveling in the dark even if we leave now."

"Then stay for the night. We've got an extra cabin," Dennis offered. "You can leave at first light."

Kate considered the offer. "The people back at the house will be worried."

"Is anyone monitoring the radio?" Bill asked.

"Yes, but probably only for the 3:00 o'clock broadcast."

Bill stood. "Then we better hurry on over to the Ham shed."

"It will give me a chance to ask around about that extra ammo for you." Dennis also got up.

Kate thought about it. "Okay. We'll stay and

head out first thing tomorrow morning."

CHAPTER 6

And I will deliver thee out of the hand of the wicked, and I will redeem thee out of the hand of the terrible.

Jeremiah 15:21

Kate and her team sat at one of the picnic tables for breakfast the next morning along with about 40 other people from the compound.

"I'm going to see if they have anything left over. I'll be back." David got up and walked toward the main cabin where the kitchen was.

Kate hugged her niece with one arm. "Did you get full?"

"Yeah, it was really good. I could tell those were powdered eggs, but the cheese made them taste so much better." Vicky leaned on Kate's shoulder.

"What was this place before?" Annie asked.

Amanda sipped her coffee. "It was like a resort ranch. All these cabins were rentals, and the lodge had several rooms as well. They had horseback riding and activities, but I think most of their business came from people hitting the ski slopes."

"So, did your friends know the ranch's owners?" Vicky turned to Kate.

She lifted her shoulders. "I didn't ask, but I suppose so."

Dennis came and took a seat next to Kate. "I found a fellow who has a pretty good stockpile of .22 ammo, but obviously he'll want something in return."

David returned with a plate of grits just as Dennis sat down.

Kate said, "I don't know what we have of value. I only brought five coins, and I spent them on the AR-15s."

David washed down his food with a drink of water. "See if he'll give you anything for that .25 auto. We only have seven bullets for the thing anyway, and it's not much more effective than a big rock to begin with."

Kate pulled the small pistol and extra bullets out of her pack and handed them to Dennis. "Would you mind asking?"

"Okay. What would you like to get for it?"

Kate turned to David. "I'm not sure what the exchange rate should be."

"Ask for 500 rounds, but we'll take 400." David continued eating.

Dennis stood up. "That might be a little steep.

Ammo is in high demand. I'd recommend asking for 400 and settling for 300."

Kate nodded in agreement to Dennis' proposal, and he left with the shiny chrome pistol.

Jan and Bill came to the table while they waited for Dennis' return. Jan gave Kate a brown paper bag. "I brought you some biscuits and venison jerky for your return trip."

"Thank you, Jan. That's very kind of you." Kate stowed the treats in her pack. "I'm sure we'll see you again soon."

Bill added, "Y'all be safe. Talk to your people. If they're interested, I think the folks up in Bryson would make room for your group."

Minutes later, Dennis returned. "I got you 300 rounds of regular .22 rounds plus fifty rounds of hollow point .22 magnum. The rifles might not take them, but that revolver will. A .22 may not be my first choice for self-defense, but if you shoot someone with one of those Magnum hollow points, they'll wish they hadn't bothered you."

"Thank you." She stashed the small package next to the food, closed her pack and hoisted it to her shoulder. Kate's group said their goodbyes and headed down the mountain toward the old ghost town.

Kate's AK-47 was folded up in her pack and she carried one of the .22 rifles. Annie's main weapon for the trip home was the shotgun. One of the ARs was broken down into the upper and the lower receiver then stowed in David's pack. He toted the second .22 rifle over his shoulder. His mother held the .30-30, while Vicky carried the other AR-15, ready to fire.

The sun was up over the mountains by the time Kate and her team arrived at the ghost town. It served to warm the air and disperse the shadows. Still, Kate led her team around the old amusement park rather than taking the more direct route through, having no desire to relive the frightening event of the day prior. Soon afterward, the group made it to the bottom of the mountain and paused behind the ghost town welcome building.

Kate tightened the straps of her pack. "Same thing as yesterday. Beat feet across the parking lot, then the footbridge, and finally the road. Don't stop running until you're at least a hundred yards into the woods. Got it?"

All answered affirmatively.

"Good." Kate looked up and down the road, seeing no signs of vehicles. "Let's go!"

Kate led the charge. By the time they reached the footbridge, Vicky and David were right on her heels, but Amanda and Annie were lagging behind by about twenty feet.

"Come on! We have to hurry!" Kate tried to motivate the stragglers.

Kate and the teens made it to the tree line. She turned to wave Annie and Amanda on. "Let's go! Let's go!"

Annie reached the woods first. "A Humvee is coming down the road. It might have spotted me and Amanda."

Amanda breathed heavily. "You should take the weapons and leave us here."

Kate tugged at her arm to get moving "No one is

leaving anybody, let's go!" She sprinted up the hill into the cover of the sparse evergreen shrubs and pine trees. Kate heard the engine of the Hummer as the vehicle came to a sudden stop on the roadside. She heard the voice of a soldier call out, "Halt, or we'll shoot!"

She turned to see if the soldiers were in view but couldn't spot them. She waved her team on and kept running. Vicky and David kept pace but it soon became obvious to Kate that Amanda and Annie would not be able to outrun the soldiers who were now already winded from the sprint across the lot and the road.

They reached a steep outcropping of rocks where David and Vicky caught up to Kate.

David leaned the .22 rifle up against the rock. "We have to go back. My mom can't keep up."

Kate shook her head. "Going back won't do your mom any good."

David unzipped his pack and quickly assembled the AR-15. "If I kill them before they take her, it will."

Kate grabbed the barrel of the rifle. "No! We're not getting into a firefight with US soldiers. Don't forget, the military is the reason we're still alive."

Vicky stepped back from the argument.

"Yeah, they're also the reason we're scavenging for guns to survive. They took our firearms and left us to be devoured by the wolves." David wrestled the barrel away from Kate and slapped a magazine into the well. "It wasn't much of a favor if you ask me. Do what you want Kate, but I'm not leaving my mom behind." He tucked the other magazine into the waist of his jeans and put his pack over his shoulders.

"David, just wait. They'll probably take her guns, then let her go. We can live with that. We have all the battle rifles," Kate pleaded.

"And if they don't let her go, then what?" He looked at Vicky. "What if it was your niece? Would you let them take her, or would you fight?"

Kate looked away, knowing the answer to the question and feeling the jagged blade of hypocrisy stabbing at her heart. She dropped her pack and retrieved the AK-47. "You'll follow my command, is that understood?"

A twinge of admiration crossed his young face. "Yes, ma'am."

"Come on. Both of you stay low and close to me." Kate led the way through the brush. "We'll take up positions and observe. If they let Amanda and Annie go, we do nothing. Those guns aren't worth the fight. But if they start walking them back toward the Hummer, we'll engage."

Kate slowed her pace as she approached the soldiers. She could hear them speaking to Amanda and Annie but couldn't make out what was being said. With her hand, she motioned for David and Vicky to get even lower. Kate identified a large oak which would provide visual concealment for her and the teens to get closer. She kept the tree between herself and the soldiers below. Once she reached the giant oak, she gently lowered herself to the ground. Kate put her finger up to her lips, signaling for absolute silence from David and Vicky. She listened closely.

"Who else are you ladies out here with?"

"No one," Amanda said.

Kate watched as two soldiers put wrist restraints on Amanda and Annie while two more rummaged through their bags.

"Why were you out here?"

"Hunting," Annie replied.

"What are you hunting for?"

"Deer, squirrel, whatever we can catch." Amanda sounded nervous.

"Did you know that it's illegal to have firearms?"

"No. Since when is it illegal?" Annie asked.

"Since Asheville was declared a reconstruction zone. The government is sinking a lot of resources into rebuilding society, and Asheville is one of the places where we're going to start."

"What does that have to do with outlawing guns?" Amanda inquired.

"The country has fallen into chaos. We have to get the guns off the street so we can make it safe."

"You're in the military, you don't actually believe that, do you?" Amanda said. "Before the attacks, some of the most dangerous cities in America were the ones with the most astringent gun laws. Criminals don't obey gun laws or any other laws, hence why we call them criminals. When you disarm decent folks, you embolden violent criminals who now know they can act as viciously as they want with complete impunity."

The soldier shook his head. "Look, lady, I'm not here to argue with you. I don't make the laws, I just enforce them."

"Not really," Amanda countered.

"Oh?"

"No, you took an oath to defend the constitution and you are in direct violation of it. At least a common thug has made no assertion of being anything other than a villain. He has some nominal degree of honor in his transparency."

The soldier snarled. "You're not helping your case here, lady."

"I'm not trying to insult you, I'm just asking you to consider what your duty is and what you're doing by disarming the American people at a time when they need to be armed."

"Okay, you can tell it to my sergeant when we get you to camp." He pushed her arm.

Annie complained, "We haven't done anything wrong! Why are we being detained?"

"You had guns. That's a serious offense." The other soldier pushed Annie.

"But we didn't even know about the law!" Amanda argued.

"Ignorance of the law is no excuse. Besides, both of you ran when you saw us. Why would you run if you weren't doing anything wrong?"

Amanda replied, "Violent gangs are running around out here. Just because you were in a military vehicle doesn't mean you're in the Army."

"What about when you saw our uniforms?" asked another. "Still didn't think we might be military?"

"Plenty of para-military types who look like you guys in these hills," Annie protested.

"Oh yeah? Which hills? Tell us where to find

these groups."

"Not anyone specific, I'm just saying," Annie said.

"You'll be saying when you get back to camp. If you know what's good for you, you won't make the interrogation team ask twice."

Kate whispered to David, "Think you can hit them from here?"

"Yep." David was already lining up a shot.

"Give me and Vicky a chance to get closer. Count to sixty, then take your shot. When they turn to fire back at you, Vicky and I will hit them from the side." Kate waved for Vicky to follow her down the hill to flank the soldiers. "Start counting now, one Mississippi…"

David nodded but did not look away from his rifle. "Two Mississippi…"

Kate walked as lightly as she could, hoping the soldiers would keep up the conversation and not pay attention to what was coming up from behind them. She pointed to a large rhododendron and looked back at her niece. Vicky nodded that she understood and followed Kate to the big green bush. Kate lay prone beneath the concealment of the vegetation and took aim. "Fifty-eight Mississippi, fifty-nine…"

POW! David's shot came earlier than she expected but no matter, she and Vicky were in position. Blood spurted from the neck of the soldier carrying Amanda's pack and rifle. He dropped to the ground. The remaining three men spun around toward David. Kate took aim at the man hauling Annie's gear. She squeezed the trigger and watched him fall. The other two pushed their hostages to the ground and went to one knee. They let off several rounds up the mountain in David's direction then turned to begin shooting at Kate and Vicky. Vicky fired three consecutive rounds, dropping another of the soldiers. The sole survivor dropped his weapon and started running.

Vicky took aim but Kate pushed her barrel down. "He's not a threat. Let him go."

David sprinted furiously down the mountain, with his rifle in tow. He followed the man out of the tree line and gunned him down before he could get in the vehicle. David rummaged through the Humvee.

Kate dashed toward him. "David! You didn't need to kill that man! We have to go!"

David carried an ammo box and a rucksack out of the vehicle and walked briskly past Kate. "They'd seen my mom's face. We had to kill them all."

"And now you're raiding their vehicle?" Kate marched behind him in anger.

David paused when he reached the place where Vicky was cutting the restraints off of Amanda and Annie. "We can't go back to the house right away. We need to give it seventy-two hours to cool off. Otherwise, we risk leading them right back to the rest of the group."

Kate did not like having orders barked at her by a fifteen-year-old but feared he could be correct. She looked at Amanda.

"He's right," she said. "If they haven't caught us by then, they'll probably limit the amount of resources they can dedicate to hunting us down after three days."

"But for now, they'll be hunting for us like rabid dogs. Let's get moving." David stomped up the hill.

"Get the guns." Kate pointed at the soldiers' weapons. "And the magazines. We might need them."

CHAPTER 7

And thou shalt remember all the way which the Lord thy God led thee these forty years in the wilderness, to humble thee, and to prove thee, to know what was in thine heart, whether thou wouldest keep his commandments, or no. And he humbled thee, and suffered thee to hunger, and fed thee with manna, which thou knewest not, neither did thy fathers know; that he might make thee know that man doth not live by bread only, but by every word that proceedeth out of the mouth of the Lord doth man live. Thy raiment waxed not old upon thee, neither did thy foot swell, these forty years.

Deuteronomy 8:2-4

Kate trudged over the mountain top and began the ascent up the next hill.

Amanda caught up to her, panting. "Kate, we have to take a break." She took long belabored breaths.

Kate looked at Annie who was also huffing and puffing. "Okay, three minutes. But we have to keep moving. We've just elevated our status from being suspicious characters to being murderers. This time, it won't be four guys. It will be an entire squadron with shoot-to-kill orders."

Kate consulted the map while Annie and Amanda rested. Vicky looked over her shoulder. "Where are we going to go?"

Kate indicated an area on the map. "If we stay along these mountains, we keep out of populated areas. This is the Blue Ridge Parkway. We've got lots of vantage points from up there. If we can get there before sunset, we can pick out our next location where we want to go."

David looked at the map and back at his mother. "It's higher elevation, which means more work for them, thinner air, and colder night-time temps."

Kate folded up the map. "I know, but any route that is easy for us is also going to be easy for a search team with a dog to pick up our scent."

"I can't argue with that." David adjusted his gear and prepared to move out.

Vicky seemed concerned. "Colder nights? We have no tents or blankets. We'll freeze if we don't find shelter."

David looked at her. "Worst-case scenario, we make a debris shelter out of twigs and leaves. Even up by the parkway, the temperatures should be above freezing. My dad made me sleep in a debris shelter in worse weather than this."

Kate said nothing, but she was glad to have the young outdoorsman along for the journey.

Amanda added, "To be fair, your dad was in the shelter with you. And if it had gotten any colder, he was going to bring you home. The car was only a half mile away."

David smiled as if remembering the experience fondly. "Yeah, that's true."

The group continued through the woods, trying to stick to game trails whenever possible. Two hours later, they came to a creek. Kate looked and listened. Seeing nothing, she said, "We'll take fifteen minutes. Drink as much water as you can and fill your containers up from the creek."

"We don't have anything to purify the water with." Vicky looked at the creek.

"That's true, but while we might get a bad case of diarrhea from drinking straight out of the creek, we will definitely suffer from dehydration if we don't have water. So, in this case, cryptosporidium is the lesser of the two evils." Kate took a long slow swig from her bottle.

"What about food?" Annie inquired. "We don't have much."

Kate pointed to the rucksack David had pulled from the Humvee. "What's in there?"

He opened the pack. "MREs. Chili with beans, chicken egg noodles and vegetables, Mexican style chicken stew, hash brown potatoes with bacon, beef ravioli, and vegetable crumbles with pasta in taco sauce. Yuck, who'd eat that?"

"We'll be fighting over the vegetable crumbles in taco sauce by the time we get home. Trust me." Kate watched David rearrange the contents of the rucksack. "We had a big breakfast this morning. My advice would be to skip eating today, and then have the biscuits and jerky tomorrow. We should save the MREs until Monday. But everyone is different, so we'll divvy up the food now and you can all make your own choices. Just remember, it will be at least Monday night before we get anything else."

"Who gets what?" David looked into the sack.

"We'll draw straws." Kate picked up a slender dry tree branch and broke it into five pieces. "Longest stick picks first, shortest picks last."

Each of them drew a twig and held it up to the others.

David asked, "What will we do with the veggie crumbles, assuming no one picks it?"

"The sixth MRE will be shared communally when we're all hungry enough for taco flavored veggie pasta." Having the third longest stick, Kate selected the hash browns and bacon.

Once the food had been distributed, Kate filled her water container and placed it in her pack. "Everyone load up. Break is over. We have to keep moving. We have some distance between us and the site of the shootout, but we've got a long road ahead." She pointed high at the mountain in front of them. "My best guess puts the Blue Ridge Parkway on the other side of that summit. It's going to be a steep hike, but we can do it."

Annie appeared tired, just from looking at the arduous journey ahead. "I thought we were trying to avoid major roadways. Why are we going toward the Blue Ridge Parkway?"

Kate led the way and began the ascent. "We're just getting up high where we can see, not necessarily following the roadway, although it will give us a point of reference for our map. But the Blue Ridge is a long winding path, the dictionary definition of *the scenic route*. With fuel resources as scarce as they are, I can't imagine many people will be using it as a thoroughfare."

An hour later, Kate's team reached the top of the mountain. She breathed in the fresh air and looked around. She could see for miles in every direction.

"It's beautiful!" Annie exclaimed. "I wish Troy could be here to see it. It's going to kill me to be away from him for three more days."

Amanda hugged her. "Just remember, we're staying away so we don't get tracked back to where your son is. This way, you'll be able to bring him up here someday and show him all of this."

Annie gave Amanda's hand a squeeze. "Thanks."

Kate hated to break up the sightseeing respite, but she had to keep her team moving. "As beautiful as it is, we're easy to spot from a helicopter up here. Let's head down a ways, and we'll take a short recess to find our coordinates."

The team diligently followed her down the far

side of the mountain. A few minutes later, the Blue Ridge Parkway came into view. Kate sat down with her back against a tree and retrieved her map. "I'd like to get to that mountain across the road. We'll have a good vantage point to see if we're being followed, and we'll have this valley between our position and the direction the soldiers will be coming if they've picked up our trail. We'll see them coming and be able to hightail it over the ridgeline and into the wilderness on the other side.

"Additionally, it will allow us to observe the parkway for motor traffic. If no one is using it, the road will make a good route back home for us on Monday. Not the entire way, but long enough to not leave footprints in the dirt and break up the trail for anyone tracking us."

"We should be able to get over there in an hour and a half." Vicky looked across the valley to the potential campsite.

David retrieved his water container and took a drink. "We'll have plenty of time to construct shelters before dark also."

"Then where will we go tomorrow?" Amanda looked at the map.

Kate pointed beyond the first mountain. "We'll follow along that ridgeline to the southwest and keep moving farther away. If we see no signs of trouble, we'll only go half a day's journey."

"Will we head back toward home on Monday?" Annie tied her boots.

Kate put her hand on Annie's shoulder, knowing she must be missing her son. "If all goes well, we'll be home Monday night."

"Good." Annie seemed re-energized by the statement. She stood up and adjusted the weight of her gear. "Then let's get going."

Once Kate's team arrived on the face of the mountain opposite of where they were, they dropped their gear around a trio of hickory trees all growing together. Kate took off her boots and rubbed her feet as did Annie and Amanda.

David looked around. "I'm going to find a good spot to build a shelter."

"One big shelter?" Kate asked. "Won't that stand out if someone is searching for us?"

"We'll be building it out of limbs, sticks, and leaves, so it won't really stick out. We need a fallen tree for each shelter so if we build multiple smaller shelters, we'll have to split up." David waited for her reply.

Vicky added, "We'll stay warmer if we're all together."

Kate thought about the options. "Okay, we'll do a single shelter if you can locate a good spot. Don't wander far."

"We won't." Vicky tagged along behind David.

Kate's stomach growled as she watched a squirrel jump from limb to limb in the trees above.

Annie seemed to know exactly what she was thinking. "Too bad we don't have silencers."

"Yeah," Amanda added. "But even if we did, we couldn't cook it. We'd give away our position with the smell of cooking meat and smoke."

Kate giggled. "I'd rather eat taco veggie pasta than raw squirrel."

The three of them laughed but quickly extinguished their amusement so as not to make unnecessary noise.

Minutes later, David and Vicky returned. "I found it!" he exclaimed.

Kate sat up and put her boots back on. "Tell me."

"It's a big oak. It took down a smaller pine when it fell. It forms a natural A-frame like you'd make to build a campfire."

Vicky elaborated, "We'll have to thin out some of the branches on the bottom side, but we can use those for the top of the shelter."

"Good work." Kate tied her boots and followed the teens to see the trees where they'd be sleeping for the night. The fallen trees were only twenty yards from the three hickories where she'd been sitting. Kate inspected them. "With all the limbs and branches sticking out along the top side of the oak, you could walk right up on it and never notice a shelter below."

"Exactly." David wasted no time. He began breaking off the lower limbs and stacking them on top of the downed oak.

"I'll bring the gear over, and we'll be right back to help you get it constructed." Kate walked back to the hickories.

Annie was looking through the scope of the M-4 rifle taken from one of the soldiers.

"What do you see?" Kate picked up another of the M-4s and looked in the same direction.

"Right between those two knobs. It's a major road. I'm thinking it must be the Smokey Mountain Expressway."

Kate searched and finally saw beyond the low hills. "I think you're right."

Annie kept looking. "It seems so far away. I don't know if it does us any good, but at least we know it's there."

"It helps us get our bearings, which is very good." Kate grabbed her pack and walked toward the shelter construction project. "Come on, let's get our little burrow put together."

An hour later, the shelter was complete, stuffed with leaves and pine needles for insulation, and barely noticeable as anything other than a pile of twigs and branches.

Kate motioned for David to get inside. "You do the honors."

His lifted chin and glowing smile showed that he was proud of the humble den. David crawled inside. "Comfy."

Vicky waited for no invitation. She was next to inspect the modest shelter.

Kate knelt down and looked inside. "It's like a big sleeping bag. Vicky, you can sleep over on this side, next to me. I'm sure Amanda will want to sleep beside David."

Vicky gave David a disappointed look but didn't argue.

"In fact," Kate said. "I think I'm going to try to get a little nap right now. I'll take first watch tonight. You guys can figure out the rest of the guard duty schedule.

"We'll roll out at first light. We have to tear down the shelter and spread out the debris before we leave. We can't leave any sign that we were here." Kate dragged her pack and weapons into the well-padded nest. Her stomach was empty and growling, but she was exhausted from the tough day and quickly fell asleep.

CHAPTER 8

For a fire is kindled in mine anger, and shall burn unto the lowest hell, and shall consume the earth with her increase, and set on fire the foundations of the mountains. I will heap mischiefs upon them; I will spend mine arrows upon them.

Deuteronomy 32:22-23

    Kate shivered Sunday morning, watching the roads below for traffic through the scope of the M-4 rifle. She'd been watching since the early morning hours but had seen no vehicles on the Blue Ridge Parkway and very few travelers on the Smokey Mountain Expressway far below her present position. She looked at her watch. "Six o'clock.

About another hour and a half before sunrise."

She crawled inside the little shelter. The body heat of her teammates was well retained by the simple hut. Kate let them sleep a few more minutes while she prayed silently for God to return them safely home on the following day.

She wanted to lie down and go back to sleep, but she knew the team needed to get moving. "Time to get up, folks." Kate gently nudged Vicky who slowly roused from her deep slumber. Soon, the others were waking, stirring gently in the tight space beneath the limbs and branches.

Kate exited the compact quarters and returned to her watch position while she ate her share of the biscuits and venison jerky. It wasn't much and she was tempted to get into her MRE, but she knew, come Monday, she'd regret it. She chugged her water to wash it all down. This gave her the temporary illusion of being full, however, she was certain that it wouldn't last.

David was the first of her team to emerge from the cramped quarters. "Could we consider stashing some of these guns? We're packing around a lot of excess weight."

Kate thought about the recommendation. "I'm in favor of lightening our load so we can move faster, but I don't want to leave them around here. I'd rather keep the extra weight than risk losing the battle rifles anyway."

"What about the shotgun and the .22 rifles? Some of us are carrying three long guns."

Kate smiled. "You're carrying three long guns. And your extra AR-15 is broken down in your pack.

I'll carry your .22 rifle on my back if you want. My biggest concern is that by stashing the guns, we create more tracks, more disturbed ground, and a dead giveaway to our direction if the stash is found out. I don't plan to go far today, and I don't want to pigeon hole us into having to return the same way we go in order to collect the weapons.

"But, we can split up the weight of the ammo. You're still carrying that entire ammo can. How many rounds do you think are in it?"

"420."

"Wow. That was fast. Did you count them all?"

"No. It's written on the side of the ammo can. And I checked to see that it was full."

"Okay. Give everyone eighty rounds to carry. That will make things a little more fair."

"It will slow Mom and Annie down if we get in a tight spot and have to run. Especially if we're going uphill."

"Okay," Kate conceded. "Give 140 rounds each to me and Vicky."

By the time the first glimmer of daylight glowed from behind the mountains, Kate and her fellow team members were ready to resume the trek. The shelter was disassembled and the debris was scattered about. They moved in a southwesterly direction keeping just below the ridgeline.

The team moved quickly for the first half of the day, but the lack of food slowed them down in the afternoon. Kate gave them a five-minute rest every hour, but by 2:00 PM all were complaining.

"Okay, guys. I haven't seen any sign that they're

on to us." Kate dropped her pack. "We'll take half an hour break, then drop down into the valley to look for water. We'll head up to the top of that mountain on the other side of the valley and look for a suitable campsite."

All voiced their approval of the long hiatus. Once the break was over, Kate led them down the hill where they quickly located a clear running stream. Everyone refilled their water containers and prepared for the final hike up the short hill. Kate's team reached the top in a half-hour.

"This spot looks good." Vicky dropped her pack and lay down on the ground using the bag for a pillow.

"Okay, you guys can hang around here for a while." Kate put her pack against a tree and rubbed her shoulders. "I'm going to see what's on the back side of this ridge. If I find a good tree for a debris shelter, I think I'd rather be on that side. It's only another few hundred feet, and it will put us out of sight for anyone tracking us from the north." She grabbed the M-4 rifle and continued over the hilltop.

Once beyond the crest, she smelled wood burning. Kate continued a little further and saw several streams of smoke trickling out of stove pipes and chimneys below. Kate counted no less than thirty dwellings on a narrow stretch of flat land beyond the hill. "Trailers, mobile homes, and one big cabin. Somebody has a compound out here." She lifted the riflescope to her eye for a closer look. "They're all armed," she whispered to herself. "Heavily armed." Kate continued to inspect the inhabitants of the makeshift village. "Rough looking crew. Nothing like the people at the ranch."

Kate quietly lowered her rifle and watched her step going back to her team. When she arrived, she told them of what she'd seen. "I think we'll keep to this side of the mountain tonight. I'd rather take my chances with trackers on the ridgeline than the people I saw over there. David, you and Vicky find us a good tree for a shelter. Amanda, you can help them. Annie, why don't you get your rifle and come with me? I'd like to spend a little more time quietly observing our neighbors."

"Be careful!" Vicky warned.

"I will." Kate led Annie to the top of the hill.

Once in position, Kate gave Annie ample opportunity to look the crowd over. "What do you make of that?"

"Mean looking bunch."

"Yeah, that's what I thought." Kate continued to watch.

Annie whispered, "Get a load of this character on the porch of the main cabin."

"Which one?" Kate directed her scope in the direction indicated but saw several men and women gathered around.

"The one with the long, slicked back ponytail, leather trench coat, and the priest's collar."

"Nice touch with the parson's hat." Kate looked at some of the women nearby. Many were scantily clad with lots of makeup, certainly not properly dressed for the cold weather.

Annie kept watching. "I wonder what denomination that minister is?"

"I don't know, but I'll bet you my share of the taco pasta that he's not a Baptist."

Annie giggled. "Judging from the congregation, your taco pasta is safe. No Baptists would ever dress like that."

A peculiar thought crossed Kate's mind. "What if he's not a *minister* but more of a ...."

Annie put down her rifle. "Reverend?"

Kate slowly stood to her feet. "I wonder if Amanda would recognize him if she saw him?"

"Only one way to find out." Annie trailed behind Kate.

Kate returned to find the other three hard at work, putting together another debris shelter. "Amanda, have you ever seen Lloyd Graves?"

"Years ago. Why?"

"Do you think you could pick him out of a lineup?"

"Probably, what's going on?"

"Did you see him? Did you see Lloyd Graves?" David ceased his work and picked up his rifle.

Instantly, Kate realized her mistake. "David, we don't know anything for sure. And even if we confirm that it's him, we're not going to do anything right now. We're in enough trouble as it is."

"He's responsible for having my dad killed!" David's face contorted with anger.

Vicky had dropped her bundle of twigs and picked up her rifle as well. "He's the reason Sam is gone, also."

Kate put her hands up in the air. "Both of you, put down the guns. If it's Lloyd Graves, we will get him. But we're five people on the run with no food and no backup. We are *not* going to attack an entire compound of murderous thugs! Even if you have no concern for yourselves or the rest of us, think about poor Troy back at the house crying because his mother has been gone two days longer than she was supposed to be. Now, imagine his pain when she doesn't come back at all.

"You both know what it feels like to lose a parent. And if you do something stupid, David, you may get to watch your mother die, just like Vicky did. Because we will not survive if you take on the Reverend out here on his turf.

"Nod if you understand!"

Vicky and David were both upset over the stern scolding but managed to affirm that they understood.

Kate hated herself for using such abrasive words, but she could not risk the two hot-headed teens taking a shot at Graves and getting them all killed. "Amanda, sorry about that. Will you come take a look?"

Amanda seemed to be fighting back tears from being reminded of the terrible loss she and everyone else had suffered. "Sure." She took David's M-4 in order to use the scope and followed Kate.

The two of them lay prone, watching the porch for some time but the man in the priest's collar was nowhere to be seen.

Kate was determined to find out. "Let's wait a little longer."

The sun dipped low over the distant peaks but still nothing. Kate counted as many individuals as she could. Her final approximation was roughly sixty.

"Whoever they are, they're up to no good." Amanda watched diligently.

Finally, the front door of the main cabin opened. The man with the collar stepped out.

"That's the man," Kate said softly.

"It sure is. That's Lloyd Graves." Amanda studied him for a while. "He hasn't changed much."

"Let's get back to our side of the mountain before we're spotted." Kate was careful not to make any excessive noise or step on any fragile branches.

When they returned to camp, the shelter was ready.

"So, what are we going to do? Are we going to get Jack and the others and come back over here?" Vicky quizzed.

"How soon do you think we'll come back? Did you mark our location on the map?" David badgered.

"Just relax!" Kate said authoritatively. "Yes, I marked his compound on the map. But I don't know when we'll come back. Whenever it is, it will be when we are completely prepared. I promise you, Lloyd Graves is a threat, and we will take care of him, one way or another." She put one arm around each of the teens. "Can you trust me on that?"

Both nodded, but neither looked fond of having to wait.

CHAPTER 9

A naughty person, a wicked man, walketh with a froward mouth. He winketh with his eyes, he speaketh with his feet, he teacheth with his fingers; frowardness is in his heart, he deviseth mischief continually; he soweth discord. Therefore shall his calamity come suddenly; suddenly shall he be broken without remedy.

Proverbs 6:12-15

Kate once again awakened her sleeping teammates. "Rise and shine. We've got a long road ahead of us, especially if we want to get home by tonight."

Annie seemed the most eager to get back. "You

think we can make it in one day?"

Kate tenderly put her hand on Annie's shoulder. "Provided we don't run into any trouble and we don't see any signs that we're being tracked, yes. I think we can."

The team seemed invigorated by the prospect of returning home. They readied themselves for the journey and tore down the shelter in half the time it had taken them the day prior. All had followed Kate's advice to keep the MREs for breakfast. Like famished animals, they devoured the meals in record time.

Kate inspected the campsite once more for signs that they'd been there, but everyone had made a spectacular effort in cleaning up after themselves. "Let's move out."

For the next several hours, the team took few breaks. Even Amanda and Annie kept pace without becoming winded. Finally, they reached a small stream just before the Blue Ridge Parkway.

Kate dropped her pack. "Okay, we'll take fifteen minutes here to rest and hydrate. Fill your water containers only a quarter full. We'll stop at another creek later but for now, I want to stay light. When we reach the parkway, we'll sprint for about 300 yards south. Doing that will break the trail for anyone tracking us but expose us to potential vehicular traffic. I want to be on the pavement for as little time as possible."

"What if we're spotted?" Annie asked.

"If we're chased, and it's a small enough crew, we'll stand our ground and fight. If the force is too large for us to take on, we'll make a run for it.

Either way, we'll have to go back into the woods and home will have to wait. We can't take a chance on bringing trouble back to the house."

Annie gazed at the dirt in despair. "Okay."

Kate knelt beside her. "But I watched the parkway the whole time we were at the first camp. I saw no traffic whatsoever. The odds of us running into someone are minimal. We'll get you home to Troy soon."

"Thank you." Annie lifted her chin.

The short break ended and Kate loaded her gear onto her shoulder. "Everyone ready?"

"Let's get this over with." Amanda tightened the straps of her pack.

Kate led the team slowly up the short incline to the roadway above. Once at the top, she watched and listened. She heard nothing. "This is it. Kick as much mud and dirt off of your shoes as possible before we get on the asphalt. We don't want to leave any clues to which way we went."

Kate checked the bottom of her boots before stepping onto the road. She picked up a small stick and cleaned between the treads. She stomped around in the shoulder gravel and took off sprinting south. The others shadowed her.

Without looking at the map, Kate estimated the team's location in relation to the ridgeline that they would follow home. She vaulted from the pavement to the roadside and called out to her group. "Come on, keep going. We're still in jeopardy of being spotted until we get over this hill."

Kate charged up the steep incline, being careful not to break any unnecessary branches which might provide an indication of which way her team was traveling. She reached the pinnacle of the short mound and looked back. Vicky and David were directly behind her but Amanda and Annie were falling behind. "Let's go, let's go!"

The two laggards pressed on and soon reached the summit.

Kate led the way over the top and down the back side of the hill. "Just a little further and we can take a break to catch our breath."

Shortly after, Kate signaled for them to sit. "Let's rest here for five minutes. Once we're farther from the road, we can take a longer break."

David retrieved his water container from his pack and finished it off. Vicky and Amanda did the same.

"How long until we get home?" Annie asked.

Kate took out her map and traced the path. "We should be about three miles from Campbell Creek. We can refill our water there. Afterward, we'll pick up the ridgeline we took to Maggie Valley, which is about another five miles. If we push hard, we'll be home before dark."

Annie was the first to stand up. "I'm ready when you guys are."

Kate's group hiked steadily for the remainder of the day. Though the trail was long, following steep inclines and precipitous drop-offs, which had to be navigated with care, Kate and her team arrived at the house in Laurel Ridge just before sunset.

With a shotgun in her hand, Rita Dean stood up from her rocking chair on the elevated front porch overlooking the woods. "They's back! Them youngins is back!"

"Great." David looked up at the old woman. "Mrs. Dean is on guard duty. We're lucky to have anything to come back to."

Pritchard came out carrying the .270. He looked down over the rail of the porch. "The prodigal children have returned!"

"Trust me, prodigal living had nothing to do with our delay." Kate trudged up the final incline to the house.

Troy came running out the basement door. Annie dropped her gear and knelt to embrace him.

Gavin was next to come out. He sprinted to Kate, looked her over, then wrapped both arms around her. "I was worried sick! Are you okay?"

"Hungry and tired, but yes, we're all fine."

Jack and Rainey came out to greet them. "We didn't know what happened to you," Jack said. "We didn't even know where to begin looking for you all. Where were you?"

"We'll tell you all about it." Kate looked up from Gavin's embrace. "But there's lots to tell and we haven't eaten much in the last three days. Let us get cleaned up and put something in our stomachs, and I'll address the group. You're all going to want to hear what I have to say."

The travelers were famished, so they didn't bother waiting for a hot meal. They ate the leftovers from the last meal eaten by the people in the house, then opened some canned goods. Kate scarfed down two cans of ravioli, a can of fruit cocktail, and an entire sleeve of crackers.

Gavin assisted Judy Hess and Kim Sweeny with

heating several pans of water so the travelers could get cleaned up before Kate's debriefing.

After she finished eating, Kate stood in the shower of the master bedroom. She had to be very conservative with the camping shower which held only 5 gallons of water. She scrubbed her hair hard, feeling grimy from going three days without properly bathing. She longed for the days of standing for hours under a high-pressure stream of steaming hot water. Yet the trip had taught her to be grateful for what she had.

The last of the hot water soon trickled out of the short plastic shower hose and Kate's less than luxurious shower came to an end. She dried off and thrilled at the sensation of putting on clean clothes. She breathed in the beautiful scent of her fresh sweater. Feeling brand new and with a full stomach, she couldn't wait to crawl into the soft sheets of her warm bed. Just thinking about it made her eyes feel heavy, but slumber was not to come just yet. The task of telling the others about her ordeal still lay before her.

Kate made her way to the living room where everyone was gathering. Judy Hess brought Kate a steaming cup of hot tea. "I thought this might make you feel better."

"Thank you." The heat of the drink radiated through the cup and into her fingers.

Jack seemed more anxious than anyone to hear what had happened. "You all made it home, uninjured and alive, so I guess things could have turned out worse."

Gavin also sounded intrigued to know how the

trip had gone. "Plus, it appears your five ounces of gold bought you more guns than you thought."

Kate took a deep breath and readied herself to relive the perilous mission. "Not exactly."

The people who'd remained at the house listened with bated breath and eyes wide as saucers while Kate told of the multiple attacks, time on the lam, and information they'd obtained while at the ranch with Bill's group.

Jack shoved his hands deep into his front pockets. "We've been listening to Radio Rick every day at 3:00, and we haven't heard anything about the nuclear reactors or the federal government's move to Asheville."

"The government broadcasts over the NOAA band didn't say anything about it either," Gavin said. "But you guys probably haven't heard the news from them."

"What news?" Kate asked.

Pritchard gave the reply to her inquiry. "Long has been shot."

"President Long?" Amanda asked.

"Yeah, but wait, the story gets stranger." Gavin stood up from his chair and walked in front of the fireplace. "Rosales is the new president."

"As in General Rosales?" Annie quizzed. "The secretary of defense? What happened to the vice president and the Speaker of the House? I'm no constitutional attorney, but even I know the secretary of defense is way down the line of succession."

Sitting back on the couch, Jack put his arm around Rainey. "Secretary of defense is sixth in line if memory serves me correctly. But, the emergency broadcasts aired on the NOAA band aren't exactly formatted like an official briefing from the White House Press Room. Let's just say they left lots to be desired for anyone expecting full transparency."

"Must have been a coup," David said.

"Maybe not according to the standard definition, but yes," Jack added. "Some type of hostile takeover of the government occurred."

"Perhaps no one else wanted the job," Judy Hess sat on the hearth. "Being made president is like being put in charge of a sinking ship."

"That ain't stopped none of 'em from spendin' billions to get elected to the Oval Office over the past decade." Pritchard wrinkled his brow.

"True," said Kate. "But the actual moment of immersion does seem to be much more imminent. Still, Mr. Pritchard is right. People who've fought their entire lives to get that high up on the food chain typically don't just cast power aside when it's handed to them. It's just not in their DNA to do so."

Gavin smirked. "I'm guessing after Long was shot, the vice president and everyone else on down got anonymous tips saying that if they had any desire to see their next birthday, nine out of ten doctors recommend abdicating the presidency."

"It's all speculation," Kate said. "Rosales is a gun grabber. He's the one who clamped down on gun rights in the big cities when the FEMA commissaries were being attacked. We can also assume he's the one who issued the directive to confiscate our guns. Knowing what level of criminal he is beyond that doesn't help our cause."

"If the news that you got from your friends up the road is true, he'll be living in our backyard soon enough." Jack stared at the fire.

Kate added, "Bill and Jan's group are thinking of moving to Bryson City to get out of Forrestal's reach."

Jack snorted. "Bryson isn't out of reach, especially if Rosales decides to hand his military commanders carte blanche."

"Any despot willing to jump over the laws of the land to seize power will stop at nothing to hold the reigns once he has them." Gavin continued to pace in front of the fireplace. "Who's to say Rosales wasn't behind Long getting shot in the first place?"

Kate stood up. "I love a good conspiracy theory as much as the next gal, but I've got to hit the hay. The last three days have been brutal."

Gavin hugged her. "I'll be along in a minute. It's good to have you home."

She kissed him. "It's good to be home."

CHAPTER 10

A wrathful man stirreth up strife: but he that is slow to anger appeaseth strife.

Proverbs 15:18

Kate gently ran her fingers across Gavin's arm Tuesday morning, being careful not to touch his injured shoulder. She smiled playfully and snuggled up close to him in the bed.

He cleared his throat and flicked his eyes toward Vicky's bed, reminding Kate that they were not alone.

Kate sighed and pulled the covers up over her shoulders. "Good morning, Gavin." She looked across the room to see her niece lacing up her boots. "Good morning Vicky."

She looked up. "Good morning, Aunt Kate. I noticed that you didn't say anything to Jack about what you saw on the other side of our last campsite."

"What's she talking about?" Gavin inquired.

"The Reverend's compound. We stumbled upon it."

"And you didn't think to tell me?" Gavin pulled away.

Kate huffed. "I was out like a light last night. I was going to tell you first thing this morning."

"What about Jack? When are you planning to tell him?" Vicky prodded.

"When the time is right. He's emotionally raw over losing Kelly."

"Everyone is emotionally raw right now, Aunt Kate. Myself included. We all want to see justice served before we lose our chance. You should talk to Jack before someone else does."

"Like who? You?" Kate sat up.

"No. I'm not the only one who knows about this compound and wants the Reverend's head on a platter. Annie Cobb lost her mother and father to that monster. The Reverend is responsible for killing David's dad who also happens to be Amanda's husband, so I'm the least of your worries."

"Then I can count on you to let me choose the time to talk to Jack?"

"I'll give you a couple of days, Aunt Kate. None of us want to see this thing dragged out any longer than it has to be." Vicky walked to the door. "I've got guard duty. I'll see you later."

Kate felt the pressure of the decision over her head. "She wants blood."

"So does everyone else," Gavin took her hand.

She sighed. "That's what I'm afraid of. That compound might as well be Fort Knox. We don't stand a chance against them. We're literally a group of widows, old people, and children; besides you and Jack of course." She inspected the bandage over his wound. "And even you are on the mend. How's that coming anyway?"

"Better, but it still hurts." He ran his hand through her hair. "You're correct about us not being in the position to attack the Reverend, but you need to trust that Jack will make the right call. And you need to do it soon before one of the others lets the cat out of the bag. If that happens, you'll lose Jack's confidence and you'll have less influence in helping him make the best decision for the camp."

"You're right. I'll go talk to him now." Kate hated to leave the soft warm bed, but she had to get this thing taken care of.

Kate got dressed and headed out to the kitchen. Rita Dean and Judy Hess were making pancakes.

"Smells great!" Kate said.

"Fix you a plate of 'em. Don't be shy." Mrs. Dean flipped two more hotcakes out of the pan.

"Have either of you seen Jack this morning?"

Judy nodded solemnly. "He walked over the hill to Apple Blossom Acres. I think he was going to visit Kelly's grave."

The big meal Kate had eaten the night prior was long gone and her stomach growled at the scent of the pancakes. "Would you be offended if I took two of these with me?"

"If I was that easily offended, girl, I wouldn't stand much of a chance of making it in this ol' world. Go on and get you some." Rita Dean shook her spatula. "We might have real maple syrup for 'em come spring."

Kate gathered a few of the smaller flapjacks. "Oh yeah? We have the right trees for that?"

"Any maple tree will make maple syrup." Mrs. Dean poured more batter into the pan. "Sugar maples are better. It takes about 60 gallons of sap to get 1 gallon of syrup from these maples around here. But only takes 40 gallons of sap to get a gallon of syrup from a sugar maple."

"I'll be looking forward to that." Kate wrapped her pancakes in a paper towel and slung her AK over her shoulder. "Thanks, ladies."

Kate prayed as she walked over the mountain top and down to her old neighborhood. "God, please give me wisdom. Help me to choose the right words, and help Jack to stay calm. I realize this man who calls himself the Reverend is an evil man and the world will be a better place if we get rid of him, but we're in no position to take him on right now. Help Jack, Vicky, and the others to not be overtaken by their desire for vengeance." She saw Jack in the distance scratching out a patch of dirt next to Kelly's grave. Kate looked toward heaven. "Thanks for getting us home. I love you. Talk soon."

She slowed her pace as she approached Jack's position. "Hey." Kate looked down to see the marking on the ground that he'd made with the barrel of his rifle. He stood in the middle of a rectangle the shape of another grave next to Kelly's. "Whatcha doing?"

"I don't know. It just seems like she got the better end of this deal." He looked at the small homemade wooden cross marking his wife's burial site.

"It's tough to be the one left behind. But Rainey needs you. So do the rest of us."

"But a guy can wish, right?" His eyes welled up. His voice cracked. "I just miss her so bad."

Kate grabbed him and pulled him close.

Jack wailed in agony of soul. "I just want to be where she is, Kate. Is that so wrong?"

Kate could see the graves of Penny, Terry, and Sam from where she was standing, she understood his pain. "No, it's not so wrong, Jack. But it's not the answer. We have to keep fighting, to honor them. We have to keep fighting for those who are still here; for Vicky, and Rainey, and the rest of our friends at the house."

"I know." He dried his eyes with his sleeve.

Kate took a deep breath in anticipation of what she was about to say. "I didn't divulge all the intel we gathered at last night's debrief."

Jack still seemed lost in his grief. "Okay."

"We located the Reverend's lair."

The statement seemed to quickly penetrate through his absent-mindedness. His expression hardened and he looked up at her. "What do you mean?"

"We found his compound. I was able to identify roughly sixty individuals. That's not counting the ones who were inside. My best estimate is that he has between eighty and one hundred people, men and women. Most of them were carrying guns."

"All combatants?"

Kate thought about the rough looking women of the camp. "I don't think that's the primary role of the females, but none of them looked like they'd think twice about killing."

Jack's eyes were red with anger. "If I kill Lloyd, the rest of them will scatter."

"That's not rational. If you kill the Reverend, another of his minions will rise up to take his place. They'll chase you down and kill you."

"And I'll go to my grave feeling satisfied."

"No, you won't. Your final seconds will be filled with regret knowing that you've abandoned Rainey in a world filled with monsters. You'll breathe your last breath wondering how she's going to get by without a mother or a father."

Jack glared at Kate, as if he were infuriated with her for taking away his dream of getting revenge and leaving the pain behind. His fists clenched around the handle of his AR-15. "I'm not going to let this demon get away with what he did."

"Nobody is asking you to. I'm only suggesting that you take your time, think it out, and wait until we have the strength to strike a decisive blow."

Jack seemed discouraged. He turned back to his wife's grave. "How do you propose we do that?"

"I don't know. But we'll figure it out. We're not the last good guys on the planet." Kate perked up to a distant sound.

"Did you hear that?" Jack looked toward the bottom of the hill.

"Yeah, it sounded like a car engine."

"In our neighborhood." Jack marched toward the street. "Come on."

Kate grabbed his sleeve. "We should go get backup."

"There's no time." Jack pulled away from her. "You can go get backup if you want. Meet me down the hill."

"I'm not letting you go alone." She tugged his jacket once more. "Let's at least approach from the woods."

He paused as if considering her request. "Okay, we can do that."

Kate led the way back to the perimeter trail. She and Jack followed it down toward the noise they'd heard. Jack shouldered his rifle. "It's the military! They're stealing Don's pickup!"

Kate looked on. "I count at least six of them. We can't engage."

"Look there's more!" Jack stayed low but continued down the path which kept them out of view from the soldiers on the street.

"Keep your voice down. We have no leaves to buffer the sound." Kate trailed close behind him. "This doesn't make any sense. They have Humvees. Why would the military be out stealing civilian vehicles?"

"No way! They're at my house and they're taking my van!" Jack leveled his rifle. "I've had too many things taken from me, Kate. My wife, my guns, my neighborhood, I can't sit back and allow it any longer."

She pushed the barrel down toward the ground.

"It's a van. I know how much you've lost, but this isn't the fight where you throw it all away. Not for a vehicle. Hardly anyone has gas, and what we do have, we need for the chainsaws so we can keep from freezing. It's just a van. Let it go."

Jack jerked the barrel of the rifle away from her hand and began marching up the hill. "Come on, let's get back to the house. We need to let everyone else know what's going on. And we need to get ready to fight, in case they come to loot Laurel Ridge."

Kate could feel Jack's anger toward her, but she didn't care. If he'd pulled that trigger, it would have been her last day on the earth as well.

CHAPTER 11

Thou shalt make thy prayer unto him, and he shall hear thee, and thou shalt pay thy vows.

Job 22:7

Kate paced back and forth on the porch overlooking the woods below, which were darkened by a cloudy moonless night.

"You should sit down. It's not like you're going to be able to see anything." Gavin sat in a rocker at the corner of the porch.

"I know. We need to pull that night vision scope out of the stash. We never should have sealed it off in the closet."

"None of us were thinking clearly when we moved over to Laurel Ridge. I'll pull it out in the morning. We've still got enough joint compound and paint to seal off the closet once more. It would be smart to stash those M-4s in the closet and pull out our weapons anyway. Getting caught with guns is one thing. Getting caught with weapons stolen from murdered soldiers is a whole other bag of worms."

"It was self-defense."

"You're preaching to the choir. I'm just telling it the way the military will spin it if they show up."

"Yeah, well, I don't think Jack is planning on letting the military come inside anyhow. At least not while he's still alive."

"What do you think?"

"I don't know." She paused from pacing. "Bill said he'd put in a good word for us if our group wanted to go to Bryson City with them."

Gavin adjusted his rifle. "I don't know about that. It would be like we're begging to go to some compound where one guy is making all the rules."

"Isn't it worth it if it means we have a reasonable chance of surviving? The military will be back and if we stand up to them, it will be the end of us all."

"Did you mention Bryson City to Jack?"

"No. It was all I could do yesterday to keep him from engaging an entire squad of soldiers. He's on a hair trigger and borderline suicidal."

"Maybe not the best person to be making decisions for our entire group, then."

She looked out at the blackness. "I don't know. Everyone is shaken up. Jack's a good guy. He's been like a rock for this community. They all trust him. I know you don't much believe in this kind of stuff but I think we just have to pray for him to come around."

"You might be surprised."

"By what?" She turned to look at him after the unexpected comment.

"By what I believe in these days."

"Explain."

Gavin took a deep breath and let it out. "It's personal."

"Too late to hide behind that. You can't set me up like that then jerk it away like Lucy with the football. Besides, I'm your wife. No secrets."

Gavin toyed with the sling of his rifle. "While you were gone, I kinda made a deal with God."

"Oh really. How did that go?"

"I had no idea where you were or what you were going through. I've never felt so vulnerable and powerless in my entire life. Every terrible thought you can imagine raced through my mind. Every day that you didn't come home, it got worse. I was going to come search for you but I didn't even know where to start looking."

He looked up at her. "I was broken, Kate. Not knowing if I'd ever see you again, kiss your lips, or hold you in my arms. I told you that I loved you, and I meant it when I said it, but when I was faced with losing you, I realized just how much I love you. The night before you came home, I fell on my face on the bedroom floor. I told God that if He would bring you home that I would never question His existence again. I told Him that I would do my best to live according to His ways and that I'd try to get to know Him through reading His book. He held up His end of the bargain. Now I have to hold up mine."

"Wow!" Her heart fluttered. "That's amazing." She sat on his knee for a while but felt her eyes getting heavy. After a few minutes, she got back to resuming her pacing.

"Come sit back down by me."

"I need to keep moving. It's keeping me warm and it's keeping me awake. We've been up for twenty hours. Aren't you tired?"

"I'll be ready to hit the sack when our shift is over."

"Which shouldn't be too much longer." Kate watched the first glow of dawn appear behind the mountains.

Suddenly, the radio sprang to life. It was Annie. "We've got movement on the road leading up to the house."

Gavin vaulted from his chair and led the way into the house. Kate followed.

Jack rushed down the stairs yelling. "Everyone up! We have a potential situation!"

Vicky emerged from the master bedroom looking drowsy but holding her rifle.

David and Amanda came from their room down the hall, also armed.

"Kate, Gavin, follow me." Jack led them through the kitchen toward the side door. "Everyone else, prepare to defend the house with your life."

Jack, Kate, and Gavin slipped silently out the kitchen door and made their way to Annie and Pritchard's guard post in the garden shed. Annie pointed at the beams of multiple flashlights coming up the road. "Looks like soldiers."

Jack whispered. "Pritchard, you and Annie cut around to the big chestnut tree and take cover behind it. We'll go down the opposite side of the road and flank them from both directions."

"How will we know where you are so we don't shoot you?" Annie asked softly.

"I'll turn on my tactical light when we're ready to engage," Jack replied.

"We're going to just take them out?" Kate inquired.

Gavin added, "If we do that, we'll have to come straight back and pack up. They'll have a death squad here in thirty minutes. We need to be long gone by then."

"I can't think of any other choice." Jack pulled the butt of his rifle tight against his shoulder.

"We could take them alive. Get information. See how far out the next platoon is," Kate said.

Jack shook his head. "I don't like it. We won't break them that fast."

"Even so," Gavin said. "It would buy us some time. If we can avoid a firefight and them calling it in, the other troops won't be looking for them until they don't show up to wherever they're supposed to be next. If we have an hour to break camp instead of thirty minutes, that could be the difference between life and death."

Jack relented, "Okay, we'll try it your way. But anything other than immediate and unconditional surrender, we open fire and take our chances with the consequences."

"Agreed." Kate got into position to follow Jack down the hill.

Jack motioned for Pritchard and Annie to move out first, then he led Kate and Gavin toward the six glowing flashlight beams. They walked as quietly as possible until they were right on top of the soldiers.

"Drop your weapons. You're completely surrounded." Jack pressed on his tactical light. Kate and Gavin did likewise.

The soldiers froze in their tracks.

"Do it now, or you're all dead," Jack reiterated his command.

All six of them complied.

"Step away from the rifles. Interlace your fingers behind your head." Jack emerged from the bushes.

The men did as they were told.

"How many other soldiers are out here with you?" Kate asked.

"Just us, ma'am," one replied.

"Just you." Gavin shined his light in the young man's face. "Why would the Army send six men out for a predawn raid?"

"We're not with the Army," he answered.

Gavin lowered the light to the insignia on the man's uniform. "That's not what the patches on your fatigues say."

"Yes, sir. We've only recently resigned our positions with that particular employer. We had no other clothing."

"Resigned?" Kate found his statement bewildering.

"Yes, ma'am. We refuse to acknowledge the new Commander in Chief. We feel he came to power in a surreptitious and illegal manner. We also believe that he is abusing his office. Thus, we do not consider our break with the organization to be desertion. Rather we see our resignation as the honorable and necessary course of action to absolve us of being complicit in what is happening with the federal government."

"Why are you in our neighborhood?" Gavin asked.

"Simply looking for a place to lay our heads for the night, sir. We were part of a search team that inspected this street after a local skirmish last week and found it to be unoccupied. We had no knowledge of your presence. If you'd be so kind as to allow us to leave, we'll be on our way and I assure you that we will not be a problem in the future."

Jack circled around all of them. "I'm not buying it."

Kate countered, "Jack, you've gone off on more tangents than I can count in the past week about how disgusted you are with the military, how all the soldiers should walk away and quit propping up this totalitarian regime. Now we actually meet six of them that had the guts to do it and you don't believe them."

"Claim to have done it." Jack inspected each man one at a time.

"You have to give them a chance," she insisted.

"I'll give them a chance. With no guns and zip ties on their wrists."

Kate looked regretfully at the man who'd been representing them. She read his name. "Is that okay with you, Sergeant Garcia?"

"You folks are the ones with the guns, ma'am."

His reply was courteous. "But with all due respect, if we weren't alone, don't you think you'd be surrounded by now?"

Kate looked around. The gentle glow of morning was bright enough to see that no other forces were in the immediate vicinity. "He's got a point, Jack."

"Then we won't have to use them as hostages or human shields when the posse arrives. But until I have more information, I'm not taking any chances." Jack lifted his radio. "David, can you run some zip ties down to the bottom of the driveway?"

"10-4. Be right there."

CHAPTER 12

Let brotherly love continue. Be not forgetful
to entertain strangers: for thereby some have
entertained angels unawares.

Hebrews 13:1-2

Kate leaned against the basement wall of the
Laurel Ridge house, watching the captives as Jack
continued with the interrogation.

Mrs. Dean and Kim Sweeny came to the bottom
of the basement stairs. Kim carried a large dish.
"Here's the food you asked us to make, Kate."

"Thank you. If you'll set it on that stack of bins,
I'll take care of serving it." Kate stepped out of their
way.

Mrs. Dean seemed much more comfortable with
the situation than did Kim Sweeny, who smiled

nervously at the six men sitting on the floor with wrist restraints.

Once the food had been delivered, Kate said, "We have to cut their restraints so they can eat, Jack."

His lips grew tight. "Okay, but ankle restraints stay on. If anyone tries anything, we gun them all down. Gavin, Mr. Pritchard, keep your fingers on your triggers and watch them close. Kate, you and Annie hand out the food; and no knives, not even butter knives."

Kate began plating the food and handing it to Annie to pass out.

Sergeant Garcia insisted on being served last and only accepted a plate after all his men had received their food.

Kate asked the sergeant, "Some other soldiers were in the neighborhood on the other side of the mountain yesterday. They were commandeering civilian vehicles."

"Let's call it what it is, Kate." Jack maintained his rigid expression. "They were stealing." Jack glared at Sergeant Garcia. "Any idea why?"

The sergeant nodded. "A third wave of Locusts hit two days ago. The viruses targeted communication and observation satellites, nuclear reactors, and military vehicles. Most of the Army's transport vehicles are trashed. The military is scrambling to keep it together right now. Colonel Forrestal issued an order to seek out civilian vehicles to maintain our mobility. We had already decided to resign, but that motivated us to walk out at our next available opportunity. The ensuing confusion also propped the door open for us."

"Military vehicles were disabled by the virus but not civilian vehicles? How is that?" Gavin asked.

Garcia finished chewing his food. "My guess is that the bug somehow infected the military's diagnostics software, hid as a Pentagon update or something. All military equipment is maintained using similar diagnostic computers. Whatever it was, it took down everything: choppers, planes, UAVs, trucks, Hummers, MRAPs, all of it."

Jack rubbed his chin. "I was starting to think maybe Rosales could have been behind the Locusts. But if he is, he cut off his own hand with that one."

Garcia added, "I don't think so, sir. I believe General Rosales is an opportunist. This latest development has been devastating to his already-fragile grip on power."

"Elaborate." Jack seemed to be softening toward Garcia.

"I'm not sure how much you folks know about what is really going on. The news bulletins put out for public consumption are a mix of half-truths and propaganda."

Pritchard interrupted. ("That ain't no different than it was 'fore them computers went down.")

Kate cut the old man off before he could embark on a tirade. "We've recently become aware of the schism between reality and what's being reported. But go ahead. Assume we only know what we've been told."

Garcia continued. "Prior to the attacks, Rosales intended on moving the federal government to Asheville. The nuclear reactors which were infected by the viruses were successfully SCRAMed but it could take decades for the rods to become stable enough to not require constant maintenance and observation."

Annie cut him off. "Rosales has changed his mind about relocating to Asheville?"

"No, ma'am. General Rosales is still relocating to Asheville, but the federal government no longer exists; at least not the same cohesive structure we had three days ago. Two other generals are challenging his claim to the presidency. General Bird has co-opted all of the top leadership in the southwest and General Holstead has assumed command of a patriot rebellion in the inland Pacific Northwest."

"A rebellion? That just started within the past three days?" Kate asked.

"It germinated back in late October when General Rosales as Defense Secretary used his expanded FEMA powers to issue the temporary gun ban on major cities. When he announced that he was stepping into the Oval Office, the patriots up there already had a special place for him in their hearts. My understanding is that it was like a bed of hot coals and the announcement was like a strong breeze which caused the rebellion to ignite into a blaze."

"What do you know about these other two generals?" Gavin asked.

"General Bird's move was a power grab, no different than Rosales'. Holstead, however, he had already issued stand-down orders to his troops concerning the growing rebellion in the northwest.

He and Rosales were going to lock horns sooner or later anyway. The latest wave of computer viruses simply accelerated the timeline."

"Then you think he's a good person?" Kate asked.

"Yes, ma'am. Once we get our footing, we intend to head up that way."

Jack relaxed his stance, but his finger was still on the trigger guard of his rifle. "To join up with General Holstead?"

"Yes, sir."

Kate watched Jack. She could tell he was thinking. "These guys have been up all day. They need to get some rest. Do you think we could let them stay in one of the houses down the street?"

Jack didn't answer her. He stared at Garcia. "Do you think Forrestal will stay loyal to Rosales?"

"Yes, sir. Rosales gave him his command."

"Do you think Colonel Forrestal will be sending troops around to look for guns?" Jack's eyes darted down the row of uniformed men.

"No, sir. He's fighting just to keep a lid on everything. We won't be the only men from his camp to resign. He'll try to hold it together until things stabilize, regroup his forces, then resume his mission."

"What, exactly, is his mission?" Annie inquired.

"To establish a secure perimeter for General Rosales' national government in Asheville. He's got all he can handle for now, but that will eventually entail rounding up the guns and subjugating the population."

Jack finally answered Kate's previous question.

"You can put them up in one of the houses, but we keep their guns for now."

"Can we cut their feet loose?" she asked.

"Go ahead." Jack turned to Garcia. "Don't mistake my hospitality for weakness. If you double-cross me, I'll kill every one of you." He left the basement and walked up the stairs.

Kate and Annie cut the restraints from the soldiers' feet. Apologetically, Kate said to the sergeant, "We've been through a lot. Jack is actually a nice guy."

Garcia looked less than convinced. "I'll have to take your word for it, ma'am."

Minutes later, Kim Sweeny came back down the stairs. She handed a set of keys to Kate. "The soldiers can use my house."

"That's very kind of you, ma'am," said Garcia. "I promise that we'll take good care of it."

"I know you will." Kim smiled. "There should be plenty of bedding in the closets. We've got five bedrooms and a pullout in the den."

"We'll walk you down." Kate signaled for Gavin to come with her. "Mr. Pritchard, can you and Annie see about getting our guests some water and maybe a few snacks?"

"We'll take care of that." Annie headed upstairs with Pritchard behind her.

Kate and Gavin escorted the men past the burned remains of the Hess house and down to the home Kim had once shared with her deceased husband, Herman. She opened the front door.

"This is a very nice home. I can't tell you how much we appreciate it." Garcia waited for his men to get inside. "I'm also very grateful for you sticking up for us."

"Sure. We'll see you soon." Kate and Gavin returned home for some much needed rest.

CHAPTER 13

Son of man, when the land sinneth against me by trespassing grievously, then will I stretch out mine hand upon it, and will break the staff of the bread thereof, and will send famine upon it, and will cut off man and beast from it.

Ezekiel 14:13

Thursday afternoon, Kate fought her impulse to snicker. "It's no different than cutting up a chicken that you bought at the store."

Vicky turned away from the squirrel she was skinning. She placed her knife on the stump and gagged. "I never bought chickens at the store and I never cut them up. The one time I watched Mom do it, the guts were already out, so this *is* different; very different."

"Give them to me." Kate finished cleaning her last animal and began processing Vicky's kills.

"I could do it if I had to." Vicky passed four squirrels to Kate. "I don't mind shooting them, but seeing the guts turns my stomach."

Kate made a small incision near the back of the neck of the next squirrel and began pulling the skin back like a jacket and trousers. "You did better than me on the hunt. I missed two. Your accuracy has really improved. It's a skill that will serve you well in this environment. If you can knock a squirrel out of a tree from fifty yards away, you'll have no problem hitting a much larger human target."

Vicky looked up at the bare tree limbs. "Squirrels don't shoot back. And a .22 doesn't kick as hard as an AK-47."

"Yeah, but the kick doesn't come until after you've pulled the trigger of the AK."

Vicky smirked. "Yeah, try telling my brain that."

"Remember what Scott taught us. The best way to train for that impulsive jerk is to practice dry firing. You have to outsmart your brain."

"I would if I had time." Vicky ran her hand over the .22 rifle. "What are we going to hunt with when we run out of ammo for these?"

"From the looks of things, we'll run out of squirrels before we run out of bullets. We spent all morning and part of the afternoon to get six. But, we can live on the chickens and rabbits which Mr. Pritchard breeds."

Gavin came sprinting down through the woods

coming from the direction of Ernest Martin's old place on top of the mountain. "Kate, your friends from the ranch want to talk to you. They're holding on the radio for you."

"Can you finish this up?" She picked up a towel and wiped her hands.

Vicky walked toward the house. "I'll find David. He'll do it for me."

Abandoning her task, Kate followed Gavin back up the mountain. "Did Radio Rick have anything informative to say?"

"Not really." Gavin picked his way up a trail that was becoming worn by regular traffic. "You know how it is. If he says anything substantive, Colonel Forrestal will find him and shut him down."

Jack was standing at the back door of the Martin house. He waved for Kate to follow him inside. "Come on, they're waiting!"

Kate hurried up the ladder to the loft behind Jack. She took the radio. "Go for Kate." She waited for the man acting as a repeater to relay her message.

"Kate, it's Bill. We need to talk."

She pressed the button on the side of the radio once more. "I'd love to, but we had … car trouble on the way home last time we came to see you." The man in the middle restated her response.

Bill snickered over the radio. "Yeah, and you hit a couple of potholes on the way here, didn't you? How about we come see you?"

Kate looked at Gavin, who'd climbed up the ladder despite his shoulder which hadn't completely healed. She then turned her attention to Jack.

He shook his head. "You can't give out our position over the radio."

"They know where we are," Kate replied.

Jack crossed his arms and looked out the loft window. "We're taking a lot of risks."

"Not knowing what they have to tell us is even riskier," Gavin rebutted. "These people were prepared for any disaster. We need to keep our relationship with them alive at all costs."

"It very well may be at all costs." Jack walked past Kate and headed back down the ladder. "Go ahead. Set it up. I'll see you back at the house."

She pressed the talk key. "When can we expect you?" The message was echoed by the repeater.

"Tomorrow morning. We'll drive up to your old neighborhood and walk over to your present location."

"See you then. Be safe." Her reply was quickly parroted by the man in between.

"We will. We know what to watch out for."

Kate powered off the radio. "We should have a nice lunch prepared for them when they come. It's the least we can do to repay the hospitality they showed us when my team went there. We can make it a grand feast. Everyone can use a distraction. We missed out on Thanksgiving, this will be good for us. Maybe we can even have Sergeant Garcia and his men up to share the meal with us."

Gavin held up his hand. "Hold your horses. I know you mean well, but emotions are still raw. Everyone won't see this the same way you do. Some people will see it as a strain on resources and a stressful event to have strangers in the camp."

"Some people, as in Jack?" She gazed out the loft window.

"I'm afraid you might get pushback from other people besides Jack. These people have lost almost everything and almost everyone." Gavin put his arm around her. "About Garcia's men, let's take it slow with that also. I'm not as suspicious as Jack, but I'm not ready to bring them into the inner sanctum either."

Kate let out a long slow breath, like a balloon being deflated. "Okay, but I'm going to make sure Bill and his team have a nice meal, even if I have to do it myself."

"You won't. I'm sure Judy, Kim, and Mrs. Dean will be more than willing to help. All three of them have been great at keeping up the laundry, meal planning, and everything else so the rest of us can focus on security, food procurement, and taking care of the animals."

Friday morning, Kate, Jack, and Gavin kept watch from the top of Apple Blossom Acres, waiting for Bill and his team to arrive. All three of them stayed deep behind the cover of the trees. Jack spoke softly. "If this thing goes sour, retreat back to the house. We can't help your friends if they've been followed and gotten themselves in trouble with Forrestal."

"Even though they've done so to try helping us?" Kate's reply was louder than it should have been.

Gavin entered the conversation as arbiter. "How about we wait and assess the situation as it presents itself. In all likelihood, being the prepared individuals that they are, they've operated with caution and we'll have nothing to worry about."

Kate affirmed her willingness to accept the terms. "Fine by me."

Jack said nothing. Rather he took another look down the road through the scope.

An hour later, Kate saw a brown Jeep Cherokee ascending the steep pavement of the subdivision. "Here they come." She saw a white, older-model, Silverado following close behind.

"Keep out of sight until we know they haven't been tailed." Jack remained still.

Both vehicles drove past Kate's position and parked beyond Mr. Pritchard's former house.

"Are these your people?" Jack inquired.

"That's them." She watched Bill and Dennis get out of the Jeep. Bobby Donovan and Vince exited the Silverado.

"What's up with Whitesnake?" Gavin chuckled. "This guy's hair is straight out of the eighties."

"Whitesnake?" Jack looked inquisitively at Kate.

She rolled her eyes. "It was the name of a metal band back in the eighties. Spandex, makeup, bandanas tied around their wrists, and hair; lots of hair."

Jack was threatening to lose the stern expression he'd worn on his face since Kelly died. "What would you know about the eighties?"

She slowly stood up. "Terry listened to those bands until well into the nineties. I'd hang out in his room when we were young. He had posters of all those bands on his wall. I thought it was cool." She brushed the leaves off her legs. "I was a little kid. I didn't know any better."

"What about the other guy with the flattop?" Jack followed Kate.

"Bobby Donovan. Everyone calls him Sarge."

"I can see why," said Gavin.

Kate put her fingers to her mouth and made two short shrill whistles, which could have been a bird call, but no particular species that she knew of.

Dennis spun around with his weapon ready to fire. The other three did also.

Kate waved her hands. "We come in peace."

Bill's look of concern melted into a smile. "Kate. It's good to see you."

"Good to see you, too." Kate led Gavin and Jack closer, then made introductions.

Afterward, both teams walked to the Laurel Ridge house, discussing recent developments on the way.

"We got some new neighbors," Kate picked her way through the trail.

"Oh?" Bill traveled near her.

Passing between two trees, she pulled her rifle close. "Soldiers from Forrestal's camp. Said they could no longer be a part to what was going on with Forrestal and Rosales."

"Yep," Sarge added. "We had a few of them boys show up over at our place. Back when I was in, we'd have all walked off the job if the government would have pulled something like this. But, this generation has been separated from history. They have no connection to the past, for the most part. At least not like we did growing up.

"The Army had me watching the commies over

125

in Korea when I should have been watching the ones in my own backyard. The pinkos took over the schools, the news, and Hollywood. It's a wonder any of these kids can think for themselves."

"You have deserters staying in your camp?" Jack inquired of Dennis.

"Twelve of them. They've helped us out with information."

Bill smiled at Kate. "You'll never guess where we ran into them."

"Let me try," she replied. "The old ghost town amusement park."

Bill laughed. "Yep."

Kate continued, "The guys who showed up here had some interesting things to say also. We'll tell you all about it over lunch."

CHAPTER 14

And I am come down to deliver them out of the hand of the Egyptians, and to bring them up out of that land unto a good land and a large, unto a land flowing with milk and honey...

Exodus 3:8a

Kate, Gavin, Jack, and the visitors from the ranch remained at the table after lunch Friday afternoon.

"You folks have some fine cooks. Your group would make a great addition to the Bryson Citadel." Bill pushed his chair back.

"We haven't received an official invitation, so what's the use in us discussing it with our group?"

Kate slid her water glass to the center of the table.

"Consider this an official invitation," said Bill.

Gavin asked, "You've talked to the guy about us?"

"I did." Bill toyed with his napkin. "Morgan asked me to meet everyone in your group. He said if I thought you would all be a good fit, that I had the authority to give an invitation."

"I didn't realize we were being evaluated." Jack sounded perturbed. "Would this fellow be opposed to meeting us? After all, the feelings need to be mutual."

Kate barely noticed Jack's annoyance. She was simply elated that he was considering the move at all. "So you would do it? You'd move?"

Jack held up a hand. "Hang on, Kate. I just made an observation. That's a decision which would require a lot of consideration and a lot of information. Even then, we'd have to put it before the group for a final determination."

"What information do you need about Bryson Citadel?" Dennis inquired.

Jack thought for a moment. "What type of housing is available? Between our two groups, we're talking about a lot of people."

"Morgan has built several small guest cabins as well as a couple of larger structures, bunkhouses more or less. You might not have your own room, but you'll have a warm dry place to lay your head at night," Bill said.

"Sounds a little bit like a FEMA camp." Gavin's brow wrinkled.

"He has 400 acres, mostly woodlands. We'll be

welcomed to build cabins, bring in trailers, or whatever else we can to accommodate more people," Sarge added.

"Trailers? So he's not running this thing like some snooty HOA?" Jack's eyes were leery.

"Not at all. I've already lined up some trailers for people in our group." Vince flipped his hair back out of his face.

"You can get trailers?" Kate asked.

"Slightly used."

"How much?" She inquired.

"Depends. What do you have to trade? Any more of those like you gave me for the rifles?"

"Perhaps. Let's say I did. Would that get me a trailer?"

"Five of them? Yeah, that would probably get you a nice travel trailer."

"What about a house trailer?"

Vince looked at the ceiling and exhaled deeply. "Moving a house trailer is a big job. What about a nice big fifth wheel?"

Kate was enjoying the negotiations. "What about 2 fifth wheels?"

"No way. Not for five."

"Suppose I had ten. Could I buy 2 fifth wheels and a small travel trailer?"

Vince looked her in the eye. "Are you ready to buy or is this all hypothetical?"

"We're trying to make up our mind about Bryson. Knowing if we can afford some type of housing besides living in the bunkhouses is going to go a long way in helping us decide," she responded.

"If you're moving to Bryson, come talk to me.

I'll make something happen for you. But I'm not going to commit to a deal like that if you're not ready to buy."

"What about cash?" Gavin looked at Vince. "How much will a trailer sell for?"

"Sorry, bro." Vince pulled his hair out of his eyes. "The dollar is backed by the full faith and credit of the United States. Since all that isn't going so well, it's basically just a piece of paper. If you've got a stash of bills, you should try to spend them if you know someone who's selling anything for them. Other than gold and silver, we're pretty much on a straight barter economy at this point."

"What about defense?" Jack directed the question to Bill.

He replied, "We've got plenty of rifles and plenty of people who know how to operate them."

"We could use more ammunition though," Sarge added. "The boys who came to stay with us say Forrestal's camp is brimming with ammo. If we ever lock horns with him, we'll have to even up those munitions numbers one way or the other."

"Sounds like you've already moved in." Kate raised her eyebrows at Bill.

"We've started the process." He nodded slowly. "We have a lot of supplies and a lot of people. We don't want to leave a giant footprint like the children of Israel moving across the desert."

She giggled. "That's understandable."

"Moving is a big process, even for a small group like yours." Bill turned his attention to Jack. "So, if it's something you think you'd consider, you should get the ball rolling sooner rather than later."

Jack seemed deep in thought. "Sarge, you said something about locking horns with Forrestal. Isn't that why you're moving to Bryson, to avoid a conflict by staying out of his territory?"

"Yes, sir. But with the federal government dissolving into the ether, Forrestal and Rosales will eventually devolve into warlords. No governmental structure means no taxes. Standing armies can survive the freezing cold, the scorching heat, they can march through the bowels of hell, but a lack of money will destroy them every time. Unless they adapt, that is. I'm betting on Rosales being the type who will adapt to his environment.

"He's already proved he has no problem taking guns. I'm sure he'd find no moral dilemma in confiscating food and provisions."

Gavin stared at the man's even flattop. "What did you mean by saying we need to even out the munitions one way or the other?"

"Exactly what it sounds like. Either we have to find more ammo, he needs to lose some or a combination of the two."

Kate needed more clarification on the statement. "Like, by any means necessary?"

Sarge looked at Dennis.

Dennis answered Kate. "You folks decide if you'd like to be a part of the Bryson Citadel. If the answer is yes, we'll talk more in depth about our plans."

Jack drummed his fingers on the table top. "If you have designs on poking the bear, that could weigh heavily on our choice."

Bill spoke politely. "Once a bear has started

going through neighborhoods and tipping over garbage cans rooting for trash, addressing the problem head-on is the only responsible thing to do. Taking action against a nuisance animal can hardly be labeled as an unwarranted provocation."

Jack pressed his lips together tightly as if he'd run out of opposing statements for the debate. "When do we need to let you know?"

"A couple of days at most." Dennis stood up.

Vince also got up from the table. "Less if you're gonna want those trailers. I need time on that."

Kate's mind was spinning. "This theoretical bear hunt; is that something that would take place only after everyone was settled in at the Bryson Citadel? Theoretically, that is?"

Bill glanced at Dennis, then back to Kate. "Theoretically, yes. But such an expedition wouldn't be launched out of Bryson. We have no desire to have such an animal causing problems for our newly established community."

Jack shook hands with the guests. "I'll talk it over with our group and have an answer to you by tomorrow."

"What about the six men staying down the street?" Kate asked.

Bill nodded. "If they walked out on Forrestal, that tells me everything I need to know about those soldiers. Please relay my invitation for them to join us at Bryson Citadel."

"I will. I suppose they'd make good bear hunters."

Bill laughed. "I suppose they would. But to be clear, those activities are strictly voluntary."

"How will we get in touch to give you our answer?" Kate asked.

"We'll come back by tomorrow afternoon," Dennis said. "If your answer is yes, we'll give you instructions on how and when to relocate. Do you have fuel and vehicles?"

Jack rubbed his chin. "Forrestal sent men to take a bunch of the vehicles from Apple Blossom Acres, but we should still have enough to get our people and supplies to Bryson."

Bill gave Kate a hug. "I'll see you tomorrow. I do hope you'll take us up on our proposal."

"Either way, I appreciate all the trouble you've gone through to make the offer." She joined Jack and Gavin in escorting the visitors back over the mountain.

CHAPTER 15

And he said, Hearken ye, all Judah, and ye inhabitants of Jerusalem, and thou king Jehoshaphat, Thus saith the Lord unto you, Be not afraid nor dismayed by reason of this great multitude; for the battle is not yours, but God's.

2 Chronicles 20:15

Monday evening, Kate carried the last box of her belongings into the fifth wheel camper at Bryson Citadel. Vicky followed her in with a jumble of hangers and plastic bags stuffed full of her personal effects. "Aunt Kate, you have to rethink the sleeping arrangements."

"It's not up to me. Sergeant Garcia and his men

went to the bunkhouse with the other soldiers. I think Mrs. Dean, Mrs. Hess, and Mrs. Sweeny have all elected to go live in the ladies' bunkhouse. We chose this camper for ourselves and told the rest of our group to do whatever worked best with the other big camper and the little one."

Vicky piled the reckless muddle of her belongings into the corner. "What the others chose will not work best."

Harold Pritchard stuck his head in the door. "You tell the youngin to take the other bedchamber. I'll take the couch. She needs her space."

"No, Mr. Pritchard, we have plenty of storage in our room. Vicky will be comfortable on the couch and can keep her clothes in our room." Kate placed the box on the counter.

Pritchard glanced down at Vicky's leaning tower of disarray threatening to fall over into the walkway. "I believe it would be in everyone's best interest if the youngin has her own room. To do otherwise may put our very lives in jeopardy should we have to skedaddle up out of here in the middle of the night. Besides, everything I brought fits in a knapsack, which can be tucked in the compartment under the couch."

"Thank you, Mr. Pritchard." Kate waved as the old man ducked back outside.

She continued packing her box into the bedroom and Vicky followed her. Kate put the box on the bed and began going through it. "Does having your own room help?"

"That's not my main concern." Vicky still appeared to be emotionally compromised.

"Okay, what's bothering you about the current arrangement?"

"Amanda and Jack will be sharing the other fifth wheel. Isn't that a sin?"

"Amanda and Jack aren't an item. Why would that be a sin?"

"Oh, come on, Aunt Kate. Didn't you recently lecture me about being naive and having raw emotions? They're both grieving the loss of their spouses, feeling lonely, and now you've shoved them into a camper to cohabitate. It's a recipe for disaster."

"I didn't shove them into anything. They decided to share the big camper because the little camper has only one bed. It's less weird for Annie to share the single bed with her 10-year-old son than it is for Jack to sleep with his teenage daughter or Amanda her teenage son. Jack is taking the master, Rainey is sleeping on the couch, Amanda and David's room has bunk beds." Kate lowered one eyebrow as she thought about the odd protest. When the real issue hit her, she felt stupid for not recognizing it sooner, even though she'd been preoccupied with the move and the coming raid. "Are you worried about Amanda and Jack or is this about Rainey and David?"

Vicky crossed her arms and looked away.

"Vicky, you have nothing to feel insecure about. Rainey is a year older than David. Girls rarely go for a younger guy. You know that. Besides, didn't you say she'd been following that boy from Sergeant Garcia's unit around?"

"You mean Philip? When Jack hears about that,

he'll shut it down so fast it'll make your head spin." Vicky plopped down on the bed. "Then she'll get closer to David because he's the only guy she's allowed to be around."

"David likes you." Despite all the other pressing matters of the apocalypse, Kate stopped what she was doing to sit next to her niece. She was the closest thing Vicky had to a parent, and she needed someone to listen. Kate put her arm around her. "You're just as pretty as Rainey, maybe even more so."

"You're just saying that."

Kate pulled her head to her shoulder. "No, I'm not. I mean it, you're a beautiful girl. I know it and David does, too."

Vicky put her arms around Kate's waist. "Thank you."

"You're welcome."

Gavin walked into the room. "Sarge is having a meeting in the dining pavilion in fifteen minutes. We're going to go over tomorrow's mission."

"We? You're still nursing an injury." Kate's eyes narrowed.

"It's been two weeks. My shoulder is fine."

Kate stood up from the bed. "We're going to be loading ammo. It's heavy. You can barely lift anything."

"I can lift a gun. Someone has to stand overwatch while the rest loads the ammo."

Vicky walked out of the room. "I've got to hurry so I can get my stuff put away before the meeting."

Gavin called out behind her. "Sorry, this mission is eighteen and older."

Vicky spun around. "What? That's bunk. I've seen more action than most of those military guys."

"Maybe so, but I didn't come up with the rule. Sarge and Dennis are running this operation and it's their call to make."

"Whatever." Vicky's voice trailed off.

Gavin turned back to Kate. "We have our own room again for the first time since the attack."

Kate bit her lip. "Yes."

His smile widened. "I'm just saying. It'll be nice."

"Mmmhmm." She blushed and continued putting her clothes away.

A brief knock at the door preceded Jack's entrance. "You guys ready? Meeting starts in five."

"We'll be right there." Kate pushed her box to the side and grabbed her gun.

The three of them walked to the pavilion.

Once there, Kate surveyed the maps laid out on picnic tables.

Sarge patted her on the back. "Good of you to come. Glad you two have your team with us."

"We're happy to be able to participate." She smiled.

"Kate, it's good to see you again. I'm looking forward to working with you." Sergeant Garcia shook her hand.

"Same here. I'm glad you fellows decided to stick around for a while."

"The pacific northwest is a long trip when fuel is hard to come by." Garcia looked at the other soldiers who'd joined up with Bill's group. "It looks like we might be able to start our own little opposition force right here."

"Maybe so." Kate turned to see who had tapped her arm.

Vince flipped his hair back. "How're your accommodations?"

"We were pleasantly surprised."

Gavin scratched his head as if thinking. "I'm normally not one to look a gift horse in the mouth, but I want to perform my due diligence in making sure we're not part of the problem. Do you mind telling me how you came about getting these trailers?"

"One of them was an older couple who needed resources. It was just sitting in their drive and they sold it at a good price. The others were at an abandoned storage lot."

"So you salvaged them, to put it nicely. Then you sell them to us." Jack's tone was less agreeable.

"I sold them to Kate, at a very fair price." Vince lost his pleasant expression. "I put my neck on the line every time I leave the camp. It's a hostile world out there if you haven't noticed. Anything sitting in a storage lot at this point is not going to be claimed, so yes, salvaged would be the proper term for it. Don't make it sound like I'm hocking stolen goods or taking advantage of people. If your morals are keeping you up at night over it, feel free to go sleep in a bunkhouse. My conscience is clear!"

Jack took a step closer to the eighties rocker. Vince didn't back away.

Kate stepped between them. "Let's take it easy. Vince, I'm happy with the deal. Jack, you don't have to like it, but we have a common enemy we need to focus on. We can't start snapping at each other."

"If I can have your attention," Sarge said. "We'll get started. We have a lot to go over."

Dennis stood next to Sarge. "We'll be working as two teams, a main assault team and a diversionary team. The diversionary team will strike first in hopes of leading the bulk of the third shift security personnel on a chase away from the compound.

"As you know, Forrestal has occupied downtown Waynesville, using the courthouse as his HQ and the county clerk building as the primary barracks. The courthouse parking garage is the storage facility for his supplies. The supplies we're most interested in is the munitions cache. Since Sergeant Garcia and his men have been so instrumental in giving the needed intelligence for this operation, I'm going to let Sergeant Garcia fill you in."

"Thank you, Dennis." Garcia stood up from the front picnic table and walked to the front.

"The only thing we have going for us is that Forrestal has allowed his troops to take over all of Main Street. They've repurposed some of the shops as living quarters, and others as recreational facilities. This means they are spread out from the courthouse on the north to Church Street on the south. A frontal attack from the south would draw all of the attention and most of the security personnel down to Church Street.

"My team would keep up that attack as long as possible before retreating. Once we do retreat, I'm confident that Forrestal's men will give chase.

"During that assault, the primary team should be able to approach the parking garage from Charles Street. Normally, the entrance has four guards. A covert strike team should be able to eliminate those four guards and allow our trucks to drive right into the garage. The munitions storage containers are on the third floor.

"Sarge is going to advise you on exact times and work with everyone on assigning individual roles, but that's the thirty-thousand-foot view. Does anyone have any questions about the general plan?"

Bill raised his hand. "Yes. The men on the other side of that line were your brothers in arms a week ago. Aren't you concerned that some of your men may have trouble initiating a lethal attack on your friends?"

Garcia's face became like steel. "That's a valid concern, and I'm glad you brought it up. The short answer is we are soldiers and we'll do what needs to be done. The longer explanation is that we didn't just walk away one night. Whispers of desertion became common when Rosales began sending troops into American cities to disarm the population. Several men left one by one. But once Rosales seized control of the Oval Office, leaving became the buzz around the camp. I only stuck around as long as I did because I was waiting to see if the leadership under Rosales would take action against his criminal act. When it became obvious to me that he was going to reign unopposed, I began soliciting others to join me in resigning. When I left, I felt I had faithfully discharged my duty of warning everyone who stayed behind that they were criminally complicit in this rogue, unconstitutional government. Everyone knows the stakes, sir. Most who stayed behind did so out of cowardice. I have no empathy for them and neither do my men."

"Good enough." Bill nodded in his chair.

Sarge said, "We'll roll out in small groups from Bryson starting at 8:00 AM tomorrow morning. We'll rendezvous at the ranch in Maggie Valley and launch our attack from there tomorrow night at midnight. Vince has the schedule for what time your group should leave from Bryson, so check with him. Get some rest. You're gonna need it."

Everyone got up and headed back to their respective housing.

Gavin walked hand in hand with Kate. He whispered, "The young thin kid at Garcia's table, that's the one that Rainey likes?"

"Yep. But don't say anything. Especially to Jack."

"Your secret is safe with me." Gavin snickered. "I wouldn't even want to be the messenger on that one."

Annie was sorting through some boxes outside of her small trailer when Kate and Gavin returned to the campsite. She looked up, "Hey, I heard about tomorrow's operation. Do you guys need me to come along?"

"Troy needs his mother. Why don't you sit this one out?" Kate smiled. "The Bryson Citadel will need some seasoned shooters to hold down the fort while we're gone."

"Okay." Annie continued picking through her belongings.

"Pssst," Gavin stood at the door of the fifth wheel, motioning with his head for Kate to follow.

She knew precisely what he had in mind. "We'll see you later, Annie. We've got to get rested up for the big day tomorrow."

CHAPTER 16

Therefore hell hath enlarged herself, and opened her mouth without measure: and their glory, and their multitude, and their pomp, and he that rejoiceth, shall descend into it. And the mean man shall be brought down, and the mighty man shall be humbled, and the eyes of the lofty shall be humbled.

Isaiah 5:14-15

Kate warmed herself by the fire Tuesday evening at the ranch in Maggie Valley. She ate from an MRE. "It's amazing how good these taste when you're hungry."

"Palatable," Gavin corrected. "Good is a stretch,

even when you're hungry."

"You two gonna be okay if I go with Garcia's group tonight?" Jack inquired.

"We'll miss you, but yeah. Go where you're needed." Kate took another bite.

Jack raked through the coals of the fire with a stick. "I haven't been very good company lately. To be honest, I'm having a hard time keeping it together."

"I know." Kate looked at the embattled man. To her, Jack was a microcosm of the entire country. He'd lost so much, yet he still had more to lose. That final thing which he held most dear motivated him to keep going when all he wanted to do was lie down and die. It spurred him on in the face of absolute adversity. His will to protect Rainey changed his very nature, caused him to become abrasive, suspicious, and callous. She hoped that he would pull through, not only survive, but learn to enjoy life on life's terms. Kate put her hand on his back. "But you're doing a really good job of it."

Gavin tossed the remainder of his MRE into the fire. "I'm going to go lie down in one of the cabins. Do you want to try to catch a nap? This is going to be a long night."

"I couldn't sleep right now." Kate gave Gavin's hand a squeeze. "If I tried, my mind would just spin up my anxiety. The best thing I can do right now is to keep myself occupied."

Gavin kissed her and stood. "You'll wake me before it's time to roll out?"

"Yeah, if I don't forget."

"Ha, ha. Seriously, wake me an hour before."

Gavin walked off toward the cabins.

Jack tossed his stick into the blaze. "I'm going to go link up with Garcia. Try to form some instant comradery. I was a little hostile when I first met them, so I need to try to smooth things over before we're all in the heat of battle together."

"I'm sure they understand. You were responsible for our community's safety."

"Yeah, but I could have been a little nicer about it." Jack waved and strolled toward the men in military uniforms.

Kate sat alone by the fire. She prayed, asking for God's protection for herself, Gavin, Jack, and the rest of her group.

Half an hour later, the solitude was interrupted. "Mind if I sit down?"

She looked up. "Bill, hey. Please, have a seat."

He looked around. "I've never seen you without an entourage around. Where are they?"

"Here and there." She watched the hypnotic flicker of the flames. "Sarge is going to be with the soldiers attacking on the south side?"

"Yep. Dennis and I will be with the group raiding the munitions cache."

"What about Vince?"

"He's on another mission."

"Oh?"

"Yeah. As you may have noticed when you were here the first time. Lots of folks in our group are past their prime."

"You all handle yourselves well." She glanced up at Bill. "Not to say that you personally are past your prime."

He chuckled. "That's kind of you to say, but it doesn't change reality. Anyway, a few of the folks in our original group depend on medication to keep them above ground. Insulin, thyroid medications, and a handful of other things that they can't do without for too long. Vince has been working on lining up some of those drugs. They're finally in, so he had to make a run."

"He's a resourceful guy." Kate stirred the fire.

"Some folks think he's a profiteer, but we're lucky to have him around."

"I've got no problem with free-market economics."

Bill laughed. "Yeah, me neither."

Dennis walked up. "Hey, Kate."

"Hi," she replied.

"Bill, I need to go over the retreat plan with you again. If they follow the trucks with the ammo, I don't think we should all return to the ranch. It might be a good idea to split 'em up."

"Let's go take a look at the maps." Bill stood. "Kate, if you'll excuse me."

"Sure." She was alone again with her thoughts.

An hour or so later, she was once again raptured from her introspection. "Aunt Kate," a whisper came.

This time, she jumped from her seat to see Vicky and Rainey standing nearby in full battle gear. "What are you two doing here?"

"I couldn't let you go without me," Vicky replied.

Rainey said, "I needed to be here for my dad."

Kate shook her head. "How did you get here?"

"We stowed away," Vicky confessed.

"Let me guess, in Philip's vehicle."

Rainey looked at Vicky sheepishly but neither of them denied the accusation.

Kate exhaled deeply to signal her exasperation. "You'll both have to wait here until the raiding party returns. There's no way to get you back to Bryson now."

"No, Aunt Kate. I'm coming with you. We've been together for everything. You can't make me sit here and worry about you while you're gone. That's a fate worse than death."

Kate tried to empathize, but she simply could not okay it. "I'm sorry Vicky. You'll both have to remain here. Come on. I'll put you in the cabin where Gavin is sleeping. Stay inside and stay quiet until we get back."

She escorted the teens to the cabin. Once inside, Gavin roused from his sleep. "Is it time?"

"Close enough. But we've got company."

Gavin looked the girls over. "What are you two doing here?"

"Long story. I'll tell you on the way." Kate waited for Gavin to get up and follow her out. She looked sternly at the girls. "Don't open this door until I return."

"Are you going to tell my dad?" Rainey asked.

"Not until we get back. He needs to focus on the mission for now. Just wait here." She pulled the door shut behind Gavin.

While they walked toward the vehicles, Gavin checked the magazines in his tactical vest. "Raising a teenage girl probably felt like the apocalypse even before the world spun out of control."

"No doubt." Kate checked her rifle to make sure a round was in the chamber.

They arrived at the staging area. The first of the other fighters were just arriving. A stocky man followed by six other well-armed men walked up. Kate looked them over. It was obvious that they'd spent a lot of money on their gear.

"Hi." The man offered his hand. "I'm Morgan."

"I'm Kate and this is my husband, Gavin." She shook the man's hand.

Gavin did likewise. "Morgan Meyer?"

"Yes. Pleasure to meet you, Gavin."

Kate said, "Thank you for everything. We just moved to the Bryson Citadel yesterday. We're friends of Bill and Jan."

"Oh! That Kate. Bill told me all about you. He called me right before the stuff hit the fan. Said some couple just about bought him out, going on about a computer virus. He told me I should make any last minute purchases I might be holding off on. I took his advice, but then when that guy from Sky National blew the whistle on Sixty Minutes, I pulled out all the stops. So, I guess I should be thanking you."

Kate looked at Gavin. "Funny how things work together."

"Yes, it is." Morgan laughed. "Why don't you two ride with us? We're in the Humvees."

"Of course you are." Kate looked at what might be the only two Hummers remaining in operation. Even the military didn't have them since the last wave of Locusts. She figured they'd been custom built for Morgan. "Let's go."

"We'd be honored." Gavin followed the man to the first flat black Humvee.

The ride to the attack was uneventful, other than the fact that Kate and Gavin were going there in style.

The convoy took the long way around, avoiding the main roads whenever possible. The vehicles parked in an abandoned lumber yard at the end of Charles Street.

Morgan looked at Kate and Gavin. "We'll wait here until the shooting starts. Then, we'll give them about three minutes to reach maximum confusion and roll in heavy."

Kate nodded and focused on her breathing. She heard the first snaps of gunfire in the distance. The frequency quickly escalated to a frenzied firestorm.

Morgan monitored his watch. "Thirty seconds more." He held his hand in the air for half a minute, then dropped it. "Go!"

The convoy raced across the railroad tracks and toward the parking garage. Once there, the vehicle doors swung open and the fighters jumped out, ready for action.

Kate and Gavin stayed close to Morgan and his men.

"I don't see any guards at the door," she said.

Morgan continued sprinting toward the opening. "They must have been drawn away by all the excitement. This might be easier than we thought."

"That will be a first," Gavin said cynically.

"Stay alert, follow me." Morgan kept his rifle ready to fire and charged into the garage. The fifty or so fighters assigned to collecting the ammunition ran in behind him.

Kate saw Bill, Dennis and several of the other people from the ranch behind her. She gave a quick salute and kept pace with the leader.

Morgan reached the second level. "Let's keep going."

Suddenly, a bright flash of light blinded Kate. The sound of a high-voltage surge pulsing through giant night time road-work lights preceded a loud voice, which echoed off the concrete interior of the parking garage. "Drop your weapons. You are completely surrounded. If you fail to comply you will be cut down with no further warning."

Kate shielded her eyes but could see nothing but dim figures of soldiers standing behind the blinding lights pointed directly at her team. She squinted to find Morgan. She could see that he was slowly putting his high-tech rifle with the expensive night vision unit on the ground.

"Put 'em down," he called out.

Kate turned back to see Bill and Dennis also surrendering their weapons. She covered her eyes with one hand to look at Gavin. "What are we going to do?"

"We've got no choice. They've got us." He slowly went to his knees, placing his rifle on the ground.

Kate also complied with the demand. "They knew we were coming."

Gavin's voice was angry. "Garcia. This was all an elaborate trap. He's been working us ever since he showed up in Laurel Ridge."

Kate hated the thought of being tricked. Even more so, she hated being captured. She'd come prepared to be victorious or die trying. She had not planned on being made a captive.

"Hands on your heads. Anybody resists being restrained by my men, you'll be shot on the spot."

Kate did not doubt the voice's resolve to follow through with that promise. Soldiers began zip tying each of the captives and leading them away, one by one. The reality of what was happening hit Kate like a ton of bricks when she watched a soldier stand her husband to his feet.

"Gavin!" she called out in horror.

"We'll get through this, Kate. I love you."

She sobbed and watched him being led away. "I love you, too."

Next, it was her turn. She felt the edges of the thick plastic bands bite into her wrists like a vise.

"Get up," the soldier said.

"Where are you taking me?"

"Just be glad you're still alive. Sedition is a capital offense. Lucky for you, we're a little short on labor around here. But, we still reserve the right to execute you on the spot if we feel like you're not giving it 100%. Keep that in mind in the coming days. It will serve you well."

"What about the men? Where are they going?"

The soldier gave her a shove to make her walk faster. "Just worry about yourself. Your old life, it's over. You just bought yourself a life sentence of hard labor. If you get tired of it, can't hack it, just let one of us know. We'll be happy to commute your sentence to death instead of life."

"But I haven't even been charged or been brought to court. How can I be sentenced already?"

"New world, new rules, lady. Justice is swift these days."

CHAPTER 17

Woe unto them that call evil good, and good evil; that put darkness for light, and light for darkness; that put bitter for sweet, and sweet for bitter! Woe unto them that are wise in their own eyes, and prudent in their own sight! Woe unto them that are mighty to drink wine, and men of strength to mingle strong drink: Which justify the wicked for reward, and take away the righteousness of the righteous from him! Therefore as the fire devoureth the stubble, and the flame consumeth the chaff, so their root shall be as rottenness, and their blossom shall go up as dust: because they have cast away the law of the Lord of hosts, and despised the word of the Holy One of Israel.

Isaiah 5:20-24

Kate was escorted to the bank on Main Street. Inside, she saw two guards sitting at a table playing cards. Her captor said, "You've got more coming."

"We've got plenty of room in the back offices." One of the guards looked over his cards. "She's clean?"

"I searched her, but you can give her another pat down if you want."

The guard ogled her. "Pat down? I was thinking strip search."

Kate shivered with repulsion.

Her captor turned. "Might be another ten or so from this raid. You two better stay on your toes until you get 'em all locked up. You'll have plenty of time for fun."

"I got ya," One of the guards stood up. "Come on girly, let's get you tucked in."

He grabbed her by the arm and pushed her to the first office on the left. "The other girls will tell you that if you don't behave, it gets worse. If you cause me any problems, you'll go in the vault. No lights in there, so make sure you're not afraid of the dark if you decide to buck the system. And in case no one else has told you, we're authorized to kill anyone who becomes violent, belligerent, or otherwise unruly." He unlatched the door from the outside, then pushed her inside. "Enjoy your stay."

Kate heard the locking sound of the large metal slide latch which had been added to the heavy office door so it would lock from the outside. She looked at six other women lying on blankets on the floor.

"You were part of the raid?" A slender dejected woman in her mid-thirties sat up.

"Yeah." Kate looked out the window. Bars covered it from the outside. "I bet those bars are just held in by concrete anchors. You could probably hammer them right out."

A rougher looking girl in her early twenties with dishwater blonde hair said, "Don't even waste your time. The windows don't open and the glass is shatterproof. They'd be in here and you'd be dead long before you started pounding away at the metal bars."

Kate turned back to the women in the room. "Why are we locked in a bank?"

The dishwater blonde said, "Banks are inherently hard to get into and hard to get out of."

"So is a jail. Are they using the county jail for the men?"

The sad, skinny woman shook her head. "The men are in a fenced-in detention center at the end of Main Street. The jail is too far away from them to keep control of for now."

"So he built a new jail?" Kate was confused.

"No," said the dishwater blonde. "Forrestal's men ran fencing around the big furniture store and the three-story bank to make them into a detention complex. Or rather I should say, Forrestal's men watched it being done. They made the prisoners do all the work."

Kate sat on the floor, trying to process what was happening. Minutes later, she heard the metal slide once more. The door opened and two women from the Bryson Citadel walked in. Kate had never met them but recognized their faces. She gave them an empathetic look of disappointment.

The guard tossed in a stack of blankets. "One blanket per prisoner. Don't touch the extras. We've got more girls on the way."

"It's getting crowded in here, Tom!" The dishwater blonde stood up to launch her complaint.

"Plenty of room in the vault, Skylar."

"Eric won't let me go to the vault."

The guard, Tom, evidently said, "Eric's shift doesn't start until 6:00 PM. He can do whatever he wants with you then. But if I hear one more peep out of you, he'll find you in the vault."

Skylar sat back down and said nothing else.

The guard warned, "Tonight's activities change nothing. Breakfast is still at 5:00 and work starts at 6:00. I suggest you ladies try to get some rest. You have a long day tomorrow."

Kate and the other women lay on the floor. She closed her eyes but despite her exhaustion, she knew she would not be going to sleep.

Twenty minutes passed and the latch opened again. In walked Vicky and Rainey. Kate's stomach sank. She put her finger over her mouth signaling for the two girls not to talk, then stood to embrace them. She whispered in Vicky's ear, "Don't call me Aunt Kate. Not even in front of the other prisoners. I'm afraid even something as small as that could be leveraged against us."

"We're prisoners. How much worse could it get?" Vicky wiped tears from her eyes.

"I don't know, Vicky." She whispered to Rainey also, "You, too. Don't say Dad. Just call him Jack if you see him."

"He's alive? You saw him?" Rainey's pained eyes sparked with hope.

"I haven't seen him. But he'll survive. That's what he does." She gave the teen girl a quick embrace. "I guess you two decided not to stay in the cabin."

Both held their heads low but said nothing.

Kate saw no point in browbeating them further. The punishment for disobeying would be far worse than either of them deserved. "They'll be waking us up for work in a couple hours. Both of you should try to get some rest."

Vicky took one of the blankets and sat on the floor. "I'm not going to sleep tonight."

"Then just close your eyes for a while." Kate curled up on the floor and pulled the scratchy wool blanket over her.

Kate must have eventually drifted off, for when the latch slid again, it startled her from slumber. She'd been dreaming that she was back at the Apple Blossom Acres checkpoint. At the time, it had seemed like a hardscrabble existence, but retrospectively, those were the good old days.

A guard brought in a tray of bowls filled with white rice. "No fighting. If I hear anyone tried to bully food from another inmate, you'll spend the next forty-eight hours in the vault."

"Rice? For breakfast?" Rainey asked.

"And for dinner." The dejected woman took a

bowl from the tray.

"What about lunch?" Vicky inquired.

The woman looked up with her trademark forlorn eyes. "We don't get lunch. I'm Lydia, by the way."

Kate passed bowls to Rainey and Vicky, then took one for herself. She watched as the women began eating with their hands and started to do the same.

Vicky put her hand on her aunt's arm. "Aren't you going to pray?"

"Oh, yeah." Kate bowed her head. "God, thank you for this food. Please watch over our friends. Keep them safe. Keep us safe. Bring us home soon. Amen."

The three of them began eating.

"That is just too sweet." Skylar rolled her eyes toward the ceiling as she ate her food.

Vicky looked at her befuddled. "What?"

"Praying. Your God has abandoned you here. If He exists at all, you should be telling Him how disappointed you are in Him."

"Well, we don't put our hope in this world." Vicky continued eating.

"Oh, pie in the sky. I see. That's convenient."

The latch slid open. "Skylar, Eric sent you something."

She stood up to retrieve a brown bag. She returned to her seat as the latch slid shut. Skylar pulled out a biscuit, which appeared to have a thick slice of sausage inside. With her mouth still partially filled with the biscuit, Skylar said, "As for me, I'm just trying to make the best of this world, because this is all there is."

"What do you have to do to get a sausage biscuit?" Rainey asked.

Skylar stopped chewing for a moment. "What do you think? Come on, you're old enough to figure that one out. Do the math. It's mostly men around here. We're a rare commodity."

Rainey crinkled her nose and continued eating her rice.

"Don't judge me. And don't let me catch you curling your nose up at me either. I'll slap that self-righteousness smirk clean off your face." She slumped back against the wall and shoved another bite of the biscuit in her mouth. "Besides, you just got here. Give it a few days of rice, rice, rice. You'll have a boyfriend or two." Her brows snapped together. "Just make sure none of them are Eric."

An hour later, the door opened again. "Exit the room, line up, and face the wall."

Kate obeyed. Vicky and Rainey stayed close to her.

"My regular crew. Come with me. We'll be cleaning the officers' barracks. New girls, go with Corporal Cannon. You'll be scrubbing down the men's detention facility. Don't try to milk it. If you're not finished by the time the men return from their work duties, you'll all sleep in the vault tonight."

Soldiers placed an ankle shackle on one leg of each woman, then led them out the door. Kate, Vicky, Rainey, and the two women from the Bryson Citadel shuffled their feet down Main Street. Kate made as many mental notes about her surroundings as possible while she was outside. She examined vehicles, the positions of troops, and tried to guess the re-purposed use of each shop that she passed.

Corporal Cannon unlocked the gate of the chain link fence. Kate passed through observing the height of the ten-foot fence as well as the coils of razor wire above. Holes in the parking lot pavement had been excavated at regular intervals to make room for metal poles to be sunk into the earth. These supported the intimidating metallic cage surrounding the furniture store and bank. If the structures had ever looked inviting, those days were gone. No one could mistake these buildings as being for anything other than what they were intended, the imprisonment and enslavement of men.

Cannon pointed to the two privates in his charge. "Brackenbury, Vahora, you know what to do if anyone steps out of line. I'll be in the office."

"Let's move it, girls!" Brackenbury watched as Vahora knelt to remove the shackles. "Broom closet is in the back. Let's get this room swept, mopped and all the trash picked up. Make it snappy, we still have to clean the second and third floors of the bank next door."

"Come on," Kate said to the others. "Let's knock this out as fast as possible. I'd rather be told to do a better job next time than get in trouble for not finishing."

Kate handed the broom to Vicky and the mop to Rainey. "You two focus on the floors. We'll get the trash and fold the blankets."

Mark Goodwin

The two teens immediately started their task. Kate called the other two women into the broom closet and passed out trash bags. "I'm Kate."

The first woman to speak had short brown hair and an athletic build. "I'm Mia." The other, a chubby blonde said, "I'm Abigail."

Mia caught Kate by the shoulder before she could exit the broom closet. "We need to get out of here before they break our will."

"Agreed," said Kate.

"We can use the broom and the mop as weapons. We'll take the guards' guns and shoot our way out."

Kate shook her head. "No. We need to lay low and observe. We need to gather as much information as we can, formulate a solid escape strategy, then make our move. If we act without a good plan, we'll just get ourselves killed."

"Dead would be better than this." Mia fluffed her trash bag.

"It's not an option for me. My husband and my friends are being held in this building. I have to get back to Bryson and help plan a rescue mission."

"My husband is here, too."

"Then you'll follow my lead, wait until we put a plan together?"

"As long as you don't take too long. I don't intend to rot here." Mia led the way out of the broom closet.

Abigail smiled at Kate and trailed behind Mia.

Kate walked around the room and began folding blankets. The old furniture store was soon cleaned and the four women were taken to the bank building. Immediately, Kate recognized that it was much cleaner than the furniture building. She noticed that Private Vahora seemed less secure than the other private and decided to make him her mark. She'd act nice, even flirt if need be, but she would use him to get as much information as possible.

The task breakdown was the same as in the furniture store. Kate walked over by Private Vahora and began straightening the blankets. "So, where are you from?"

Vahora seemed surprised by the question. "Me? Oh, ah, Georgia."

Kate continued her work. "Georgia is a big state. What part?"

"Columbus."

"That's nice. It's a big military town, right?"

"Fort Benning is just south of there, so yeah, kind of."

Kate continued quietly to see if he'd keep the ball in play.

Finally, the private said, "What about you?"

"Atlanta," said Kate.

"Wow, big city."

"Big mess now. It's just a burned out shell."

"Pretty much like the rest of the country."

"Yeah, right?" She giggled. "Speaking of messes, the guys staying in this building are much neater than whoever is sleeping at the furniture store."

"This is the stockade."

"What's that mean?"

"The colonel wants the military deserters and the civilians kept separate. We keep the military guys in here. They're used to living in close proximity to one another, and they're accustomed to keeping their quarters clean. I guess it just goes to show that you can quit the Army but the Army doesn't quit you."

Kate forced herself to laugh at the clunky comment. "You're clever."

Vahora seemed pleased with himself. "Yeah, I was the class clown in school."

"I bet you were." Kate tried to balance her energy between getting the job done on time and continuing to chat up Private Vahora.

The girls eventually finished cleaning the two buildings and their shackles were replaced before returning to their own detention facility.

On the walk back, Corporal Cannon walked close to Kate. "You know, if you're going to make friends with someone, it should at least be someone in a position to help you out. Privates barely get enough food to feed themselves. Bosses, on the other hand, have access to whatever they want."

Kate glanced at the key ring jingling from the corporal's belt loop. She'd obviously set her sights too low. She'd been offered the bait but she wasn't going to bite just yet. "You mean like a sergeant or a lieutenant?"

Cannon's face showed his annoyance at having failed to get his point across. "That's the general idea but a corporal is only one pay grade below a sergeant. And you won't see too many lieutenants consorting with prisoners."

"Oh, okay. Thank you for that information." Kate looked at the insignia on Cannon's uniform. "Corporal Cannon."

She watched him suppress a smile at the thought. She batted her lashes at him, then ignored him the rest of the way back to lockup.

CHAPTER 18

And I said unto them, If ye think good, give me my price; and if not, forbear. So they weighed for my price thirty pieces of silver. And the Lord said unto me, Cast it unto the potter: a goodly price that I was prised at of them. And I took the thirty pieces of silver, and cast them to the potter in the house of the Lord.

Zechariah 11:12-13

Kate was awakened from her nap by the harsh snap of the latch. "Dinner." A soldier brought in another tray filled with bowls of rice.

"Is Eric here?" Skylar asked.

"Yeah, come on out, Sky." The soldier held the

door open for her.

"You girls can fight over my rice. I won't need it." Skylar waved. "See you in the morning."

Another soldier stood in the doorway. He looked at Vicky and Rainey. "It's fried chicken night. If either of you girls want some, just let me know."

Rage flashed through Kate's brain. She stood up. "They're not even eighteen, you sicko!"

"Excuse me." The soldier snarled.

The other soldier said, "You better watch it, David. You don't want Colonel Forrestal to find out you're hitting on teenage girls."

Kate reiterated the warning. "If it happens again, I'll make sure he finds out."

"Yeah, you do that. Once he knows they're here, he'll add them to his personal staff. The only reason he doesn't want us bothering them is because he wants them all for himself, the greedy dog." David slammed the door and hit the latch.

Kate looked at Mia. "You're right. We have to get out of here fast." She turned her attention to Rainey and Vicky, both of whom looked petrified by the exchange they'd just heard.

"But after dinner," Kate said, "I'm going to do something I should have done a long time ago."

The women in the cell scarfed down the modest portions of plain white rice. Kate chugged a glass of water, then addressed her niece and Rainey. "Jiu-Jitsu takes lots of time and practice to ever get proficient at it, but I think I can teach you one move that will get you out of a sticky situation. Each class usually only focuses on one move or a series of related moves, so this isn't much different."

"You're going to teach me Jiu-Jitsu? Here? Now?" Vicky looked bewildered.

"I'm going to teach you one move." Kate lay on her back. "Vicky, get on your knees, between my legs."

Vicky complied. "Okay."

Kate continued, "As you can imagine, if a guy is sitting where you are, he thinks he's on his way to where he wants to go, right?"

Vicky looked worried. "Uh-huh."

"Unless he's taken Jiu-Jitsu, or watched a lot of MMA fighting, he has no idea what's coming next. Mentally, he's totally disarmed." Kate quickly wrapped her legs around Vicky and pulled her forward, locking her ankles behind her back.

"This is called the guard position. Technically, it's a defensive position, but you can launch a variety of offensive attacks from guard. We're only going to work on one for now." Kate put her hand on the back of Vicky's neck, pulled her head down to her chest, and wrapped her right arm around Vicky's neck. She grabbed her right hand with her left hand. "Up until this point, if you're sort of playing along with the guy, he probably just thinks you like to play rough. But, if you put your arm around somebody's throat, they usually have a pretty good idea that they're about to get choked. Once you're here, you need to close the deal fast."

Kate released the grip of her ankles and put her left foot on Vicky's hip. She pushed out and used her left leg to lift her hips. She let go of Vicky's neck. "Did you feel that pressure?"

Vicky's face was purple and quickly went to red, then slowly returned to its normal color. She nodded as the other women looked on in shock and amazement.

"Can you teach me that move?" Mia asked.

"Yeah, everyone who wants to learn, team up with a partner. We'll drill through this for the next hour or so. Keep in mind, I didn't put any pressure on Vicky's neck. If I had, she would have been asleep in a few seconds."

("What's this move called?") Vicky teamed up with Rainey.

"The guillotine," Kate replied.

"That makes sense." Vicky wrapped her legs around Rainey and pulled her forward.

Kate watched. "Good, now pull her head down and wrap your arm around her neck."

On the other side of the room, Mia had her legs around Abigail and her head pulled to her chest. "I can't quite reach around her head."

Kate looked at her hold. "If you have shorter arms or if you're fighting a bigger opponent, you'll have to release your guard first and push out with your foot on her hip. But until you're ready to make that transition, you need to keep your legs wrapped around her tightly."

Mia pushed out with her foot and easily got her arm around Abigail's neck.

"Good," said Kate. "Run the drill five times, then switch; person on the bottom gets on top. Once you think you have it down. The person on the top will start trying to fight their way out of the hold. Ladies on the top, tap your partner to let them know when you feel the choke."

Kate worked with them for the next hour. She demonstrated the proper technique several more times. Not only was she helping the others by teaching them the valuable move, but she was also keeping her own skill set sharp in case she needed it.

Late that night, Kate was awakened by a gentle nudge. She turned to see Lydia's crestfallen eyes in the pale glow of the security lights coming in the window. "Hey, what's up?"

Lydia whispered, "Are you thinking of trying to escape?"

"Why?"

"If you are, I want to go with you. I can't take it here much longer."

"Then be ready. You'll know when it's time."

"You'll wake me if it's at night?"

"I probably won't need to, but yes, I'll make sure you know it's time to go if it's not obvious."

"Thank you."

"You're welcome." Kate rolled back over to get more sleep.

The next morning, Kate ate her breakfast next to Lydia. "I guess Skylar came back in the middle of the night."

Lydia whispered. "Yes. She gets in around 2:00 AM usually. That's when her boyfriend's shift ends."

"Boyfriend, huh?"

Lydia lifted her shoulders. "That's what they call

it around here."

"How many guards are on at night?"

"Three."

"So with Skylar's boyfriend gone, that leaves only two?"

"Yep. We're locked up from 6:00 PM to 6:00 AM anyway. We can't really cause any trouble during that time."

"How long have you been here?"

"Two weeks. I ran out of food. I was going through a neighborhood of mostly abandoned homes, looking for something to eat. The Army rolled in while I was there. If I had to do it over, I would have ran, even if that meant getting shot in the back. Of course, a lot of the men who were here two weeks ago wouldn't have shot a woman in the back for trying to find food."

"What do you mean by men who were here then?"

"Defectors. A lot of them left in the past two weeks. Forrestal is hanging on by a thread. That's why he lets the guys get away with whatever they want. I suspect it will get worse as time goes on. Right now, they sort of bargain for it, like with Eric and Skylar. But soon, I suppose they'll just take what they want, from who they want, when they want. Most of the men with any honor have walked off."

Mia sat close enough to hear the low conversation. "You said you thought it was one of the defectors who set us up."

Kate looked at the thin industrial carpet where she sat. "I don't know what to think. If it wasn't him, I can't imagine who else it could have been. But until I see Garcia walking down Main Street in shackles, he isn't fully exonerated in my mind."

"Sergeant Garcia?" Lydia asked.

"Yeah, you know him?"

"Yes. He was preaching to all the other men. Saying the government was corrupt and illegitimate, telling them that if they stayed they were complicit in Forrestal's crimes and that a rebellion was rising, which would shut down Rosales and everyone who stuck by his side. He was the talk of the camp. He cut out just in time. Forrestal would have made an example out of him."

A pang of guilt hit Kate in the gut.

Mia said, "Sounds like an exoneration to me."

Kate twisted her mouth to one side. "The way things went down, it sure didn't look good for Garcia; very coincidental."

"Coincidence or not, you can't deny Lydia's testimony."

"I suppose you're right." She looked up at Mia. "Then who sold us out?"

"I guess we'll find out when we get out. If we don't, it won't matter anyway."

"How do you figure we'll find out?"

"Cui bono, right?" Mia said.

"Cui bono?"

"Yeah, it's Latin; legal doctrine. It means who benefits. Who stands to gain from a crime?"

Kate's blood began to boil. She knew exactly who stood to gain, or at least who stood to profit. "We have to get out of here. The person who set us up is still on the loose. If he double-crossed Bryson

Citadel once, he'll do it again. We have to stop him."

"Time for work, ladies." Corporal Cannon held the door open. "Line up. Face the wall."

Kate and the others assumed the position while they were shackled like animals being led to the grindstone.

Cannon walked next to Kate. "Did you think about what we talked about yesterday?"

"How could I not?" she toyed.

"So, what do you say?"

"About what?"

"I've got access to a little office on the first floor of the bank building. Maybe we could steal away and get to know each other a little better. I brought some extra French toast from breakfast this morning."

Kate wrinkled her nose. "I'm not that kind of girl."

"Oh, I guess I got the wrong impression." Cannon looked angry.

"I mean, I'm not the rendezvous-in-an-office-for-a-piece-of-toast kinda girl."

"Then what kind of girl are you?"

"Eric takes Skylar out of the cell all night. I'm assuming they go back to his place, have a nice dinner, relax, take it slow. Maybe a drink or two. You know, that kind of thing."

"Eric works third shift."

"You're a boss. Can't you get someone to switch with you?"

"What, like work a double?"

"If you think of hanging out with me as work,

then maybe I'm the one who got the wrong impression."

Cannon grimaced. "I'll see what I can do."

"Let me know." Kate waited for Private Vahora to remove her shackles, then went to work with the other girls.

After work, the crew returned to the holding cell in the back. Cannon approached Kate. "Guess what?"

"Tell me."

"I'm working third shift tonight."

"Great. Did you get us something to drink?"

"What do you like?"

"Something hard, whiskey, tequila."

"I think I can do that. See you at six?"

"See you then." Her stomach churned, nervous about the encounter.

Vicky overheard the conversation. "What are you doing?"

"We're getting out of here tonight. Make sure you're ready."

"What time do you think we'll leave?"

"I'm aiming for ten o'clock. It will be cold, dark, I can't imagine very many soldiers will be out milling around by then."

"Please don't get caught," Vicky begged.

"Trust me, I don't want to." She bit her fingernail, anxious with anticipation about the plan.

CHAPTER 19

And Jael went out to meet Sisera, and said unto him, Turn in, my lord, turn in to me; fear not. And when he had turned in unto her into the tent, she covered him with a mantle. And he said unto her, Give me, I pray thee, a little water to drink; for I am thirsty. And she opened a bottle of milk, and gave him drink, and covered him. Again he said unto her, Stand in the door of the tent, and it shall be, when any man doth come and enquire of thee, and say, Is there any man here? that thou shalt say, No. Then Jael Heber's wife took a nail of the tent, and took an hammer in her hand, and went softly unto him, and smote the nail into his temples, and fastened it into the ground: for he was fast asleep and weary. So he died.

Judges 4:18-21

Kate heard the latch open outside the door Thursday evening. The guard placed the tray filled with bowls of rice on the ground. "Skylar, come on out. You too, Kate."

Skylar snarled at Kate. "Boy! That little goody, goody routine didn't last long."

Kate felt ashamed even though she had no other way to save Vicky and Rainey. "We all do what we have to in order to get by."

"That's what I've been saying all along." Skylar sauntered down the hall, then paused. "But tell me, was it all just a ruse? Were you playing hard to get to make yourself more attractive?"

"I don't give away my secrets." Kate saw Cannon standing by the door.

Skylar took Eric's hand. "Well, kudos to you."

Kate felt a surge of panic as she walked up to the corporal. "Ready?"

"Yeah, we'll go out the back. Nobody really says anything, but it's not smart to advertise."

"Sure." Kate kept her distance from the man. "Where's your place?"

"The back office of the funeral home."

This operation kept getting creepier. "Really?"

"Yeah, but it's private. No one else wanted to sleep there."

"The place right next to the men's detention

center?"

"Yep, you walk by there every day."

Kate considered the possibilities. The risks kept escalating, but so did the potentials for reward.

Cannon opened the door to his eerie flat in the rear of the funeral parlor. Her heart beat in her chest like the kettle drum of an orchestra leading to a crescendo. She walked in to see a mishmash of strange furnishings. An antiquated couch appeared to have been pulled from the parlor's lobby. Its faded red crushed velvet covering was pushed against the back of the couch with large-diameter cloth buttons. The sofa would have been very much at home in a haunted mansion. A dresser against the wall looked as if it had been part of a display in one of the shops along Main Street.

Cannon's bed took up a space in the room which was probably once occupied by a desk. The bed was covered by an olive drab sleeping bag, which had been unzipped and spread out. Next to the bed, the last relic of the office remained. A hideous, beige, single-wide, metal filing cabinet acted as a nightstand. Atop the cold steel furnishing sat a fat white candle, another item which had likely been liberated from a shop window, and a bottle of Dewar's.

"I didn't know what kind of whiskey you liked," Cannon said nervously.

"Scotch is fine." Kate surveyed the atrocious quarters. "Do you have anything to eat?"

He passed her a Styrofoam container. "We had roast beef. I can trust you with a steak knife, right?"

She sat on the dilapidated couch and opened the

box. "You have a gun. I'm pretty sure that outranks all dinner utensils."

His laughter was tense. "Yeah, right? Still. If you don't mind, I'll take it when you're done."

"Sure." Kate took her time eating the meal. It was the first thing she'd had besides rice in two days. She'd need the energy for phase two of her escape.

Cannon poured himself a shot of Scotch in a coffee cup. He took a sip, then poured a cup for Kate. She commented, "Nice whiskey mugs you've got there."

"Yeah, it's all they had in the kitchen here." He took a long gulp and winced as if it was too strong.

"Sip it, we've got all night, right? I mean you don't have to get home to your wife or anything, do you?"

He seemed to lighten up instantly. "No. I have to have you back by 2:00. It's an unwritten rule that you don't keep a girl out on the next guy's shift."

She felt repulsed by the fact that they had standardized protocols for this sort of thing. "You boys run a tight ship."

Kate left the empty box on the couch and took the coffee cup. She put it to her lips and pretended to take a sip as she strolled around the room. When she turned around, Cannon was taking off his BDU jacket. She put the coffee mug on the metal nightstand and lay back on the bed. "Easy there tiger." Still fully dressed, she opened her legs. "Let's take it slow. Come over here and let's get to know each other a little better."

He nodded anxiously and crawled up onto the

bed. Once he was on top of her, she ran her fingers through his hair and pushed his head down. She locked her legs around his back, slowly, gently, like an anaconda constricting its unsuspecting prey. He tried to turn his head to kiss her torso, but she was already slipping her arm beneath his chin. She put her left foot on his hip and arched her back.

"Hey! What are you doing…"? His muffled voice trailed off. He tried to squirm out of her grip for a moment, but then his body fell limp and heavy. She rolled his listless torso over on the bed and slid out from under him. Kate quickly retrieved the steak knife from the Styrofoam box. "On second thought, you probably shouldn't trust me with sharp objects." She took a deep breath, steeling herself for the grotesque task at hand. She plunged the knife into his eye, shoving it deep into his brain. She let the instrument of death remain lodged in his eye socket, not wanting to produce any more blood than necessary.

Kate unbuckled his belt and unzipped his trousers. "You probably would have enjoyed this part." She tugged at the legs and eventually had them off. She quickly changed into Cannon's BDUs and put on his boots. She stuffed her clothes under the bed and rummaged through the room looking for one more item of clothing. She opened the bottom drawer of the beige filing cabinet. "There you are!" She retrieved a slightly wadded camouflage BDU cap. She shook out the wrinkles, put it on her head and tucked her long blond locks beneath.

She glanced at the dead man on the bed. "What

to do with you?" The solution came to her instantly. "Ah. I'm in a funeral home. They must have a gurney for just such a task." Kate found a flashlight in the top drawer of the filing cabinet and searched for the door to the basement. She quickly located the stretcher and bounced it back up the stairs. Kate carted it to the bedside, rolled Cannon over onto the transport vehicle, and wheeled him into a back room filled with coffins. "Take your time. Pick out one you like."

She closed the door behind her and headed for the back office. Kate searched Cannon's footlocker finding a box of 9mm shells for the pistol on her belt and an ammo can of 5.56 for his M-4 rifle. She tucked as much as she could fit into the side pockets of the BDU pants. She adjusted her cap and headed out the door into the night.

Kate followed the same back street that she and Cannon had taken to get to his quarters. Wall Street ran behind the local businesses on Main and kept her out of sight until a small alley led across the road, directly to the bank. She sprinted to the door and walked in calmly.

The single remaining guard glanced up from the video game on his phone, then quickly back down. "What's up?"

"You're holding two teenage girls. Colonel Forrestal wants them remanded to his custody."

"I bet he does." The soldier continued the game but was positioning himself to get up. "Do you have the paperwork?"

"No, would you like me to tell him he needs to come down here himself? Where are the rest of the detention guards?"

"On break, that's okay. I'll get 'em." The man put his phone on the desk. "Games are all these things are good for now."

"How do you keep it charged?"

"Solar chargers. We found some in that prepper store right behind here." He motioned toward the rear of the bank and made his way toward the office used for a holding cell. He pulled the latch and opened the door. "Two young girls, come on out. You're going with Corporal..." He turned to look at Kate's name badge. "Cannon?"

Before he could complete the equation formulating in his brain, Kate smashed the butt of her rifle against the bridge of his nose, sending him backward into the cell.

"Everybody out. Mia, get his uniform off of him. It looks like it should fit you." Kate waved the others out of the room.

"He's gonna wake up." Mia unbuttoned his BDU jacket.

Kate handed the M-4 for Vicky to hold. "Maybe not." She knelt down and put her hands around his neck. She watched him turn blue and continued to squeeze.

The girls rolled him over so Mia could get the jacket off and Kate continued choking the soldier. Mia finally had his uniform on and her boots laced up. "I think he's dead, Kate."

Kate stood up and latched the door of the cell just to be sure.

"Where are we going to go?" Lydia asked.

"Mia and I are going to act like we're escorting

the rest of you across the street and into the alley. From there, we'll take you to Cannon's. I've got an idea to get a couple more guns and a couple more uniforms. We're gonna need them."

CHAPTER 20

With her much fair speech she caused him to yield, with the flattering of her lips she forced him. He goeth after her straightway, as an ox goeth to the slaughter, or as a fool to the correction of the stocks; till a dart strike through his liver; as a bird hasteth to the snare, and knoweth not that it is for his life.

Proverbs 7:21-23

Kate ushered the women into Cannon's abode.

Vicky looked worried. "Where's the corporal?"

"Picking out a casket. Here, hang onto the rifle. Mia, give yours to Rainey. They know how to run them if we get into a pinch." Kate grabbed the bottle of Scotch. "Mia, come with me. We're going to get our husbands out."

"Whoa!" Mia handed her rifle to Rainey and checked the chamber of her pistol. "You told me to slow my roll, now I'm going to return the favor. Take a breath, tell me what you've got in mind, and let's go over this."

Kate looked at the other women as she laid out her plan. "Discipline is on the decline around here. I think we can use that to our advantage. I'm going to lure the two guards watching the entrance to the civilian men's facility away so we can break in and rescue the men."

Abigail shook her head. "That's just the two at the gate. What about the ones inside? Do you even know how many there are?"

"We'll bring those two back here and have a little conversation with them. They'll tell us how many guards are inside," Kate retorted.

Lydia's eyes darted around the room nervously. "What if someone finds the guard at the bank dead? What if someone comes here looking for Cannon?"

"No one should be checking in here nor at the bank until 2:00," said Kate.

"Theoretically." Mia crossed her arms.

Kate gave an optimistic smile. "Theoretically."

Mia examined Kate's attire. "I don't like this, but I'm willing to give it a try. We'll bring the guards back here if we can. But, if we can't free the men without a firefight, we head back to Bryson and gather more troops. I don't like the thought of leaving my husband behind any more than you do, but getting ourselves killed won't do them any good either."

"Agreed." Kate fished a few strands of hair out of her cap and let them dangle in her eyes. She unbuttoned the top button of her BDU jacket and grabbed the Scotch. "Come on, and try to look like you're in the mood to have fun."

Mia followed her out the door and also unbuttoned her top button. "Sorry, I don't have any glistening blonde locks to tease the boys with."

"You'll do fine." Kate walked around the side of the funeral home and up to the gate. "Hey!"

"Hey yourself," the first guard answered.

"My friend and I got a bottle and got ourselves all worked up for a party."

Mia took the Scotch, removed the top and had a swig. "Then we realized that we forgot to invite any guys." She handed the bottle to the first guard.

The two guards looked at each other like they'd just hit the lottery. The second guard said, "We wrap up here at 2:00."

Kate snatched the bottle back. "2:00? The liquor will be gone, and I'll be passed out by then. We'll find somebody else. Sorry to bother you."

"No shortage of guys around here, that's for sure." Mia sauntered off, swinging her hips.

"Ladies, ladies, hold on!" said the first guard. "You'll have to forgive my friend here. He's a little slow."

"Oh?" Kate paused and looked back.

"Yeah, I'm the resourceful one." The guard took out his radio. "Ted, I need you to cover us. Me and Jimmy are going on break."

"Break? It's 8:30. You don't have a break until

11:00."

"I know, listen, we might be gone a while. I'll make it up to you."

"Give me a minute."

Shortly thereafter, two guards emerged from inside the old furniture store. The first shook his head. "You better hope Forrestal doesn't hear about this."

"Or what?" The soldier lifted his chin in defiance. "He'll bust my chops? I'll jump ship like Garcia and the rest of them. This thing is falling apart, Ted. Everybody is doing whatever they want. Don't be such a square."

Ted replied, "If you jump ship like Garcia, you'll end up in the stockade like Garcia."

The soldier put his arm around Kate, took the bottle and began walking away. "Garcia is in the stockade because he came back. If I leave, you'll never see my face again."

Ted yelled out, "Whatever, you owe me for this."

Kate and Mia led the two men back to Cannon's quarters.

"Funeral home?" The soldier took a drink and passed the bottle to his companion. "You chicks are kinda wild."

Mia ran her finger across his lips. "You have no idea."

Kate opened the door and let the men walk inside.

Jimmy looked around. His eyes widened. "How many girls are here?"

The butt of Vicky's M-4 struck the first guard in the nape of the neck knocking him to the ground.

Jimmy turned to look and Kate put her arm around his throat. She put her hand on her own bicep and put the opposite hand around the back of his head. She squeezed steadily, arched her back and lifted up with her hips. Jimmy stopped moving and she gently lowered him to the ground. "Get their clothes off of them. Tie them up." While the other women stripped the guards of their BDUs, Kate rummaged for materials to restrain the two men. "Here's a belt."

"I got duct tape!" Mia held the silver roll in the air.

"Perfect." Kate watched with her pistol drawn, making sure neither would come to and cause trouble before being properly bound.

Jimmy started to come around first. "Hey! What's going on?"

Kate knelt down beside him. She grabbed his hand and bent his wrist as far as it would go.

"Ah! You're hurting me!"

"How many men are still in the furniture store?"

"Six. I mean four."

She pressed harder on his wrist. "Which is it? Six or four?"

"Four. There were six, but two of them are covering for me and Bruce."

"Think he's telling the truth?" Mia asked.

"I'll find out. And if you're lying to me, I'll kill you." Kate maintained the pressure on his wrist. "How many are guarding the stockade?"

"Twenty."

"Twenty?" Kate inquired. "Why would Forrestal put more than twice as many men on the same size facility?"

"Because they're soldiers. Some of them have SERE training. Plus he's afraid Garcia will pull some Jedi-mind-trick stuff and get them to defect if he has any less."

"It makes sense," Abigail said.

Rainey tapped Kate on the shoulder. "The other one is waking up."

Kate pressed the interrogation. "Is the stockade on the same radio frequency as the furniture store?"

"Yes."

Kate put her arms around the man's neck and head once more. "You've been very helpful." She squeezed and the man passed out.

She looked at Mia and the others. "Let's see if he gives us the same answers."

She slapped Bruce in the face. "Wake up, wake up!"

Bruce looked around at his captors. "You're not going to get away with this."

Kate grabbed his arm and twisted it behind his back. "Don't worry about us. How many guards are left in the furniture store?"

"I'm not telling you anything."

Kate ratcheted his arm further behind his back.

"AHHhhhhh!"

Kate pulled his socks off and shoved them in his mouth. She gave his arm one more good wringing as his face contorted in torment.

She pulled the socks out of his mouth and looked at the beads of perspiration on his forehead. "You're gonna tell me. It's just a matter of how much you want to endure before you start talking."

"Six! Okay? Please!"

"Good. How many are in the stockade? Guards, that is."

"Look, I don't know. I don't work over there."

Kate shoved the socks back in his mouth. She grabbed his foot, put it under her left armpit, crossed her left hand over her right wrist, dropped her left shoulder to the floor and pushed his stomach with her foot.

Even through the socks, she could hear his scream. She released the pressure and sat up. "I can do this all day. Are you ready to talk?"

His nostrils flared with each breath, his eyes begged her not to do it again. He nodded vehemently.

Kate pulled the socks out of his mouth. "Speak!"

"Twenty men. Colonel Forrestal is worried the soldiers will try to overpower the guards if he doesn't have enough of them on."

"Good. Are they on the same frequency as the guards at the furniture store?"

He watched her fearfully, as if wondering what part of his body she would attack next. "Yes!"

"Thank you, you've been very helpful." Kate pulled his head into the crook of her elbow and crossed the fingers of both hands.

"No, please, not again. I'll tell you what you want to know."

"This won't hurt." Kate rocked her elbow toward the ground and Bruce went out cold.

She dropped him to the floor. "Let's get this mess cleaned up before they come back around."

Kate sprinted out of the room to retrieve the

gurney.

She walked into the storage room and tipped the gurney, rolling Cannon's corpse onto the linoleum floor. "Sorry you didn't see anything you like. They've got some nice black plastic bags you might be interested in. I'll have someone bring one over."

Kate wheeled the cart back into Cannon's quarters. "Get them up on the cart."

"Where are you taking them?" Lydia asked.

"To the trash." Kate didn't feel like elaborating.

Abigail seemed hesitant in helping Mia lift Jimmy onto the stretcher. "You're going to kill them?"

"Sooner or later. Either I put them down now, or wait until we fight Forrestal next. If I do it now, you don't have to worry about one of them shooting you the next time we come. So, what do you think?"

Vicky and Rainey hoisted Bruce onto the gurney, stacking him atop Jimmy. In unison, the teens said, "Kill 'em now."

Kate shoved the cart out the door. "If you insist."

Once back into the storage room, she bent down and extracted the steak knife from Cannon's eye. She fought back a gag reflex and quickly cut into Bruce and Jimmy's jugular veins. The sight of the pulsating eruption of blood sent her over the edge and she lost the roast beef dinner she'd eaten shortly before. Kate wiped her mouth, composed herself and returned to the bedroom.

Once inside, she found a bottle of water and rinsed the vomit out of her mouth, spitting it into the waste can.

"It's done?" Vicky asked.

"Yeah, it's done."

Mia looked at her with a slightly worried look, as if she thought Kate might be a little too violent. "We can't take on 26 soldiers with radios. As soon as a firefight begins, every soldier in the camp will be on top of us in a matter of minutes."

Abigail stood behind Mia, as if using her for a shield. "I agree with Mia, don't be mad at me."

Kate thought about the odds. She looked at Vicky and Rainey. She knew she needed to get them home and if she attacked the prisons, that probably wouldn't happen. "Okay. Who can fit into Jimmy and Bruce's uniforms?"

"I can fit in Jimmy's," Lydia volunteered.

"Can you run an M-4?" Kate asked.

"No," she replied.

"Vicky, Rainey, you two put on their BDUs. Roll up the sleeves and pant legs if you have to. The women who will be posing as prisoners can carry pistols concealed. Anyone packing an M-4 should be wearing a military uniform." Kate handed her pistol to Lydia. "Point and shoot. Don't point it at me."

Lydia nodded and tucked the pistol into her pants.

"Let's get ready to move!" Kate looked out the window.

CHAPTER 21

I cried to thee, O Lord; and unto the Lord I made supplication. What profit is there in my blood, when I go down to the pit? Shall the dust praise thee? Shall it declare thy truth? Hear, O Lord, and have mercy upon me: Lord, be thou my helper.

Psalm 30:8-10

Kate continued watching out the back window for foot traffic. "We've got a long walk. We'll never make it to Bryson tonight, but we've got a place we can lay low over in Laurel Ridge. We've got food, supplies, blankets; enough for all of us."

She looked at the women behind her. "Who knows the neighborhood streets around

Waynesville?"

Lydia looked at the other women as if waiting for someone else to speak up. "I guess I do, fairly well, anyway."

"Good," said Kate. "We need to take the back streets, pass the compound on the north side and get to the mountains on the other side of 74. From there, we should hit Mauney Cove if we just keep heading northwest. I can get us to the house once we get to Mauney Cove."

Lydia peered out the back window. "We should go northeast to Marshall Street, use the cover of the trees. It's out of the way, but it limits our chances of being seen."

"Marshall will get us out of town?" Kate asked.

"It will take us to the tracks, which will get us far enough south to not worry about running into any of the soldiers. We can then get across the creek and walk through the old neighborhoods to get to US-74. Once we cross the highway, we'll be home free."

"Good enough." Kate examined the face of each woman on her team. "Ready?"

They all nodded or answered in the affirmative.

"Then let's go. If we're stopped, our story is that the four of us with uniforms caught the others snooping around. We're taking them to the bank for questioning. If that doesn't work, we'll have to shoot our way out."

"Aunt Kate?"

"Yes, Vicky?"

"Should we pray before we leave?"

Kate felt ashamed that she'd not thought to ask

for God's help. In all the killing and conniving, she'd allowed herself to revert to (relying on her own strengths.) "Yes, Vicky, I suppose we should." Kate bowed her head. "God, thank you for bringing us this far. It's easy to get lost in the darkness. I pray that you'll guide us with your light, both in the spiritual realm as well as the one we can see and touch. Watch over us Lord and bring us home safely. Amen." She opened the door. "Lydia, after you."

Kate hurried Lydia along to keep the entire procession moving fast. "Let's pick up the pace."

The group progressed quietly through the trees and shrubs, circling behind an abandoned nursing home.

Kate pointed at a street sign which read, *Boundary Street.* "Where does this go?"

"It takes us to the tracks, but in much closer proximity to the courthouse complex." Lydia paused.

"But we'll only be two blocks away when we reach the tracks anyway."

"That's true," Lydia said.

"I think it's worth the risk. Circling back is going to burn time. Once they discover that we're gone or when they start tripping over bodies, they'll sound the alarm. I'd like to be as far away as possible when that happens."

Lydia turned down Boundary. "You're the boss."

"Roll your feet to make less noise on the pavement." Kate led the group in a sprint down two blocks of a residential street. She paused when they reached Branner Avenue. She could see ten soldiers milling about, guarding the entrance to the parking garage only a block away. Kate waited for the entire group to reach her position. "We have to be quick about crossing Branner. If we're spotted, they'll gun us down. When I give the signal, I need everyone to run as fast as you can. Don't stop until we hit the tracks."

Kate held her arm in the air and waited. "Go!" she whispered loudly and dropped her arm.

All the women ran as fast and silently as possible. Kate slowed the pace when they reached the railroad tracks, not wanting anyone to trip or to get overly winded; however, she continued to push the women for a steady speed. They crossed the creek at Depot Street and followed Chestnut Park west.

"Do you think we can slow down a little?" Abigail was panting.

"We'll take a more leisurely gait once we cross the highway and get into the woods." Kate dropped the tempo of her stride slightly but wanted to get out of harm's way. "Remember, breathe in your nose, out your mouth."

Abigail fought to regulate her respiration by following Kate's advice.

The women eventually reached the highway. Kate listened closely for approaching traffic but heard none. "Alright, everybody, go! Fast as you can!" Kate positioned herself behind the stragglers. "Move! Move! Move!"

Once on the other side, Abigail looked as though she were ready to pass out. "How much ..." she gasped, "further?"

"From my old cabin, it was roughly five miles to downtown. We've already covered part of that. I'm guessing about three miles. But it's through the woods at night with no flashlights, so it will be a slow trek."

Abigail smiled between her heavy breathing. "I can do slow."

The crescent moon above offered little light to illuminate the long trudge through the woods. Kate, Vicky, and Rainey took the lead, stomping down fallen limbs and traversing brambles.

An hour later, they reached Mauney Cove. Kate turned to the women behind her. "We're through the worst of it. We'll be on pavement or well-worn paths from here on out."

"Unless Forrestal's men catch up with us," Vicky added. "Then, it's back to the woods."

Kate nodded her agreement. "Yep."

The hike to the top of Apple Blossom Acres was steep, yet they eventually made it. From there, it was only a short march through the woods to the home in Laurel Ridge where Kate still had an adequate cache of food and weapons. She located the hidden key, and let her group in.

"Vicky, Rainey, and I will take the master since that was my old room. The rest of you can take any room where you feel comfortable. I'll dig out some MREs in a few minutes."

Later that evening, Kate snuggled up on the bed. Vicky shared the king size bed with her aunt and gave her small mattress on the floor to Rainey. Kate put her hands behind her head and looked at the clock on the wall, which read 2:00. "If they haven't figured out that we're gone by now, they will soon. Cannon, Jimmy, and Bruce should all be good and stiff by now."

"Aunt Kate, you're sorta freaking me out."

"How so?"

"You used to be so much more serious about stuff. Now, you're kinda flippant about everything."

"I spent most of my life dealing with anxiety issues. Deep down, I was afraid; afraid to die, afraid of what people thought of me. Things are tougher now than they've ever been, but I'm not afraid anymore. Maybe we'll get through all of this, but the reality is we could go at any time. Ever how long I have left, I'm not going to spend it being afraid or worrying. It won't buy me any more time. It will only serve to devalue what I have remaining.

"And forgive me if I'm becoming less remorseful every time I have to rid the planet of another dirtbag. I'd much rather they left me alone.)

"But no, they stole our guns, looted our neighborhood for vehicles, locked us up, were going to turn you and Rainey over to some pervert to be his pets, and are planning to work my husband to death in a concentration camp. Call it a lack of compassion, or empathy fatigue, whatever; but I don't feel bad anymore about killing people who are trying to destroy me and the people I love."

Vicky hugged her. "Okay. I can handle that. I just thought maybe you were coming unglued or something."

"Far from it." Kate held her niece's hand tenderly and soon drifted off to sleep.

The next morning, Kate was up at sunrise. "Vicky, Rainey, come on. Up and at 'em, girls."

"I think I just fell asleep like five minutes ago." Rainey's eyes were puffy.

"We need to get to Bryson. We have to put together a rescue mission to get your dad and all of our friends out of Forrestal's work camp."

"We're walking all the way to Bryson?" Vicky asked.

Kate looked out the window, down the hill toward Kim Sweeny's house. "Maybe not."

After waking the rest of the women, Kate, Vicky, and Rainey strolled down to the old Sweeny residence. Kate broke out a small pane of glass in the basement door. She gingerly reached inside and flipped the deadbolt. Kate opened the door which led to the garage.

"That would definitely beat walking." Vicky walked past the Escalade and ran her fingers over the hood of the black Mercedes AMG GT.

"Vicky, Rainey, why don't you girls go upstairs and see if you can locate the keys. Check the drawers in the kitchen cabinets and any furniture in the living room."

Kate pulled the release to manually open the garage door. She remembered that fuel had been salvaged from the Mercedes for Molotov cocktails in the fight against James Dean and hoped that it still had enough gas to get them to Bryson. She waited at the bottom of the stairs for the girls to return, recalling the awful moments when Gavin lay in that very spot clinging to life.

"Found 'em!" Vicky scampered down the stairs dangling the keys. "Can I drive the Mercedes?"

"You're fifteen, you have no license, and it's not even my car. So, no. You can't drive."

"Kim abandoned it, and there are no laws to say I need a license. What happened to your philosophy about making the best out of the time we have left?"

Kate considered all the teenage joys which Vicky and Rainey had been robbed of by the unyielding waves of Locust attacks and subsequent societal meltdown. "If you scratch it, you owe Mrs. Sweeny a new car."

Vicky's eyes swelled with unbelief. "Are you serious? I can drive?"

"Probably not, but I'm going to let you do it anyway." Kate took the keys of the Escalade from her niece and got in.

Kate giggled as she watched Vicky gun the gas and stomp the brakes up the hill to the house. The other women were soon loaded into the Escalade and Kate got into the Mercedes. Lydia rode with Kate and the girls while Mia drove the Escalade.

Kate called out the window to Mia. "It's about thirty-five miles to the Bryson Citadel from here. We've got plenty of gas to get there. Once we're on the highway, let's try to keep the speed around a hundred while we're on the straightaways. Obviously, we'll have to slow it down for the curves in the mountains. We shouldn't have to worry about a convoy surprising us from behind if we're moving that fast."

She rolled up her window and looked at Vicky. "Think you can handle that?"

"Oh yeah!" Vicky gripped the steering wheel. She was more excited than Kate had seen her since the world melted down.

CHAPTER 22

Thou hast defiled thy sanctuaries by the multitude of thine iniquities, by the iniquity of thy traffick; therefore will I bring forth a fire from the midst of thee, it shall devour thee, and I will bring thee to ashes upon the earth in the sight of all them that behold thee. All they that know thee among the people shall be astonished at thee: thou shalt be a terror, and never shalt thou be any more.

Ezekiel 28:18-19

Kate's group rolled up to the front gate of the Bryson Citadel. The men guarding the entrance were older as all of the younger men had been captured in the mission to Waynesville.

"Step out of the vehicles with your hands up!" Eight men leveled rifles at Kate and her group.

Kate slowly got out and lifted her hands skyward. One of the men recognized her from the ranch. "Hold on fellas. That girl is friends with Bill and Jan."

"Mia!" Another man recognized Mia when she stepped out. "These are our people. Guys, lower your rifles. Let 'em through."

Kate addressed the man who'd recognized her. "We just escaped from Waynesville. I need to speak to whoever is in charge."

"That would be Mandy Meyer," he said. "But she's in an important meeting at the pavilion right now and cannot be disturbed."

"That's Morgan's wife?"

"Yes," he replied. "How are the men?"

"Colonel Forrestal has them in a work camp. We were set up. We have a mole in the Bryson Citadel. Forrestal's men could be coming here any minute. I need to speak with Mandy right away."

The lines in the older man's face deepened. "Okay, I'll escort you up there."

Kate looked at Vicky. "Find Mr. Pritchard. Tell him what's going on and spread the word to Annie, Amanda, and the others. Make sure you let Jan know that Bill is still alive."

"I will." Vicky got back in the Mercedes and drove through the gate.

Kate walked up the hill toward the pavilion with the old man. "What's your name?"

"Henry Kaufman. You're Kate, aren't you?"

"Yes, sir." Kate saw a woman flanked by six guards speaking with another person, who seemed to have a separate security detail. The person she was speaking to had a long gray ponytail draped over a leather trench coat.

"Oh no, what is he doing here?"

Henry put his hand on Kate's shoulder. "Mandy is pulling out all the stops to get everyone back home."

Henry approached the pavilion. "Mrs. Meyer…"

She cut him off. "I thought I said that I wasn't to be disturbed, Henry."

"Yes, ma'am. But I think you're going to want to hear this. Kate here and the women who went on the mission to Waynesville have escaped."

Mandy stood up with astonished eyes. "You're Kate?"

"Yes, ma'am."

"Oh, you poor, poor dear!" She embraced Kate. "I'm Mandy. I'm in charge during my husband's absence. Let me wrap up my meeting, and I'll be with you right away."

She glared at the Reverend still seated at the wooden picnic table. "Let me tell you a little something about the man you're meeting with. He attacked our community. He killed almost everyone, including my sixteen-year-old nephew. Most of the women who came here with us are widows because of this monster. If you know what's good for you, you'll kill him right where he sits."

The Reverend's guards drew their weapons and so did Mandy Meyer's security personnel. The

Reverend held up his hands. "How about we let cooler heads prevail here. Every story has two sides. If you're the young lady I think you are, I believe you murdered my brother."

Mandy asked, "Is that true, Kate?"

"His derelict brother attacked my home in the middle of the night!"

The Reverend quickly countered, "My understanding is that he was slighted in a deal by someone from your group. I feel remorseful that things escalated to the point that they did, but no one is innocent in this thing. Being a man of God, I'm willing to let bygones be bygones; bury the hatchet so to speak."

"A man of God? You're a meth dealer, a bandit, and a cop killer."

"Kate, that's enough!" Mandy shouted. "I can't have you derailing my negotiations. The Reverend is here to help me rescue my husband. We've all done things since the Locusts came that we regret. Desperate times call for desperate measures. Henry, will you please escort Kate to the main cabin? I'll be with you as soon as I'm finished here."

Kate reluctantly let Henry lead her away. "Yeah, here's another familiar saying. The first rule of holes says when you find yourself trapped in a pit, stop digging. I swear that you'll never regret anything as much as making an alliance with this depraved villain!"

"Henry! Take her away, now!" Mandy pointed in the direction of her large luxury cabin.

Kate sat on the rocking chair and fumed as she

waited for Mandy Meyer to arrive. When she finally did, Kate sprung from her chair.

"Sit down!" Mandy barked. "You just don't know when to stop, do you?" She put her hands on her hips. "Do you think I'm stupid? Do you think I don't know the nature of the man I'm dealing with? Do you think I'd choose this path if I had any other option?"

"Ma'am, with all due respect, this won't end well."

"Listen here! My husband has been captured and the bulk of our security team is with him. Things are about as bad as they can get, so I'm running a last-ditch effort here."

"My husband is locked up there, too. So are most of my remaining friends. But the Reverend is as bad, possibly even worse than Forrestal. You can't do this."

"This is my property, my compound, my rules, and my call. I can do whatever I see fit to do. If you don't like it, you're free to leave. But if you want to work with me to get your husband and friends back, you'll fall in line right now. Can you accept those terms?"

Kate could not accept those terms, but like Mandy Meyer, she was down to her last desperate option to rescue her husband. She looked at the expensive reclaimed barn wood planks on the deck of the cabin. "Yes, ma'am."

"Good. I'd rather have you as a friend than an adversary, Kate, but we're doing this my way."

"I have something else I need to tell you."

"Go on."

"When we got to Waynesville, Colonel Forrestal was waiting for us. You have a mole in the camp."

Mandy looked out over the property. "I figured that. It was those soldiers. Forrestal sent them out as spies."

"That's what I thought at first. But I overheard too many conversations while we were being held as prisoners. I think the mole is still here. Probably still feeding information to Forrestal. You have to root out the mole before you announce any plans to free the hostages."

"Who do you think it is?"

"Vince. He was supposed to go on the mission with us. He was in all the planning meetings, so he knew exactly how the attack would take place. Then, at the last minute, he had another matter to see to."

"I know about that. He was trying to secure much-needed medications for some of the people here."

"Did he?"

"I think the deal fell through, but that doesn't make him the mole."

"I think you should have him detained."

"Kate, the world around us may be melting into chaos, but the whole reason we built the Bryson Citadel was to preserve civility and rule of law in case of some event like the Locust attacks. We don't lock people up over innuendo and suspicion. We spent a lot of time putting this community together, and we were thinking about the end of the world long before it ever came."

"It's your decision, but I hope your high-minded

concept of what the apocalypse is supposed to look like doesn't cost our husbands their lives." Kate picked up her rifle and walked off. "At least try to keep Vince out of the loop until after we've planned the rescue mission."

Later that afternoon, Kate sat by a campfire built near her group's campers. Annie and Troy Cobb, Amanda and David McDowell, Pritchard, Vicky, and Rainey Russo all sat around the blaze warming themselves.

Amanda put her hand on David's arm. "So, I guess this one will be an all-hands-on-deck sort of thing."

Kate snapped pieces off of a twig and tossed them into the flames. "Yeah, we need everybody who can pull a trigger for this one."

David hugged his mom. "We'll be alright. You know Jack and Gavin would come to get us if we were the ones being held captive."

"I know."

Troy Cobb looked at his mother. "Can I come? I can pull a trigger."

She tousled his hair. "I know you can. But someone has to keep an eye on the camp. Mrs. Dean, Mrs. Hess, and Mrs. Sweeny all need someone strong to look after them."

He looked disappointed. "That's a load of garbage. I don't even have a gun."

Annie's face showed that she was considering something she did not want to do. "Okay. Let's go get you a rifle and go work on your marksmanship."

"Really? I'm coming with you?" He jumped up

from his seat.

"No. But I'm not going to leave you here unarmed."

"Okay." While not nearly so ecstatic, the ten-year-old boy seemed to accept the bargain.

Kate watched Annie lead her son into the camper, to do something no mother should ever have to do.

Pritchard chewed on a length of straw. "I ought to've went the first time. Maybe I could've wrestled you'ns out of them vermin's grip."

Kate was in no mood to argue with the old curmudgeon. "I'm sure you would have, Mr. Pritchard. But you'll still get your chance."

Vicky's lips were pressed so tightly together that she had a white ring around her mouth. "I can't believe Mandy Meyer is bringing Lloyd Graves."

Rainey's eyes also burned with vengeance for the death of her mother. "Accidents happen in battle. Bullets going every which way, people get confused, friendly fire incidents."

"Accidental shootings are a two-way street," Kate counseled. "The Reverend's forces outnumber us two-to-one. If you take a shot at him, you'll have two of his guys taking shots at you. Don't think they won't notice. I want him dead as much as anyone, but let's wait for the right time."

"Here comes ol' Jezebel herself." Pritchard cocked his chin up in the direction of Mandy Meyer and her approaching entourage.

"Why would you call her Jezebel?" Amanda fought a grin.

He spoke low enough for Bryson Citadel's

acting administrator to not hear. "On a counta her bringing that no-good Lloyd Graves into the camp. He's a prophet of Baal if I ever seent one."

Kate stood up when the woman arrived.

Despite their earlier exchange, the woman was cordial. "Kate, can I have a word with you up at the pavilion?"

"Sure." Kate slung her rifle over her shoulder and followed the woman and her security detail.

Mandy Meyer spoke while they walked. "I've decided to take your advice about Vince. He has a line on some firearms on the other side of the mountain, some militia group outside of Chattanooga who bought a lot of guns but not much food."

"You sort of need both to get by in this day and age," Kate commented.

"Yes, we do," Mandy replied. "Anyhow, he'll be leaving this afternoon and isn't expected back until after we've executed the operation to bring back our men. We lost a lot of weapons in the failed raid on Waynesville, so we legitimately need the rifles. If he is a mole, I don't think he'll suspect he's being sent away."

"May I ask what you're offering in exchange for the guns?"

"Mostly provisions, long term storage foods. We've got plenty to see us through until we can begin producing our own food. Plus some gold and silver coins."

"If he is the mole, you've got a good chance of never seeing him again. He could take the thirty pieces of silver he sold us out for, everything he's pilfered by selling goods to the residents, plus that haul, and simply disappear."

"I've considered that possibility. It's a much more desirable outcome than having him tip our hand about the rescue mission."

Kate adjusted her rifle strap. "What about my other recommendation?"

"To leave the Reverend out? Not going to happen." Mandy offered a stern smile. "I assume those people sitting around the fire with you are your assault team?"

"Yes. We have one other girl coming with us who isn't there, Annie Cobb."

"Still, your group is a miniature representation of the entire Citadel. We're essentially a smattering of old people, widows, and children. Not only are we going against trained soldiers, but we're vastly outnumbered. And attacking a fortified position, I might add. It simply can't be done without the Reverend's assistance."

"What does he stand to gain?"

Mandy's eyes showed her uneasiness about the arrangement. "We'll be split into two groups. It's basically a reverse plan of attack, which we tried before. Only this time, an attack against the munition stores will be the diversion. The Reverend's men will lead that leg of the assault while we use it for cover to free the men."

"So Graves gets to keep all the ammo he can take. To him, we're bleeding off some of Forrestal's defenses to fight the rescue mission."

"One hand washes the other," Mandy said grimly.

Kate countered, "Until one hand thinks it would be better off alone, and that hand just so happens to be the one holding the meat cleaver."

"Don't think I haven't considered that, Kate. But we have to get the guys home, and I don't see any other way."

"Is that all Graves gets out of the deal?"

"We're issuing him a small stipend of gold and silver coin."

"Once the fox knows you've got more eggs in the hen house, you can bet that he'll be back."

"We'll cross that bridge when we come to it."

"Okay."

"So you agree?" Mandy looked at Kate.

"No, but you're calling the shots, and I'll do what I have to in order to rescue Gavin."

"Good enough." Mandy Meyer waved her hand at the picnic table when they arrived. Mia, Abigail, Jan, Henry Kaufman, and several other people she didn't recognize were sitting around a hand-drawn map of Waynesville. "I'd like you to be part of the planning team."

"I'd be honored," Kate said as politely as possible.

"I think you know some of the people." Mandy put her hand on Kate's shoulder. "I'll introduce you to the rest."

After introductions were made, Kate and the others worked on formulating the rescue mission, which was to be carried out the following day.

CHAPTER 23

For wickedness burneth as the fire: it shall devour the briers and thorns, and shall kindle in the thickets of the forest, and they shall mount up like the lifting up of smoke. Through the wrath of the Lord of hosts is the land darkened, and the people shall be as the fuel of the fire: no man shall spare his brother.

Isaiah 9:18-19

Kate watched the breath come out of her mouth like a puff of smoke and dissipate in the cool, dry, night air. She led her team up Walnut Street toward the detention complex just before midnight Saturday. Lydia, Mia, and Abigail had joined up with Kate. The vehicles were parked in the staging area, an old concrete plant roughly two blocks from the prisons. Each person on the team carried two pistols and one extra rifle in addition to their main battle rifles. These were to be distributed to the captives upon their release.

They drew closer to the complex. Kate directed her group off the street and into the concealment of the homes in the residential neighborhood leading up to the objective point.

Lydia knelt next to Kate at the corner of a house where they could both see the internment complex. "I don't know how much good I can do. I'm really not a very good shot."

Kate patted her hand. "It's okay. If you do nothing but hand off those weapons to the men coming out of the prison, you alone could change the outcome of this operation."

Lydia nodded. "Thank you, Kate. I needed to hear that."

Vicky and Rainey held their rifles tight against their shoulders. Both girls looked eager to get on with the fight.

"If that rascal, Lloyd Graves, backs out, we'll be in a mess for sure," Pritchard whispered from behind Annie Cobb.

"Either way, we're going in." Kate turned to look at her team. "Are we all agreed on that?"

"I'm not going home without my husband," Mia said.

"I'll see this through to the end," David added.

His mother nodded her approval. "Me, too."

Just then, Kate heard the first shots being fired

from the direction of the parking garage. "You might not be able to count on the Reverend, but you can count on his greed."

Vicky and Rainey positioned themselves to sprint toward the chain-link fence.

Kate held her arm up in front of the teens like a gate holding back a pair of racehorses. "Wait for my signal. We need to give Forrestal's troops time to respond to Graves' attack." Kate pointed at the two guards on the far side of the furniture store's parking lot. "Mia, think you can hit one of those guards from here?"

"Absolutely." She raised her rifle.

"Annie, can you hit the other one?"

"No problem." Annie also took aim.

"Good, on my count. Once they're down, I'll storm the compound and clip the fence. Vicky and Rainey will cover me, then I'll give the signal for the rest of you to follow once I have a hole cut." Kate took a deep breath. "Three, two, one."

Annie and Mia's rifles snapped. Kate saw the guards drop and bolted across the street before the men even hit the ground. Rainey and Vicky knelt at Kate's side watching for enemy troops while Kate snipped between each link of the fence. She dropped the bolt cutters and held her rifle at a low-ready position while slipping through the fence opening. She waved for her team, but they were already coming. Kate peeked in the front door of the furniture store to see the other six guards scrambling nervously. She saw one talking on his radio and overheard his voice calling for the two downed guards at the gate.

"Ted, pick up. We need to know if you guys are okay out there!" said the voice over the walkie.

Kate whispered to her team. "They're about two seconds from calling it in. We have to move now. Shots have to be exact. You have friendlies all around your targets. Pritchard, Abigail, jerk the doors open. Everyone else, pick your target carefully and eliminate them."

Kate went to one knee right in front of the doors. She looked through the sights of the rifle. "Go!"

The doors flew back. Kate saw the first hostile. Several prisoners were behind him, so she tucked even lower. If the bullet passed through his head, it's upward trajectory would take it too high to be a threat to the hostages. She pulled the trigger, dropping the guard.

Another of the guards yelled, "Watch out!" Before he could level his weapon, he'd been taken out by Vicky.

Mia and Rainey each killed another soldier leaving only two more for Kate's team to contend with.

"Bring me a gun!" one of the hostages called out.

Lydia ran toward the man, with a rifle held out.

"No! Wait!" Kate yelled.

It was too late. Lydia was cut down by one of the surviving guards. However, she fell close enough for the hostage to take the rifle still in her hands. The other prisoners stripped weapons from the dead guards and soon killed the remaining two troops.

Kate saw Gavin across the room. She ran toward him, headlong into a sea of desperate men pushing against her to escape. Vicky and Rainey managed to stay with her. She embraced Gavin with both arms.

He kissed her on the head. "Come on, we've got to get out of here."

Kate passed him her extra rifle. "Where's Jack?"

Gavin chambered the M-4. "He was shot."

"Shot?" Rainey's face turned pale white.

Gavin grabbed each of her shoulders. "No, Rainey, as far as I know, he's still alive. He was hit in the leg during the diversionary attack. They took him to the prison infirmary, which is in the bank building next door. But, I'm going to be honest, they don't do much to treat prisoners."

"Then we have to get over there now!" Rainey didn't wait for anyone else. She began the march toward her father's last known location.

"Are you guys liberating the stockade?" Gavin tried to keep up with Rainey.

"Mandy Meyer's team is trying to get in there, but they have more guards than the furniture store." Kate held her rifle close while she jogged out the doors.

Vicky pointed ahead. "There's Bill and Sarge!"

Kate grabbed Rainey's shoulder and steered her toward the two familiar faces. "Come on, we're going to need all the help we can get if you want to save your father.

"Do you guys have guns?" Kate asked when she arrived.

"Some gal handed me a .45." Sarge held up a large framed semi-automatic pistol. "It's better than a sharp stick, but if you've got an extra rifle, that'd be nice."

Rainey handed her extra AR-15 to Sarge while

Vicky gave hers to Bill.

"Jack is in the stockade. We have to get to him," Kate explained.

Bill racked a round into the chamber of the AR-15. "Lead the way."

Kate waved her arm in a circular motion, signaling for Amanda, Annie, David, and the others to rally around her. The rest of her team fought through the confusion to get to her. "Mia, go find your husband. The rest of you, we've got to get Jack. Come on!"

Mia nodded and hurried off toward the exit.

When they got to the doors of the bank building, the last of the captive soldiers were just leaving.

"Kate!"

She looked up to see Sergeant Luis Garcia.

He said, "You're going the wrong way!"

"Jack is still inside, in the infirmary."

Garcia's face looked bleak. "The remaining guards are holed up in the infirmary. I don't have any idea how you'd get in there. Even if you did, you risk killing anyone you're trying to save."

Rainey pushed past him. "I'm gonna try, if it's the last thing that I do."

Kate looked at Garcia. "Will you help us?"

He sighed. "Got a gun for me?"

Sarge handed him the .45. "Don't ask for my rifle. You ain't getting' it."

"Philip, hang back. You're coming with me." Garcia turned to go back inside.

"Anyone has a gun for me?" asked the young soldier in Garcia's charge.

Rainey quickly surrendered her sidearm to

Philip.

"The infirmary is on the third floor. Come on, the stairwell is this way." Garcia led the group.

Kate jogged to keep up. "How many guards are still alive up there?"

"Probably around thirty."

"Thirty? I thought Forrestal only assigned twenty to the stockade altogether."

"Yeah, that was before they had a jailbreak over in the women's prison."

Kate grimaced. "Great. Any ideas on how to get in there?"

"It's just an office building. We can kick through the drywall if we have to. Only problem is that's going to draw a lot of fire." Garcia sprinted up the stairs, two at a time.

Once on the third-floor landing, Kate looked through the small pane of glass in the fire door. "That metal medicine cart, think it will stop a bullet?"

Garcia peeked in. "Not 5.56. But it might slow some of them down. What are you thinking?"

"I could push that cart toward the glass double doors to the infirmary. Another team could slip into the adjacent office space and open fire into the wall."

"You'll hit my dad or one of the other patients." Rainey objected.

"Not if we keep the bullets high." Kate stepped aside to let Rainey look through the window. "All the patients are lying on mats directly on the floor."

"Then I want to be one of the people on the other side of the wall, so I can make sure everyone is shooting high enough." Rainey seemed adamant.

"Okay, Vicky, you, Pritchard, Amanda, and David go with Rainey. Annie, Mia, and the rest of you, follow Sergeant Garcia's lead. He'll storm in to do the clean up after I make my run at the guards with the medicine cart."

"Good plan," Gavin said. "But I'll push the cart."

"No, Gavin!" Kate protested.

"It's not up for debate." He pushed past her and crawled to the cart. Once there, he opened fire at the glass doors and ran recklessly toward the infirmary with only the thin layers of metal to stop the bullets.

Rainey's team tucked low and slipped into the adjacent office space. They hastily took prone positions to lower their profiles for the return fire which would inevitably come. Rainey was the first to begin shooting.

Kate watched in horror as bullets ripped through the thin metal cart, many of them, continuing through Gavin's body. "Gavin!" Kate screamed at the top of her lungs and led the secondary charge through the double doors to the infirmary. Gunfire erupted in every direction. Kate dropped next to her bleeding husband but continued shooting while the rest of her team rushed into the room.

Bullets tore through the drywall from Rainey's team, killing and confusing the soldiers inside. Kate lost track of everything going on around her. She focused on finding targets, shooting, and changing magazines when empty. The exchange of shots moderated to an occasional pop then died off completely. Kate took one last survey of the room before turning her attention to Gavin.

His eyes were closed, and he was covered in blood. Her mouth hung open, not knowing what to do. "Gavin, please, don't leave me. I love you so much."

Garcia dropped down right beside her and began cutting away Gavin's shirt and trousers. He handed Kate a box.

"What's this?"

Garcia kept working. "It's a medical kit. It might be the sorriest excuse for an infirmary on the planet, but they do have a medical kit. Start pulling out those bandages. Stuff gauze into the open wounds and then bandage over them. Pull the bandages tight. Don't worry about cutting off circulation, we have to stop him from bleeding out."

Kate did as she'd been instructed. Annie put her gun beside Kate's foot. "Let me help."

"You have medial experience?" Garcia's gaze caught Annie's for a moment.

She gave a brief smile. "Some."

Kate worked feverishly. "Let's save the introductions for later."

Both broke away from the other's stare to patch up the holes in Gavin's body as rapidly as possible.

"We can't take him outside like this." Garcia pointed at the blankets over by the beds.

Kate sprinted to get the woolen covers and hustled to cover him. She watched as Rainey, David, and Vicky carried Jack past her position. Jack looked at Kate when they took him by, but she could tell he was in bad shape. Pritchard and the others helped the remaining patients down the stairwell.

Garcia hoisted Gavin over his shoulder. "Kate, you and Annie cover me. I'll get him where he needs to go."

Kate grabbed her gun and looked around to make sure no one was being left behind. Abigail and Sarge were both lying motionless on the floor. "Wait!"

Annie quickly went around to each of them checking for pulses. "They're gone, Kate. We can't do anything for them."

Garcia's eyes looked pained. "We need to go now."

Kate led the way down the stairs, ready to neutralize any hostiles they might encounter on the way. Her mind was consumed by her concern for Gavin on the way back to the vehicles, but she still felt terrible for those who'd lost their lives in the rescue mission.

CHAPTER 24

(Be anxious for nothing,) but in everything by prayer and supplication, with thanksgiving, let your requests be made known to God; and the peace of God, which surpasses all understanding, will guard your hearts and minds through Christ Jesus.

Philippians 4:6-7 NKJV

Kate rocked on the front porch of a guest cabin at the Bryson Citadel. A wool blanket shielded her upper torso from the chilled night air. Her legs were cold, but she welcomed the discomfort. The icy breeze was the only thing keeping her awake. Upon construction of the compound, one cabin had been allocated as a medical facility. However, it could not accommodate all the victims of a mass casualty event like the rescue operation, and the guest cabin next door had been repurposed as a secondary trauma facility. She prayed silently, begging God to spare Gavin once more.

Annie walked out on the porch and pulled off blue nitrile gloves, which were heavily soiled with blood.

Kate leaped from the rocking chair. "How's it going?"

"We've got him stabilized. It looks like none of his organs were hit. The metal cart didn't stop a single bullet, but it may have slowed down the velocity."

"Why would that matter?"

"Less velocity means a smaller wound channel, less trauma. We picked out some fragments also. A few of the bullets broke upon impact of the cart. Those very well could have killed him if he'd had no cover at all."

"Can I see him?"

"We've got him sedated right now. The best thing he can do is sleep. To be honest, we're working with a limited amount of elbow room. You'd be helping us out and probably yourself if you'd just go home and get some rest. Come back in the morning. Maybe he'll be awake, and things will have calmed down around here."

"How's Jack?"

"He still has a bullet in his leg. We have to get his fever down and the sepsis under control before we can even consider extracting the projectile. He obviously had very little treatment in the infirmary. I'm guessing he'd have gone into septic shock by tomorrow if we hadn't gotten him out. From there, he'd have been dead in a matter of hours."

"But we got to him in time?"

"We'll have to see how his body responds to the antibiotics. We should know by tomorrow."

"Thank you, Annie, for everything you're doing. Are you sure you'll be okay?"

"I'm fine. They're keeping the coffee flowing in there. But look in on Troy for me, if you don't mind."

"Sure. See you in the morning." Kate dragged her feet back to the trailer and collapsed on her bed.

Early Sunday morning, Vicky shook Kate's arm. "Are you awake?"

"I am now," she said without looking up from her pillow.

"Some man is outside. He wants to talk to you."

"Some man?"

"Yeah, I think it's the guy who runs this place."

"Morgan Meyer?"

"Maybe."

Kate looked around for something to put on, but then realized she was still wearing her clothes from the night before. She navigated out of the bedroom and to the door, looking through puffy eyes. She blocked the light of the sun with her arm and squinted as she looked outside. "Yes?"

"Kate, good morning. I wanted to thank you for your part in getting us out of there. My wife said you were instrumental in the planning process."

"Sure. But aren't you tired? I mean you guys had some pretty primitive accommodations. Weren't you enjoying being home in your own bed?" Seeing that she was a guest on the man's property, Kate went above and beyond the call of duty in finding a polite way to tell him not to bother her this early in the morning.

Morgan smiled. "I was, and I wouldn't be so rudely interrupting your sweet slumber if I had no more pressing news than the conveyance of my gratitude."

Kate knew she didn't want to hear what was coming next. "Go on."

"We're having a meeting at the pavilion in half an hour. Sergeant Garcia thinks Colonel Forrestal will mobilize his troops for a counterstrike rather quickly. Perhaps as soon as today. We need to get a plan together, and I'd like you to be in on it."

"You'll have coffee and donuts?"

He laughed. "Will you settle for coffee and pancakes?"

"Just this once."

"Then I'll see you at the pavilion in thirty." Morgan Meyer waved his hand as he walked away.

Kate closed the door and rested her weary head against the jamb.

Vicky leaned against the wall of the trailer. "So it's still not over."

"Evidently not." Kate walked to the bathroom. She poured some water from a jug into a wash pan to wash her face.

Vicky followed her. "How are we going to stand up to an entire battalion?"

Kate knew she'd sound insincere if she tried to soft-pedal the seriousness of the situation. "I'm not sure. But if you had asked me how we were going to get Gavin and Jack home, or how we were going to survive any of this, I would have told you the same thing. God has seen fit to get us this far. We have to trust Him."

"Mom, Dad, and Sam all trusted God. It didn't help them."

"Yes, it did." Kate paused what she was doing long enough to give her niece a hug. "He brought them through the hard times. Now they're home. Taking it easy, enjoying heaven, and waiting for the day that we can all be together again."

"I miss them, but I'm not ready to die." Vicky swallowed hard. "After Sam was killed, I thought I was. I'm not afraid to. I trust Jesus, but I don't want to go right now, and I don't want you to either."

"The feeling is mutual. I'm going to do everything I can to keep that from happening." Kate picked out some clean clothes and changed out of the previous night's attire.

She marched across the property to the pavilion. Morgan and Mandy Meyer were both present. Mia sat beside a man who Kate guessed was her husband. Bill and Dennis were at the table representing the residents from the ranch. Sergeant Garcia and the young private named Philip were also there.

Morgan brought Kate a Styrofoam cup of coffee. "Pancakes will be around in a minute." He walked to the chalkboard at the end of the pavilion, which acted as the focal point for the meeting. "Sergeant Garcia, I'm going to let you take the floor. You know more about our enemy than anyone else."

"Thank you." Garcia walked to the board and

drew a circle on the far right side of the board. "Colonel Forrestal has approximately five hundred men in Waynesville." He drew a smaller circle on the left. "We have roughly one hundred. Out of that hundred, about twenty are either too old or too young to be effective in battle. Another ten are confined to bed rest in the infirmary. We might have seventy potential shooters. That number is really cutting it close as I'm using eighty as the cut off point for the elderly and thirteen as the cut off point for children. Outnumbered and outgunned doesn't even come close to describing the severity of our situation.

"The way I see it, we have two options. Hunker down and wait for them to mow us over, or hit them before they hit us.

"The advantage to hunkering down is that we have the high ground. We can select a fortified position, like the main cabin and pick off several of our attackers when they approach. The drawback of that plan is we have nowhere to retreat if the fortification is overrun."

Bill added, "With five of them to every one of us, we will be overrun."

"Probably so," Garcia continued. "That brings us to our second option. We attack them. The upside is that we'll have the element of surprise. The downside, they'll be defending from a position of strength."

Morgan Meyer added, "We still have the issue of them being an overwhelming force."

"Yeah," Garcia looked down at the piece of chalk in his hand. "There's that."

Mandy Meyer stood. "Regardless of which avenue of certain death we choose, I think we should admit that this is a suicide mission unless we're willing to solicit assistance from the Reverend."

"Lloyd Graves is a bad apple." Bill crossed his arms.

"I agree with you completely," Mandy confessed. "But most of you would still be rotting in prison if he hadn't sided with us."

"You mean sided with his chance at a profit." Kate wasn't arguing the fact that they may indeed have to hire the menacing thug to help them survive the coming onslaught, but she wanted to make sure everyone understood that the Reverend was not acting out of the goodness of his black heart.

"Yes, Kate. He's a mercenary. Unfortunately, we're in dire need of a hired gun at this particular juncture." Mandy turned to her husband.

Morgan Meyer stared at the concrete floor of the pavilion, as if he'd never in his life been at such a loss for a solution.

Kate studied the chalkboard, knowing a more practical solution must exist. "What if we had a third option?"

Garcia held out the piece of chalk, as if he were eager to be rid of the overbearing responsibility that accompanied it. "Sure, go ahead."

Kate stood and took the chalk but asked for permission from Morgan. "May I?"

"Please." He waved his hand, but his downcast face showed that he expected little from the pretty blonde girl.

Kate formulated the idea from only a spark to a complete proposal while she stalled in front of the chalkboard. "What if..." She drew a third circle, between the other two. "...we set up an ambush site? They have to take US-74."

"Not necessarily. It's only a couple miles out of the way to take US-19," Bill said.

Kate refitted, "A couple of miles, but lots of ups and downs around winding mountain roads. I can't imagine a military commander choosing that path if he had a better alternative."

Garcia leaned against one of the picnic tables. "She's right. Forrestal will take 74."

Morgan picked up the map from the table and gave it to Kate. "Where would you set up your ambush?"

She studied the map. "Sergeant Garcia, what do you think?"

Dennis glanced at the map. "Anywhere you hit US-74, you'll have 4 lanes of traffic, plus wide shoulders to block off. It provides them lots of space in which to maneuver. That will make it tough for us to fix them."

Garcia rubbed his forehead with his fingers. "I can't completely discount what Bill said about them taking US-19. Forrestal could be anticipating an ambush. If so, he might take US-19 because he knows we'll be looking for him on 74. Heck, he could split his forces, send one contingency down each road figuring one will hit the camp and the other can take on the ambush. He'd still have us outmanned by nearly three-to-one."

Kate looked at the map like a doctor helplessly

watching her patient die. Suddenly, a solution came to her. "I got it! We stage our ambush on Alarka Road."

Mia shook her head dismissively. "They'll be in our backyard by then."

"They'll be close, but it still provides us enough of a buffer that the Citadel can be evacuated if we're overrun." Kate examined the map more closely.

"Evacuate? To where?" Mandy Meyer seemed annoyed by such a useless proposition.

Kate looked up at her with humorless eyes. "If the main attack force has broken through, the elderly and children left in the camp will have to choose between making a run for it into the woods or being made into slaves by a depraved despot. It's not much, but it is a choice that they won't have if we sit here until Forrestal arrives.

"Setting the ambush on Alarka Road also alleviates our concern over which road he'll take and it creates a smaller kill zone, giving his troops less room to maneuver."

"She's right." Garcia looked at Morgan, Dennis, and Bill.

Morgan nodded. "Set it up. Mandy, I suppose you know how to reach the Reverend over the radio."

Her face looked sullen. "I do. But he's going to need an incentive."

"Offer him whatever gold and silver we have left. If we don't survive this, it won't be worth anything to us." Morgan took his wife's hand.

"What if he wants supplies?"

"Whatever it takes. We can't pull this off without

his help."

Kate hated to hear those words, but as unsavory as they were, she knew them to be true. "What do you need from me?"

Morgan replied, "Kate, start marking out some attack positions at the proposed ambush site. Garcia, help her out with that. If you have a couple of men you can spare, send a team on up ahead to watch and radio us when the first vehicles start to arrive.

"Bill, Dennis, have your people start dropping trees and dragging them into the road on Alarka. Then get some tractors with log chains stashed where they first turn onto Alarka. We'll need a team to block the retreat also. Have the trees felled and waiting for them."

"If all it takes is a tractor and a log chain to block the road, they'll be able to clear it with the same instruments," said Dennis.

Morgan countered. "Take the keys to the tractor and the log chains when you leave. That'll slow down Forrestal's men in clearing a path for retreat." Morgan clapped his hands. "Let's get this plan rolling folks, Colonel Forrestal could be loading his vehicles as we speak."

Kate hurried back to the trailers to gather her team.

CHAPTER 25

Therefore sent he thither horses, and chariots, and a great host: and they came by night, and compassed the city about. And when the servant of the man of God was risen early, and gone forth, behold, an host compassed the city both with horses and chariots. And his servant said unto him, Alas, my master! how shall we do? And he answered, Fear not: for they that be with us are more than they that be with them. And Elisha prayed, and said, Lord, I pray thee, open his eyes, that he may see. And the Lord opened the eyes of the young man; and he saw: and, behold, the mountain was full of horses and chariots of fire round about Elisha.

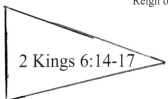

2 Kings 6:14-17

Late Sunday evening, Kate, Vicky, Pritchard, and Rainey returned to the trailer.

"Now what?" Vicky plopped down on the couch.

Pritchard opened the cupboards and selected some canned goods. "Get some vittles in you. Sleep if you can. Be it early in the mornin' or late of a evenin', we've got to be ready when these devils come."

"But why are we here? We should have stayed at the ambush site." Vicky put her hands in the pockets of her hoodie.

"We've done everything we can to get the trap set and our positions ready." Kate sat next to Vicky. "It could be days, even weeks before Forrestal comes. Sergeant Garcia has sentries posted at all the possible avenues of approach. We'll have at least a twenty-minute warning before the colonel reaches the ambush site. Mr. Pritchard is right, we need to be rested and nourished when the time comes."

"I'm going to go check on my dad while I can." Rainey headed out the door.

"Take your rifle and assault pack. We have to be ready to go at a moment's notice," Kate replied. "I'll meet you down there in a minute. I want to see Gavin before I go to bed."

Kate opened a can of beef ravioli and began eating it cold, straight from the can.

"I'm fixin' to build a fire." Pritchard looked at her. "Why don't you wait and let me heat that up for you?"

"I need to go see Gavin. And, I need to get some rest. I'm running on about three hours of sleep."

"Alright then." Pritchard began dumping various cans of ingredients into a saucepan. "Vicky, come on outside with me. Help me get a fire going. We's fixing to cook up a mess of hobo stew."

"What's that?" Vicky wrinkled her nose and followed the old man outside.

Kate wolfed down the food, snatched her canteen off the counter, and headed toward the infirmary.

She saw only one woman acting as a nurse. "Hi, have you seen Annie Cobb?"

"She's gone to her trailer to get some rest. She was about to fall over she was so tired."

"Yeah, I'm sure." Kate looked inside the cabin.

"Is there anything I can help you with?"

"You have a patient named Gavin. Can you tell me how he's doing?"

"He's progressing fine. He just woke up a little while ago. Last door on the left."

"Thanks." Kate made her way to the back of the small residential cabin, which was being used as a hospital. She walked in the bedroom to three small cots set up in a U-shape. Gavin lay on the center cot, flanked by two men Kate didn't recognize. The one on the right was asleep. The man on the left watched Kate walk into the room. She smiled at the man on the left, then knelt beside Gavin's cot. "Hey," she whispered.

He rolled to the side and opened his eyes. "Hey, yourself."

She took his hand. "That was a stupid move you

pulled back there."

"You're the one who came up with the idea." He gave a weak smile. "Did you get Jack?"

"Yeah, we got him. All the other patients, too." She looked down at his hand. "Sarge and Abigail were killed."

He closed his eyes. "Forrestal will be coming."

"We figured as much. We've set an ambush. Garcia has patrols watching for his approach."

Gavin held out his hand. "Let me have your pistol."

"No Gavin!" She quickly realized how loudly she'd responded. Kate looked at the sleeping man, but he'd not been awakened by her outburst. "No. You need to rest. I thought you were dead. They pulled an entire magazine's worth of bullets and fragments out of you. You are gonna sit this one out."

His face looked grave. "I don't even think I could stand up. You don't have to worry about me getting out of bed. But be realistic. Whatever your plan is, you're outnumbered. Forrestal may eventually come here. I at least want to take a few of those guys with me."

Kate couldn't stand to see Gavin in such a vulnerable state. She hated the thought of leaving him to go fight. "If the worst happens, I'll come back here. The ambush point is on Alarka Road. We'll make our final stand together."

"I'd like that." His voice was frail. "But either way, I'll still need a gun."

She swallowed the knot forming in her throat. She unholstered her pistol and handed it to Gavin.

"I'll be back. I promise."

"I'll be right here." He attempted another anemic smile.

"You get some rest." Kate kissed him on the head.

"I love you." Gavin closed his eyes.

She slowly stood to leave. "I love you, too."

Kate walked out of the room and quietly pulled the door shut.

Rainey came out of the room across the hall.

"How's Jack?" Kate asked.

"His fever is down. His body is reacting well to the antibiotics." Her response was anticlimactic.

"That's good news, right?"

"Yeah." She looked at the wooden floor of the cabin.

"Then what's wrong?"

"They have to take his leg below the knee. He went too long without treatment."

Kate hugged the teen girl. "I know it's rough, but be grateful that he's alive. They weren't sure if they could save him last night."

Rainey dried her eyes with the cuff of her sweatshirt. "I know. And I am grateful. But this world is so hard to survive, even if you have all your hands and feet. This puts him at a serious disadvantage and makes it more likely that he'll get killed."

She sniffed and dried her eyes again. "Oh, what am I talking about? Chances are that we'll all be dead by morning anyway."

Kate held her shoulders firmly. "Rainey, we're not going to give up yet. Your dad has done everything he could to keep you safe. But right now, he needs you to not lose hope. The only possible way any of us can live through what's coming is if we all keep it together and fight like we've never fought before. Can you do that for me, for your dad?"

"I think so." Rainey nodded.

"Good." Kate put her arm around her and walked her toward the door. "Let's get you something to eat, clean ourselves up, and get some sleep."

"Okay." Rainey walked back to the trailers with Kate.

"We've got a massive line of vehicles moving westbound on US-74." Morgan Meyer's voice came over the radio. "They're moving fast. We have about fifteen minutes before they're in the kill zone. Unit leaders, get your troops mobilized. This is it!"

Kate abruptly awakened from her deep slumber. She grabbed the radio. "Roger that. Unit Echo is in route." She had no idea how long she'd been asleep, didn't bother to look at the clock. Kate stuck her feet into her boots, grabbed her rifle and her assault pack and threw the door open. "This is it! Up and at 'em!"

Not wanting to be alone, Rainey had slept in Vicky's room. She was the first to answer the call. Pritchard still lay on his back on the couch, mouth open and snoring loudly.

Kate slapped the bottom of his feet. "Mr. Pritchard! Wake up!"

He awoke startled by the unexpected assault against his feet. He kicked against the arm of the couch, flailed his arms and rolled onto the floor. "What's a matter with you, smackin' my feet, girl? Ain't you got no sense?"

"It's time to go, Mr. Pritchard." Kate looked past Rainey. "Vicky, this is it!"

"I'm up!" she responded.

Kate hurried out the door and into the night air. She banged on Amanda's trailer door. "David, Amanda, it's time!"

"Coming!" Amanda's voice called from inside.

Annie emerged from her trailer, a rifle slung over her back.

Troy tugged at her free arm. "No, mama! Don't go."

Kate couldn't bear the look on Troy or Annie's faces. "Annie, we're going to have untold casualties pouring into the camp. You can do more good by staying here."

Annie looked perplexed, as if she felt a mix of guilt and relief. "Are you sure?"

"Positive. But keep that rifle with you. Troy, do you think you can be brave today?"

He nodded.

"Your mom is going to need some help at the medical center. You might see a lot of blood, but something as simple as handing your mom a bandage or getting some water could help save somebody's life."

"I can do it."

"Good." Kate looked at the boy's innocent face. "And take your gun; just in case."

"Best get a move on. We ain't doin' no good hangin' about the camp yakkin' like a bunch a hens." Pritchard hurried Kate along.

Kate put her hand up at the cantankerous old man. She whispered to Annie, "It's possible that Lloyd Graves could end up in your care if he were to be injured during the fight. You should think about how you'll handle that situation before it arises."

"Say no more. I'll take care of Graves if he's brought into the infirmary."

"Make sure it looks like he died from his injuries." Kate promptly led her team to the vehicles which were shuttling the troops to the ambush site.

Kate helped Mr. Pritchard step up onto the rear bumper of a pickup truck. Kim Sweeny and Judy Hess stood nearby.

"We want to come. We want to fight with your team," Kim said, a bolt-action deer rifle slung over her shoulder.

Kate looked at the two housewives, untrained, untested, and both in their sixties. She knew this was no environment for them, but if she turned them down, they'd probably die anyway. "Are you sure? No one will think any less of you if you stay back and guard the fort."

Judy Hess held a shotgun. "We're sure."

"Okay, then we're honored to have you as part of Unit Echo." Kate helped the two women into the back of the truck.

Once everyone was in, the truck bed was tight. Pritchard spoke words of encouragement on the short ride to the objective rally point. "The King of Syria was told that the prophet Elisha was warnin' Israel ever time he was a goin' up to attack. So, that ol' devil called for his army to run and fetch Elisha. When Elisha's servant looked out, there was all the Syrians surroundin' the city. Well, he got a feared and pitched the awfulest fit you ever saw, tellin' Elisha that they was about to die. Elisha prayed that God would open his servant's eyes that he might see how many more soldiers was on their side. He did and the servant looked again. He saw the angel armies of God with horses and chariots of fire!

"I want every one of you to believe that we serve the same God as Elisha. We ain't alone in this. You just need to open your eyes and see that all the angel armies of heaven is right here with us. Jesus, himself, is amongst us, too!"

Kate had seen scores of her friends and family members die in the months since the Locusts first arrived. She was not naive about the fate that awaited them. Yet she hoped that God would provide a miracle for her group. Anything less and Colonel Forrestal's troops would annihilate every last one of them.

CHAPTER 26

Woe unto them that decree unrighteous decrees, and that write grievousness which they have prescribed; to turn aside the needy from judgment, and to take away the right from the poor of my people, that widows may be their prey, and that they may rob the fatherless! And what will ye do in the day of visitation, and in the desolation which shall come from far? to whom will ye flee for help? and where will ye leave your glory?

Isaiah 10:1-3

Kate used a flashlight to direct her team. "Judy, Kim, take that big oak. Use it for cover until the soldiers begin coming up the hill and into the forest. Once that happens, you'll have to relocate to another position. Shoot and move. If you stop doing either one of those things, the enemy will close in on you, and it's game over."

Kate shined the beam at Vicky and Rainey. "You two are behind that fallen locust with me. Pritchard, you, David, and Amanda, take that outcropping of rocks. The rocks are low, so they'll only provide cover if you're lying prone. Do you think you'll be able to get up fast enough when the troops come at us?"

"Girl, I ain't no invalid. I can outrun most of these young bucks around here." He pointed his light toward the adjacent unit of soldiers who'd defected from Forrestal's camp. "I could probably whoop a good many of 'em too."

Kate stitched her brows together. "Hopefully that won't be necessary."

Garcia held his arm over his eyes to block the light coming from Pritchard's flashlight. "You should keep your beams low. The light travels in the darkness. We wouldn't want to tip them off."

Pritchard clicked off his light and mumbled under his breath as he stomped off to his position.

Garcia and Phillip walked over to Kate. Garcia inspected her team's positions. "Looks good. We're Unit Alpha, right next to you. Call us if you get in a tight spot."

"Thanks," said Kate. "The Reverend's men are ready?"

"I hope so." Garcia glanced across the road toward the adjacent hillside. "With friends like those…"

Kate looked in the same direction. "We sure don't need any more enemies."

Looking at Rainey, Phillip held his rifle snug against his shoulder. "Good luck. Take care of yourself."

Rainey blushed and looked away to conceal the uncontrollable grin invading her face. "You, too."

"Come on." Garcia put his hand on Phillip's shoulder. He called out to Kate as he walked away, "See you on the other side."

Kate knelt behind the downed locust tree next to Vicky. She looked past her niece to Rainey. "Your dad doesn't need two legs to make that boy wish he'd never been born."

Rainey smiled wide. "I know."

Morgan Meyer's voice came over Kate's walkie. "The convoy just turned onto Alarka. Lights out and radio silence until after the operation has commenced. Find your targets and hold your fire until I give the command."

Kate looked to confirm that everyone on her team had shut off their flashlights and were ready to fight. She positioned her M-4 atop the tree, took a deep breath, and waited. She noticed that Vicky's rifle was pointed up, toward the opposite hillside. "The action is going to be on the road below."

"Just seeing if I can spot the Reverend. Making sure he is where he's supposed to be."

Kate gently put her hand on the barrel of Vicky's gun and pushed it down. "Stay focused. One enemy at a time."

"Here they come!" Rainey whispered loudly.

Kate saw the first set of headlights racing toward the roadblock of trees in the pavement below. "Get ready. Hold your fire."

The first vehicle was a heavy-duty Ford F-350. The driver came upon the downed trees too fast and skidded sideways when he slammed the brakes. The truck careened into the barricade of large pines. The vehicle behind the F-350 hit the brakes too late and crashed into the back of the pickup. The third vehicle stopped just short of the second's bumper. Soldiers got out of the trucks.

A man from the sixth vehicle back could not see the roadblock from his location. He left his truck running and the door opened as he stepped out of the driver's side. "What's going on up there?"

"What's the holdup?" Another yelled.

"Tree in the road," called a soldier from the third vehicle.

A soldier who'd come from the second vehicle clicked on his light and began scanning the opposite hillside where the Reverend's fighters were positioned for the attack. "Keep your eyes open. This could be an ambush."

Kate lined up the reticle of her night vision scope on a soldier in the bed of the fourth truck, assuming everyone else would be aiming for troops already out of the vehicles.

"Commence!" Morgan's voice flashed over the radio and rifle fire echoed from both hillsides, raining down a barrage of lead upon the stalled convoy.

"Ambush!" The soldiers on the road below dove for cover. Some dropped to the ground and hid beneath the vehicles. Others got back into the cabs of the trucks.

Kate dropped the first troop in the bed of the pickup and moved on to the next. She killed three of them before the other three bailed out of the bed to seek cover under the truck. She quickly found another target in the passenger's side of a box truck cab. She eliminated him then moved to the box, surmising that the cargo area was filled with more men who'd come to murder everyone she cared about.

A few stray flashes of gunfire erupted from below the trucks, but it was obvious that they were shooting blind. "Back it up! Get out of here!" Several voices from Forrestal's convoy pleaded with the trucks near the back to make room, but it was no use. They were trapped from that side too, with no escape from the kill zone.

"We have to get up into those woods!" yelled a soldier. "We have to fight back."

Kate changed magazines and patted Vicky on the shoulder. "Get ready to move. We'll hold this position until they're halfway up the hill, then we'll leapfrog back to our secondary location. Vicky, you go first. Rainey and I will keep up the cover fire. Yell *set* when you're in place. Rainey, you go next, then you two will cover me while I move back."

"Got it." Vicky kept shooting.

Kate sprayed the road below while the soldiers attempted to exit their vehicles without being hit.

"This is an absolute massacre! We might actually win!" Rainey changed magazines and continued shooting.

The asphalt below was littered with dead bodies and coated in blood. Indeed, the assault was going much better than Kate ever could have imagined, but she was hesitant to share in Rainey's premature celebration. "Concentrate on the fight, it isn't over until it's over."

One of the soldiers below called to the men getting ready to charge up the mountain toward Kate's team. "Other side! We've got an opening!"

Kate glanced up only for a second to see what the man could be referring to. Instantly, she noticed that no muzzle flashes were coming from the opposite hillside. The troops ran into the cover of the trees.

Sergeant Garcia stooped low as he weaved through the trees and bushes to get to Kate. "The Reverend is gone. He pulled out."

"We killed almost all of them," Vicky replied.

"All but about fifty or sixty," Garcia held up a pair of night vision goggles.

"Almost the perfect number for mutually assured destruction," Kate scanned the woods on the other side of the road with her scope. "Graves had this planned all along."

"We have them outnumbered by about ten or twenty," Garcia said. "At least the Reverend waited until we had the upper hand before backing out."

"Which ensures our survivors will be easy prey for him after the smoke clears." Kate was furious. "One way or the other, I will kill that man."

"You have to live through this first," Garcia reminded. "Gather your team and follow me."

"Where are we going?" Kate asked.

"We have to flank the troops on the other side before they have a chance to get organized." Garcia headed back to his men.

"Kim, Judy, Pritchard, all of you, follow me." Kate waved to her team. She led them to Sergeant Garcia.

Garcia pointed down to the road. "We'll work our way toward the roadblock, moving in a diagonal direction. We'll circle around the pines, cross the pavement, and get into those woods. Once we get there, I'll verify that none of them are to the right of us, then we'll hike up to a flanking position." He looked at Judy. "I need one person to run down to Morgan and tell him what we're up to. Ask him to keep suppressive fire on their location, even if he doesn't have a shot. The important thing is that he continues harassing them, so they won't notice my team sneaking up on them from the side."

Judy nodded. "Okay, but why can't you just call him on the radio?"

"The enemy is probably monitoring the airwaves."

"Oh, right."

"Get going. We don't have any time to waste." Garcia patted Judy on the back. "Everyone else, follow me."

Kate trailed behind Garcia and his unit. Sporadic gunfire rang out from both sides of the road. Her group soon reached the road beyond the pine blockade, then began ascending the hill where Forrestal's men had taken up positions. Kate turned back to see Kim Sweeny and Amanda McDowell struggling to keep up. Kate sprinted ahead to catch up with Garcia. "How much higher are we going?"

"I want to get beyond the ridgeline; circle around from the back side of the hill. Then we can swoop down like an eagle for the kill."

"Sounds good, but I'm afraid some of my team can't make the hike at our current pace."

Garcia looked back. "Then put them behind those mountain laurels over there. I can put them to use. We'll have them open fire to create a diversion when we're ready to pounce. Do they have radios?"

"Amanda does. I'm sure David will stay behind with her."

"Okay, get them in position and hurry back."

Kate kept her eyes on the forest floor and bounded down the mountain. She quickly passed on the instruction to Kim and Amanda. As she'd suspected, David stayed with his mother.

Fighting to regain the ground she'd lost, Kate's thighs burned and her lungs ached. "Great, now I'm the one who's winded," she whispered to herself. Eventually, she caught up to Garcia. The team crested the hill and followed the back side of the ridgeline. Garcia led them to the top and had everyone crouch low. He looked through his night vision binoculars once more. "They're right below us. Everyone find a target. Kate, tell your diversionary team to light them up."

Kate spoke softly over the radio. "Amanda, have your team open fire."

Garcia waited for Amanda's team to get the enemy's attention then gave the order. "Fire!"

POP, POP! Kate dropped two enemy combatants early on and kept shooting. They seemed confused as gunfire rained down upon them from all sides. Kate continued scanning for targets but found fewer and fewer. She knelt beside Garcia. "Why is Morgan's unit still going through so much ammo?"

Garcia also appeared perplexed by the continued high rate of gunfire on the opposite hill. "I don't know."

Just then, Morgan's voice came across the radio. "We need help over here. They're right on top of us!"

Kate realized exactly what had happened. "While we were flanking them, they were flanking our people."

Garcia shook his head. "Oh no! Come on! We have to get over there!"

Kate looked at Vicky, Rainey, and Pritchard. "Are you guys ready?"

Vicky and Rainey nodded.

Pritchard was breathing heavily. He waved his hand. "Y'all get on over there. I'll be along directly."

"Okay, come on girls." Kate led the charge down the hill. Gunfire came from every direction, but mostly from across the road where Morgan's unit was.

She heard a loud thud from behind her and turned to look. "Vicky!" Kate's heart sank. She turned to check on her. Vicky was lying on her back. Blood and dirt soiled her face. "Vicky!" Kate let her rifle hang from the sling and took a pack of gauze from her pocket.

"I'm okay, Aunt Kate. I just tripped on a tree root."

Rainey looked on in horror. "But you're bleeding!"

"Yeah, I think I hit my head on a rock." Vicky touched the shallow wound on her head.

Kate passed the gauze to Rainey. "Stay here. Take care of Vicky."

"I will." Rainey blotted the cut on Vicky's forehead.

Kate bolted down through the woods, determined to get back in the fight.

"We're stuck." Garcia and his men were pinned down, immediately inside the tree line and could not get across the road. "Just you?"

"Yeah, last of the Mohicans." Kate looked for a way across.

"Any ideas?" he asked.

She looked at the three-car pileup near the roadblock. "We could crawl beneath those vehicles. That would get us close."

"Yeah," Garcia snorted. "Close to being shot."

"I can't think of anything better."

"You're right. It's our best play." He waved to his men. "Let's go."

Kate mimicked the forward crawl that Garcia and his men performed to get beneath the trucks. They cradled their rifles in the crooks of their elbows and slinked under the vehicles.

Garcia paused at the edge. "I'm going to roll out and open up on them. The rest of you make a dash for the tree line."

Kate waited for Garcia to come out from beneath the F-350 then she darted for the trees.

Gunshots rang out overhead. Soon, all of

Garcia's men were in the woods.

Kate looked to see Sergeant Garcia sprinting for cover. A shot echoed in the hills, blood spurted from his leg, and he tumbled to the pavement. "Philip! Cover me!"

Phillip and the other men peppered the trees where the shot had originated and Kate ran back to get Garcia.

She put her arm under his. "Come on. You're almost there."

"Ahh!" He shrieked in pain but managed to stand up.

Kate assisted him for the last few feet to cover, then sat him down easily. Garcia looked up. "Thanks, but you have to keep going." He turned to the young private. "Philip, you're in command. Listen to Kate. She might not be a soldier, but she knows what she's doing."

"Yes, sir." Philip pushed forward up the hill toward the gunfire.

"I've got four enemy troops, straight ahead." Kate took cover behind a big tree.

Philip dropped down right beside her. "I see them. Everyone, on my mark."

Kate took aim.

"Fire!" Philip and the other men opened up.

Kate also let the bullets rip through the woods.

Philip lowered his weapon. All became quiet. "Anybody got anything?"

Kate looked all around. "Nothing. No enemy, none of our guys."

Philip motioned for his men to stand up slowly. "Okay, let's advance."

Kate stayed close to the unit. She heard a twig snap nearby. She patted Philip on the shoulder who gave a hand signal for his men to stop and go down to one knee.

Suddenly, four troops popped up from the brush and fired on Kate and the other men. Kate fell to the ground and rolled down the hill. She caught herself and scurried behind a heavy tree trunk. She came from the other side and engaged the four enemy fighters. They all fell one by one. Philip quickly found the four fallen hostiles and placed two more rounds in each of their heads.

Kate looked around. "Where is everyone else?"

"We are everyone else." He remained vigilant looking through his scope.

She looked at the other men who'd been with them. All lay motionless on the forest floor.

Kate stayed close to Philip as they proceeded to search the dark woods. "I saw something. Behind those rocks," she whispered.

Philip nodded and walked silently in that direction. The two of them slipped up close to the position by keeping a large oak between them and the source of the movement which Kate had noticed.

Philip looked at Kate. He held up three fingers and dropped them one by one.

She nodded to let him know she understood it to be a countdown.

When Philip's last finger dropped, they each emerged from opposite sides of the tree.

"Wait!" Kate put up her hand when she saw Morgan Meyer with a bloody, bandaged arm cradling the body of Mandy.

She dropped down to check on Morgan. "Are you okay?"

"Flesh wound. In and out. But Mandy is gone."

"I'm sorry. Where's the rest of your unit?"

"Get down!" Philip pushed Kate to the forest floor. "Someone is coming!"

Kate positioned her rifle for another battle. Philip did likewise.

She heard the footsteps on the other side of the rock from where they were hiding. She took up the slack in her trigger.

A figure emerged from around the rock.

"Bill!" Kate called.

Bill jumped and put his hand over his chest. "Kate?"

Jan and Dennis came into view.

"Are you okay?" Jan asked.

"I'm not shot. But all three of our units have been nearly destroyed."

"Ours, too," Jan said sorrowfully.

"Have you seen anyone from Bravo?" Morgan inquired, still holding Mandy.

"Just Mia. She's next to Ethan's body," Dennis said.

"Where's the enemy?" Kate asked.

Bill looked behind him. "We were all the way up at the other roadblock, and we didn't see any hostiles between here and there."

"Maybe we got them all," said Philip.

Kate looked at the sky. A faint hint of daylight was crawling across the darkness. "We've got a lot of people who need medical help. Does anyone know where those tractor keys are and that log chain?"

Bill held up the key. "I stashed the log chain by a stump near the tractor."

"Good. If you'll clear the path, we'll start getting the wounded down to the road."

Dennis pointed at the F-350. "If the keys aren't in that Ford, they'll be with one of the bodies nearby."

"Jan, can you and Dennis help Morgan? I need to go find my niece." Kate walked cautiously down the hill.

"Sure," Jan answered.

Philip said, "I'll assist Sergeant Garcia."

"Okay, I'll see you back at camp," Kate kept watch for any stragglers still lurking about in the woods.

CHAPTER 27

A man's heart deviseth his way: but the Lord directeth his steps.

Proverbs 16:9

Kate stood next to Annie Cobb while she dressed the wound on Morgan Meyer's arm. "We should hit them now."

"No way." Morgan winced in pain. "We need to recuperate, rest up, put a plan together."

"Giving the Reverend time to do the same." Kate crossed her arms.

Morgan said, "We don't even know where his camp is. No one knows. Vince managed to obtain a radio frequency for the man. That's the only way we were able to make contact. Mandy met with him here once. All the other times we've spoken with him were over the airwaves."

Kate looked at Annie. "We actually might know where his camp is."

"That should hold you, for now, Mr. Meyer." Annie inspected the bandage. "Kate, we're inundated with casualties. Some of these people may not make it for the simple reason that the medical staff is overwhelmed. I want that monster dead as bad as you do, but you have to exercise discretion here. Give us some time to catch up before you bring in any more injured, please."

Morgan reiterated her plea, "Many of the injuries are superficial. The chance to mend for a day or two would allow several of us to get back in the fight; myself included."

Kate clenched her jaw. "If anyone here at the Bryson Citadel is left alive in a day or two, I've misjudged the Reverend altogether. He suffered no losses at the ambush. His people probably went back to camp and celebrated the near obliteration of all their enemies. If we hit them right now, we might be able to catch them sleeping off a hard night of drinking and revelry."

"I don't want to hear any more about it." Morgan stood up from the exam table. "I'm going to bury my wife and get some rest. I'll see who might be able to participate in a raid, and we'll start putting a plan together tomorrow morning. Go home, Kate."

Kate complied with the order but did not respond to Morgan. She stomped off from the infirmary toward the trailers. Passing the bunkhouse, she saw Philip.

"Kate!" he called.

"Hey, Philip."

"Did Rainey and Vicky get back okay?"

"Yes, thanks for asking."

"What's the plan? Are we just going to sit around and wait for the Reverend to attack?"

"According to Morgan Meyer, that's exactly what we're going to do."

"What do you say?"

"I think the Reverend's camp is likely boozing it up right now. They probably have their guard down. They think both of their enemies are all but destroyed, so that makes them the apex predator. Sharks and lions don't spend a lot of time standing guard. What are your feelings on the matter?"

"My thoughts exactly."

"Glad to hear someone recognizes our situation. A lot of good it does. We can't pull off a mission like that by ourselves." Kate continued walking toward the trailers.

Philip walked with her. "A mission like what?"

"Sneak into the camp, kill Graves, and get back out." She sighed. "I'm sure another depraved lunatic would take his place, but it would give the rest of them pause. It would show them that they can be touched."

"Do you know where he is?"

"Yes."

"We could get in and kill the Reverend," Philip replied.

"Sure, but unless you're a ninja, you won't make it out alive."

Philip looked up with sad eyes. "If we sit around here and wait to be attacked, we're dead anyway."

Kate considered what the young man was saying. Philip wasn't even twenty years old, yet he displayed such bravery. Could she allow herself to shrink back? "So, you and me, huh? A two-person suicide hit squad."

"Unless some other people want to come along."

"Let's keep the death toll at a minimum. Promise me you won't say anything to Vicky or Rainey."

"Your secret is safe with me. What about Dennis and Mia?"

"I suppose." Kate thought about the suggestion. "It increases our odds of success, but I feel like their blood will be on our heads for bringing them along."

His sorrowful eyes met hers. "Kate, I don't mean to sound morbid, but they're dead already. Unless we do something, everyone at the Bryson Citadel is gone. If a few of us are willing to go a little sooner, maybe we can change the outcome for the rest."

She thought about Gavin and Vicky, how she'd do anything to save them. "Okay, see if you can find them. If so, put the question to them, but you have to keep it quiet. Make sure no one else overhears you. Meet me at my trailer in half an hour. Get something to eat and hydrate. We'll have to move soon."

"Yes, ma'am." He turned toward the cabins where Dennis and Mia were staying.

"And don't call me ma'am. You make me feel old."

"Yes, ma'am," he laughed and broke into a sprint.

When Kate walked into the trailer, she saw

Vicky on the couch with her foot up and sock off. Her ankle was swollen and discolored. "Looks bad. You should go to the infirmary."

"I'm taking care of it for her." Rainey seemed to be fabricating a bandage by tying together torn pieces of cloth.

Vicky pulled the leg of her jeans up so Rainey could begin wrapping the ankle. "The infirmary has enough to deal with. No one should be there unless they have a bullet wound."

Kate looked at the gash on Vicky's head, which could probably have used a couple of stitches. "I appreciate your compassion for others, but you really need to let Annie take a look at you after they get caught up."

Kate pulled three MREs out of the cupboard, handing one to Rainey and another to Vicky. "You girls should eat, get cleaned up and try to rest. We don't know when we'll have to fight again."

Vicky tore into her MRE. "I'm not even old enough to drive, but I've already lost count of how many times I've had to wait, not knowing when the next impending attack would commence."

Rainey tied off the bandage and opened her pouch to begin eating. "Yeah, right?"

Kate thought nothing of the food she was eating. Her mind struggled as if treading water, awashed in a sea of melancholy. She figured this was the last time she'd share a meal with Vicky. She had so many things she wanted to say, pieces of motherly advice she wished to impart. However, she could say nothing that would tip her hand about the mission.

Pritchard barged through the front door abruptly and startled Kate. Instinctively, she put her hand on the handle of her rifle. "Mr Pritchard, you made it back!"

He held a pair of crutches in his hands. "Of course I did! Somebody had to look after the youngin' here whilst you was off galivantin' about the camp."

"I was just checking on the injured. Seeing what I could do to help out."

"Yeah, that's what Annie said." Pritchard passed the crutches to Vicky. "This is the last pair they had. Other folks are gonna need them soon, so best get to mendin' right quick like."

Vicky placed the crutches beside the couch. "Thanks, Mr. Pritchard."

"Y'all didn't see fit to wait for me to eat?" Pritchard made his way to the cupboard.

"We didn't know you were coming," said Kate.

"Don't make no difference no how." Pritchard took one of the MREs. "These are the foulest vittles I ever ate. I've had two-week-old opossum taste better than this."

With that comment, Kate lost her appetite. She put the remaining food on the counter and sat next to Vicky. She put her arm around her niece and pulled her close. "You get some rest. I want you to know that I love you."

"Thanks, Aunt Kate. Where are you going?" Vicky looked puzzled by the sudden display of affection.

Kate stood up quickly so as not to give herself a chance to get emotional. "I'm going to go look in on Gavin again."

"You just came from there!" Pritchard scolded. "Quit pesterin' the boy if you want him to get better. Sometimes a man just needs to be left alone for a spell."

Kate hugged the irascible old man despite his unsolicited advice. "I'll make sure he gets plenty of rest, Mr. Pritchard." She turned her attention to Rainey. "Take care of Vicky. Make sure she stays off that foot."

Rainey replied, "I will."

Kate went to her room and hastily reloaded her magazines.

Pritchard followed her in. "You figuring on a fight?"

"The Reverend will probably be back to finish us off sooner rather than later. You should get ready, too."

"Don't reckon he'll want to put his heels up for a minute? Take in the victory at havin' hoodwinked us into killin' off his foe?" Pritchard extracted a lost morsel of food from his beard and put it into his mouth. "Graves pert near wiped us out, too, with that contrivance. Two birds with one stone, so to speak. I can't see no reason he'd be in such a hurry to finish us off."

Kate didn't look up from her task. "You can't guess what Lloyd Graves is going to do by projecting the actions of a reasonable man upon him, Mr. Pritchard."

"Maybe not, but I might be able to postulate about what you're a fixin' to do."

Kate froze momentarily but did not make eye

contact. "Mr. Pritchard, you've been very kind to me since we've met. Nevertheless, I've not asked much of you since our initial acquaintance. But I have one favor to ask of you right now."

"Go on then."

She turned to look him in the eye. "I need you to tell me that you'll watch over Vicky."

"She don't need me lookin' after her. She needs you for that."

"I'm doing the best thing I know to do for her." Kate shouldered her assault pack. "Please, Mr. Pritchard."

The lines around his eyes showed deep concern. He gave a shallow nod.

"Thank you." She put her hand on his chest for a brief moment and headed out the door. "Take care." Kate forced a smile to Vicky, then turned away before a tear formed in the corner of her eye.

Philip stood outside the door. "Is Rainey inside?"

"Yeah, but you can't go in there. They'll know something is up." She hated to rob him of his final goodbye, but it could be no other way.

Philip lowered his gaze. "I understand."

Mia and Dennis stood behind Philip.

"You know where we're going?" Dennis asked.

"Yeah. We need a vehicle." Kate started walking toward the front gate. "I left an Escalade down by the road."

"Lead the way," Mia fell in line behind her.

CHAPTER 28

That which is crooked cannot be made straight: and that which is wanting cannot be numbered.

Ecclesiastes 1:15

Kate continued driving past 441 on US-74 out of Bryson.

Dennis sat in the back seat. "You should have taken 441 north to US-19. Didn't you say the camp was between Cherokee and Soco Falls?"

"Yeah, but it's one road in and one road out. They'll have guards posted at the entrance to the compound. We'll come in the back way." Kate had studied the map of the Reverend's lair many times since stumbling upon it. She knew exactly how to approach.

"Over the mountains?" Mia asked. "We'll lose our advantage if they're all out of bed by the time we get there."

"The back side isn't so bad. Pinnacle Park has a trail that goes to the top. It's a three-mile hike to the top from the parking area." The rest of the team could come along or stay behind. Kate was not deviating from the path in her head.

"What about the way down into his camp?" Philip asked.

"It's dense brush. But we can pick a path down."

"I hope it's not booby-trapped," Dennis added.

Kate grew tired of hearing the complaints. "I'll take the lead. If something happens to me, you three just get inside and kill Graves. Remember, you all signed up for a suicide mission. No one should expect this to be easy."

"It doesn't have to be easy," Dennis said. "But if I'm going to die, I want the mission to succeed."

"It will succeed." Kate tightened her jaw. "It has to."

"Can we get to the Reverend's cabin without passing by any of the trailers?" Philip looked at her.

"Yes. It's the dwelling farthest from the road," she replied.

Mia said from the back seat, "I hate to be the bearer of bad news, but we've got company."

"Company?" Kate's heart raced. Not with fear this time, but with concern that she wouldn't reach the objective.

"Two Hummers."

Kate growled, "Forrestal?"

"No," said Dennis. "I pulled Forrestal's corpse

264

out of a vehicle after the ambush. Besides, military Humvees aren't operational. This has to be a civilian."

"Morgan." Kate shook her head. "He's going to try to stop us."

"Just keep driving." Philip looked at the side view mirror. "The worst he can do is follow us to Pinnacle Park."

"But why would he be in two vehicles?" asked Mia.

"My guess is that he's brought an entire group with him," Kate answered.

Philip smirked, "Does he think he's going to change our minds with an intervention or something?"

"I suppose that's what you do when your friends display self-destructive behavior," Kate sighed.

Mia's voice was somber. "We're not smoking meth, we're trying to save the community."

"When we arrive, everyone just get out of the truck and follow me straight to the trail. Don't even acknowledge them." Kate increased her speed.

The team soon arrived at their destination. The two Humvees rolled up right beside the Escalade.

"Remember, no eye contact." Kate stepped out of the truck and slipped her arms in the straps of her assault pack. Out of the corner of her eye, she saw Morgan Meyer, Pritchard, Amanda, and David exit the first Hummer. They also seemed to be gearing up for a fight.

Kate knew they were not prepared to use lethal force to stop her team. "Come on, let's go." Kate hustled into the woods.

She heard Bill's voice behind her. "Kate, wait up!"

She turned to see Bill, Jan, and Kim Sweeny sprinting past the other members of her team. "Bill? What are you doing here? You're not going to stop us."

"Stop you?" Bill took long strides to keep up. "Why would we want to do that?"

Kate paused. "Then why did you come?"

"To help. You can't take on the Reverend's entire compound with four people."

Kate turned back to the path and continued her ascent up the mountain. "We're not taking on his entire compound. We're just going to hit his cabin. My mission is to kill Lloyd Graves. You shouldn't have come. Everyone on my team knows they're not going home. We've accepted that."

"Maybe we can change that."

Kate glanced over her shoulder. "Seven more people won't make a difference. You're cannon fodder. David is only fifteen, and he needs his mother. The Citadel is brimming with orphans already. Turn around and take them home."

"Eleven against a hundred is better odds than four against a hundred. We're coming with you, like it or not. And even if we die, we will make a difference."

She turned to Bill once more. "If you die? It's not a question of if. Either you turn around, or you will die. That is an absolute certainty."

"We all knew the risk before we came."

Kate huffed. "I guess I can't stop you if you've determined to follow me like a bunch of lemmings."

"No, you can't. So, we might as well come up with a plan that incorporates all of us."

Kate fumed for the next several hundred feet. However, as she followed the well-worn trail, she came to accept the circumstances for what they were. "Okay, maybe we could set up sniper positions in the woods above the cabin."

"That's better." Bill seemed pleased that Kate was coming around.

"When we hit the main cabin, we'll eventually have to start making some noise. Once that happens, the rest of them will come pouring out of the trailers to assist the Reverend. Your team can pick them off as they emerge. Even if you see them pass by a window, take a shot. Those trailers are paper thin. The walls won't stop anything but birdshot."

"We can handle that. Maybe we can buy your team enough time to accomplish your objective and get back out. If we cull the herd sufficiently, perhaps we can regroup and retreat back over the mountain. We can divide into two teams. One team can put down suppressive fire while the other team pulls back. We can take turns all the way back over the mountain." Bill briefly put his hand on her shoulder. "You've got a lot to live for, Kate. This doesn't have to be a suicide mission."

"I appreciate your optimism, Bill, but we're taking on a hundred people. Let's be realistic."

"If the opportunity presents itself, I'm going to call a retreat for my team." Bill seemed unwilling to give up hope of living through the operation. "I'd be happy if you join us when that time comes."

Kate thought it over as she pressed herself to

keep climbing the hill, but she couldn't imagine it would ever work out the way Bill hoped.

Morgan, Pritchard, and Kim Sweeny were the last three people to reach the top of the mountain. Kate observed the camp below through her rifle scope. "Not much activity. I guess they really tied one on after they pulled out of the ambush."

Mia looked through a pair of binoculars. "Do you see any guards?"

"Two men sitting in chairs behind the gate." Dennis peered through his scope.

Kate lowered her rifle. "Morgan, Bill, Jan, and Kim, you four should circle along the ridgeline to the left. Mr. Pritchard, you should take David and Amanda to the right. Morgan, your team will have the best shot of the two guards. You should keep your reticles glued to them. When the shooting starts in the cabin, they'll be your first targets to eliminate."

She waited for nods of agreement from all of them. "We need to get going. They'll be waking up soon."

Navigating down the mountain and through the brush, Kate had the peculiar feeling of going to slay a colony of vampires. It took her team nearly twenty minutes to descend.

"Are you guys ready?" She looked Mia, Dennis, and Philip in the eyes.

"I'm ready." Mia was the first to answer. "I'm looking forward to seeing Ethan again."

Philip looked through the last few rows of trees to the cabin. "Every man that signs up for the military knows this day might come. I guess I've been ready since I put my name on that line."

Dennis crouched low behind a tree. "I've been given more time than most since the Locusts came. I'm thankful for that. I'm not itching to go, but if it's my time, I'm willing to accept it."

Kate felt proud of her team. "That skinny window is most likely a bathroom. It will be the easiest to break out without waking someone."

"That's unlikely," said Dennis. "Even if you can smash it out without setting off an alarm and get inside, I can't get through that window. I doubt Philip could squeeze through either."

"Once we're in, Mia or myself will come around and open the back door." Kate stared at the final obstacle between her and the Reverend.

"Shouldn't we at least check to see if it's unlocked?" Philip asked.

"It's the apocalypse." Kate shook her head. "It won't be unlocked."

"I wouldn't be so sure about that," said Dennis. "This isn't Atlanta. People don't lock their doors around here."

Philip added, "Especially if you're an apex predator with no enemies. Why would you?"

Mia whispered low, "Plus, it's probably being used like a barracks. People are coming and going all the time."

Kate rolled her eyes. "We'll stop by the back door and check to see if it's unlocked. Afterward, Mia and I will proceed to the bathroom window. We'll pop it out and slip through. Mia will come around and open the back door. If you guys hear rifle fire before we get there, just shoot the lock."

"I can't ask for more than that." Dennis got into position to move.

Kate led the team quietly up on the back deck. Expecting nothing, she turned the knob. To her surprise, the door opened. She looked to see an I-told-you-so expression on Dennis' face and signaled for him to go in first. Dennis paused and motioned toward the living room with the barrel of his gun. Kate drew her knife and held it with her left hand. She glanced in the direction Dennis had indicated to see a man lying on his back, snoring loudly. She cautiously approached the couch. She hoped his rhythmic log-sawing wasn't the key to other hostiles in the house staying asleep. Kate positioned her knife above his esophagus and turned away as she let the blade glide across his throat. The man jerked and snorted, trying to sound an alarm, but nothing came out but a guttural gurgle. He clutched his bleeding throat and rolled onto the floor.

With the bloody knife, Kate directed Dennis to lead the way down the hall. He came to the first bedroom and gently nudged the door open. Kate looked inside to see a man and woman passed out next to a nightstand with an empty tequila bottle on top. She slipped inside and removed the pistol on the nightstand as well as the shotgun leaning up against the corner. She pointed to her eyes, then to Dennis, then the couple, indicating that she wanted him to keep the gun on them until she and the remainder of the team could check the rest of the first floor. Mia and Philip walked past Dennis with their rifles leveled toward the other two rooms. Philip pushed open a door and stood guard while

Kate removed the weapons of another sleeping couple. Mia gently turned the knob of the last bedroom. Kate entered finding a single ruffian out cold with an overflowing ashtray on the bed.

She readied her blade and quickly slashed at the man's throat. His eyes opened in terror. He grabbed her arm and pulled her toward him. Kate fell onto the spurting fountain of red fluid. She looked to see Mia ready to shoot but held up her hand for her to stop. The first echo of gunfire would spell the end of their stealth attack.

The man's grasp on Kate's wrist grew ever weaker and finally released. Kate used the blanket to wipe the blood off of her face and arm. She took a few deep breaths and motioned for Mia to follow her. She pointed at the knife in Philip's sheath. He nodded that he understood and followed Kate into the next bedroom. Mia stood guard while Kate stood over the woman and Philip over the man. Kate looked to see that he was ready, then mouthed the word "*Go!*"

Both plunged their blades downward and swiped at their respective target's jugular veins. A brief struggle ensued then the couple returned to motionless silence. Kate and Philip repeated the tactic on the last couple, then Kate led her team to the stairs. With Dennis on point, the team proceeded up the staircase with rifles ready.

They came to a door at the top of the stairs. Kate gently turned the knob. She looked inside to see Lloyd Graves lying alone in the middle of a king size bed. She tiptoed softly into the room. Her mind raced, unable to believe that the plan had actually worked. She knew she should simply stab him and continue to eliminate as many of his followers as possible, but she couldn't kill him without letting him first see her face. Kate motioned for the others to follow her in. On his nightstand was a walkie-talkie and the largest semi-automatic pistol she'd ever seen. She picked it up to move it away from her victim and glanced at the inscription on the side. *Auto Mag* .44 AMP. Kate placed it on the floor and kicked it under the bed.

Against her better judgment, she decided to put her hand over the Reverend's mouth as she put the sharp edge to his throat. His eyes sprung open like a mouse trap.

She looked deep into his soulless optical organs. "Shhhhhh. Remember me?"

Graves dared not move.

"You killed a lot of people close to me. Friends, family, you've made more than your share of orphans and widows. You had to know this day was going to come. Now it's your turn. If you ever really believed in God, now would be a good time for you to start begging him for mercy." She pressed the blade to his neck.

CHAPTER 29

The preparations of the heart in man, and the answer of the tongue, is from the Lord. All the ways of a man are clean in his own eyes; but the Lord weigheth the spirits. Commit thy works unto the Lord, and thy thoughts shall be established. The Lord hath made all things for himself: yea, even the wicked for the day of evil.

Proverbs 16:1-4

"Okay, you've had your fun," said a familiar voice. "Put the knife down."

Instantly, she regretted her delay. Kate looked up to see Vince with his arm around Mia's chest and a pistol to her head. Two young females stood on either side of Vince. Each of them had shotguns pointed at Philip and Dennis.

"Just kill him, Kate." Mia held her rifle, helplessly unable to shoot her attacker. "None of us expected to go home anyway."

Realizing that Mia's life wasn't his best source of leverage for the negotiation, Vince quickly aimed at her thigh. "Maybe not but, I'll shoot to maim both of the girls. And oh, what fun they'll have with the boys around here." Vince kept a tight hold of Mia.

"I was wondering where these people got all the trailers." Kate did not let go of the knife. "I came here to fulfill a mission; I think I'm willing to risk it."

"Maybe for yourself, but what about your friends here?" Vince watched her like a poker player trying to read his adversary. "Put down the knife, Kate."

Kate slowly drew back the blade. The Reverend snatched the weapon from her hand and pushed her to the ground. His eyes blazed with fury over being attacked in his sleep. He picked up the walkie-talkie. "Everybody, wake up. We're under attack. Get to the main house ASAP!"

The Reverend slung his radio across the room, then took the rifles from Kate and the others. He peered at Kate with hatred and rage. He ran his thumb across the smear of drying blood on her cheek. "I'm guessin' I'll have a mess to clean up when I get downstairs. But don't you worry little gal, you'll pay for this."

Gunfire broke out all around the cabin. The radio on the floor near the wall came to life. "They've got snipers all around! They're tearing us up!"

The Reverend smashed Dennis in the head with the butt of his rifle. He took the radio from Dennis. "Everyone from the Bryson Citadel, listen up. I've got your friends in here." Graves pulled the trigger and shot Dennis in the head. He pointed at the two girls assisting Vince. "Open that window and toss him out of it. I want the ones up in the woods to know I'm serious."

The two rough-looking females followed the order.

The gunfire from the surrounding forest grew silent. The Reverend pushed the talk key on Dennis' radio once more. "The fellow who went out the window got the good end of the deal compared to what I'll do to the rest of them. The little soldier boy here, I'll cut off his arms and legs, then send him back to your pathetic village as a reminder of who you're dealing with. The girls, well, I won't have to be nearly so imaginative with them, if you catch my drift. So, unless you're all ready to die and sentence your friends to lives of living hell, put down the guns and come on down here."

Mia looked at Kate, shaking her head. "He's going to kill all of them anyway, and I can only imagine what he'll do to us. This is our last chance to fight."

Kate hated the situation but knew Mia was right. With a brief nod, she set into action a chain of events that would alter the future.

Mia grabbed the pistol from Vince. As she attempted to wrestle it from his hand, the gun went off and killed one of the girls standing next to him.

Seeing the threat Mia now posed to his own life, the Reverend aimed the gun at her and fired. The bullet pierced her chest but continued on to Vince who was still standing behind her. With his fading breath, Vince said to the Reverend with astonishment, "You shot me!"

"Just business, Vince. You of all people should understand that." Graves turned the rifle toward Philip who was fighting the other girl for control of a shotgun. The Reverend let off several rounds. Kate dropped to the floor behind the bed and crawled beneath. She grasped the handle of the giant semi-automatic pistol. From under the bed, she could see the Reverend's feet. Estimating where his body was, she took aim into the mattress above her and began firing. The huge weapon barked out round after round, with such aggressive recoil that it threatened to jump from her hands. Yet she held tight and continued to fire. Finally, Lloyd Graves toppled to the floor, his head facing beneath the bed. She could see the devastation from the rounds of the .44 Auto Mag. The Reverend's body was pocked by bloody craters. His head was nearly severed from his body by one of the rounds that had hit his neck. Kate pushed out from under the bed and scrambled to the nearest battle rifle.

She looked around to see Philip pushing the dead girl off of him. He was coated in blood but seemed to be conscious. "Are you hit?"

He gripped the handle of the shotgun with one hand and ran the other across his blood-soaked body. "I don't think so." He looked up at Kate, who still bore the stains from her attack downstairs. "Are you?"

Kate likewise did a rapid self-inspection. "No. It's not my blood." She looked outside. "They're coming. Get ready."

Philip placed the shotgun in the corner and grabbed the nearest M-4. He took a knee and prepared to shoot toward the staircase. "I'll hold back the ones who get inside if you can pick off the hostiles coming toward the house."

"Roger that." Kate knocked out the glass of the window and pushed the talk key on her radio. "Morgan, Pritchard, we killed Graves and are in control of the cabin. But we can't hold it for long without your help."

"That's all we need to know," Pritchard replied.

Kate took aim and began firing at hostiles who were streaming out of the trailers toward the cabin. Philip's rifle spat out a steady bombardment of bullets behind her.

"Let me know if they get too thick for you!" she called.

Philip yelled back. "I could use a hand. I need to switch magazines."

Kate rolled on the floor, coming to a halt in a prone position with her rifle pointed at the stairway landing. She waited to see the top of an enemy's head before shooting. She pulled the trigger and he fell backward as did two more who crested the level of the upstairs floor. "I'm getting low myself, Philip!"

He slapped the bottom of his magazine and hit the bolt release with the palm of his hand. "Okay, I've got this." Philip resumed shooting while Kate switched magazines. She crawled back to the window. She took the targets closest to the house and worked her way back.

Morgan's voice came over the radio. "We've got a bunch of them trying to flank us. Pritchard, watch out, they're probably all…" POW! A gunshot rang out over the radio and Morgan's transmission was cut short.

Kate took a brief hiatus from shooting to put a call over the radio. "Mr. Pritchard, Bill, get your teams down to the house if you can. We can make our stand here."

"We's a-comin'. Don't shoot me when I get there!" Pritchard called.

Kate emptied two more magazines as did Philip.

"Don't shoot! We're coming in!"

"That's Bill!" Kate called to Philip.

"Come on up!" Philip yelled.

Kate continued to watch for more hostiles approaching the house from the trailers. She turned to see Bill and Jan rush into the room, winded. "Where's Kim?"

Jan's eyes fell to the carnage strewn about the room. "Dead."

Kate ached inside for her friends who were being massacred before her very eyes. "What's it like out there?"

Bill changed magazines. "Not good. We've probably dropped thirty or forty of them total."

"We killed a few before we ever got upstairs." Kate looked out the window. "Could we say we've killed half?"

Bill slapped the bolt closed on his rifle. "That

would probably be a very optimistic estimate."

"How are you guys set for ammo?" Philip used the lull in the fighting to assess his remaining magazines.

"I've got three magazines left." Jan looked at her rifle. "This one is about half full."

"Two more," said Bill.

Kate jumped to her feet. "Jan, Bill, can you cover the window?"

"Sure." Jan hurried to replace Kate. Bill quickly followed.

Kate pulled open the nightstand to find an extra magazine for the .44 as well as a box of shells. "This is something." She tossed them on the bed and searched the closet. Inside were an AK-47 and a chest rig filled with loaded magazines. Green metal ammo cans were stacked near the door. She assumed they would be filled with 7.62 rounds. "This is what I'm talking about." Kate took the rifle and swiftly distributed her remaining 5.56 ammunition amongst the other team members.

"We've got more coming!" Jan began shooting out the window.

Kate returned to her previous position to back her up. Kate, Bill, and Jan each dropped one hostile but two others got past. Kate tapped Jan on the shoulder. "Help Philip! They'll be in the stairs soon."

"Hold your fire!" Pritchard yelled from downstairs.

"Watch your back! We've got enemy coming in the house!" Kate replied.

Immediately, her voice was drowned out by an

exchange of gunfire below. The shots soon fell silent.

"Mr. Pritchard?" Kate called.

"It's clear downstairs," David said. "We're coming up."

Amanda was first to enter the room. Next, David helped Harold Pritchard in the door.

"Mr. Pritchard, you're shot!" Kate wailed.

"Just a scratch." His torso was soaked red and his breath shallow.

She knew he was trying to keep the attention off of himself. "Lie on the bed."

"Oh, I ain't ready for all that just yet." He waved his hand in the air, then readied his rifle.

Kate looked up at the surrounding hills. "I can't get a shot, but I see them all coming down from the mountains. They're going to try and pin us in."

"I wasn't long for this world anyhow." Pritchard put his hand over the blood coming from his stomach. "I might ought to hold 'em off whilst the rest of you'ns clear out."

"I appreciate the offer, Mr. Pritchard, but we've got nowhere to go," said Bill. "We're surrounded."

Pritchard sat on the bed and put his back against the wall. He changed magazines. "Then we best get on up to Glory and let them devils get on to wherever it is that they're a-goin'."

Kate nodded her agreement but was not looking forward to the final confrontation. "Philip, David, you two should run downstairs and try to scavenge some 5.56 ammo from the deceased hostiles. Pick up any AK-47s you see laying about also. We've got plenty of bullets for those."

"The first wave of them are coming," said Bill. "You better make it snappy."

Kate exchanged her tactical vest for the loaded chest rig and rushed the AK to the window. Immediately, she joined Jan and Bill in cannonading the avenue of approach to the cabin.

"Hurry!" Amanda stood at the top of the stairs motivating her son to finish his task swiftly.

Kate kept up her barrage against the coming onslaught of enemy forces but heard Philip and David's panting voices when they reached the landing of the stairs. "We got guns and ammo," said David.

"But they're closing in from the woods," added Philip. "They'll be upon us in no time."

"Then make that stairway the most dangerous place on earth!" commanded Kate.

"Aunt Kate?" The radio on Kate's belt suddenly came to life.

She dropped down behind the wall to change magazines and answer the call. "Vicky? How are you transmitting this far? Where are you?"

"We're on top of the mountain."

"No, Vicky! You have to go home. How did you get here with a sprained ankle? And who are you with?"

"Never mind all of that." The radio crackled. "Where are you?"

"In Graves' cabin. We killed him, but his gang is about to overrun us! They're coming through the back." Kate let the radio sit on the floor and unleashed a volley of shells out the window.

"They're in the house!" Philip yelled between

the deafening rounds exploding from his weapon.

POP, POP, POP! Kate watched three hostiles who'd taken cover from behind trailers or vehicles fall to the ground.

"That was Vicky!" Bill said with hopeful excitement.

Amanda and David continued to assist Philip in defending the hallway at the top of the stairs.

The radio delivered yet another transmission. "Aunt Kate, we've got the back entrance to the cabin covered. You can get out and make a run for the top of the mountain. We'll cover you."

Kate switched magazines and thought about the option. She looked at Pritchard. "You'd never make it up the hill. I'm not leaving you."

"Don't be stupid, girl! I ain't gonna make it no how. You've got to get up that mountain and get that girl out of there before they flank her like they did us."

Bill put his hand on Kate's shoulder. "He's right. You should go now."

"What about you?" she asked.

"I'll stay here with Mr. Pritchard. I'll hold them off. You lead Jan and the others to safety."

Jan scoffed. "Bill! Have you lost your mind? I'm not going anywhere without you. Remember what I told you years back?"

"What was that?" Bill looked at her curiously.

She put a fresh magazine in her rifle and took aim at a hostile poking his head out from around a corner. "For better or for worse."

"I'll stay with them," Philip added. "You get Amanda and David out of here."

Kate turned to Amanda. "I'm going to stay also. You should take David."

David sat on the floor feeding fresh rounds into an AK-47 magazine. "I'm not going anywhere. We came here to back you up and to kill off this camp of thugs. I'll leave when we're finished."

"Then let's finish it." Kate tucked the .44 Auto Mag in her waist and looked at Philip. "What do you say we take the fight to them?"

"I thought that was the plan all along." Philip checked the chamber of a pistol he'd picked up downstairs. He stuck it in the back of his pants and shouldered his rifle.

"Can I get a couple of those?" Kate pointed at the topped-off mags near David's leg.

"Sure." He handed her the ones which were already full.

"Philip, follow my lead." Kate pressed the talk key on the radio. "Vicky, I'm coming out the back, but we've got some things to clean up down here before we can get to the mountain. Cover me if you can."

"Roger that!" came the voice over the radio.

Kate pressed the button once more. "And try not to shoot me. We'll be moving fast."

"Whatever," said the annoyed teenager on the other end.

"Create a distraction!" yelled Kate as she and Philip stormed down the stairs.

CHAPTER 30

And the Lord spake unto Moses, saying, "Speak unto Aaron and unto his sons, saying, On this wise ye shall bless the children of Israel, saying unto them, The Lord bless thee, and keep thee: the Lord make his face shine upon thee, and be gracious unto thee: the Lord lift up his countenance upon thee, and give thee peace. And they shall put my name upon the children of Israel, and I will bless them."

Numbers 6:22-27

Gunfire rang out in every direction. "I'd say this

qualifies as an official war zone." Kate peeked out from behind the edge of the log cabin.

"I agree." Philip looked over her shoulder. "Two combatants, edge of the first trailer. They're focusing on the snipers at the top of the mountain."

"They're behind the trailer. We can't get a clear shot." Kate looked down the open sights of the AK-47.

"But we can make an educated guess." Philip took aim.

"On three," said Kate. "One, two, three!" POW, POW! The two rifles snapped in unison. Kate watched the weapons of both hostiles drop to the ground.

"A group of them are taking cover in the trailer closest to us." Kate pointed ahead.

"You want to barnstorm it?"

"I had something a little more subtle in mind."

"Like what?" Philip asked.

"Let's crawl up underneath and shoot from below."

"I'm game." Philip trailed close behind her as she tucked low and hurried across the short open space between the cabin and the first trailer.

Kate crawled beneath and rolled onto her back. Philip followed.

Kate pointed out the sounds of footsteps, which indicated the locations of the enemy above. She drew the Auto Mag and held up three fingers. She dropped one finger at a time until all were gone. Then, with their pistols, she and Philip ripped holes through the thin flooring above. Kate paused to listen for more footsteps. She looked at the thin shafts of light streaming through the bullet holes over her head.

Philip wriggled to the side, avoiding a steady stream of blood trickling from one of the openings near his face. "I think this dwelling has been vacated."

"We're on a roll. Let's keep going." Kate inched her way out and squatted low to observe the source of more enemy gunfire. "There's one!" She saw a bullet strike a hostile rushing toward the cabin. "Never mind."

Rounds ripped through the thin trailer siding where she was hiding. Philip pushed her to the ground and returned fire. "Get down!"

Kate turned to see three enemy fighters fall after being struck by bullets from Philip's gun, but not before he caught multiple rounds. "Philip!"

"I'm good. Just keep going." He gasped for air.

She knew he was anything but good, but she had no other alternative than to keep fighting on her own. She saw a group of five men go into the tree line, heading up toward the top of the mountain where Vicky was. "I'll be back."

The echo of sporadic gunfire lingered in the hollow between the ridgelines. Kate tailed the five men as quickly as she could without being spotted. She knew wherever Vicky was, she would be in no condition for running if she were flanked. She had to catch the men before they reached the top of the mountain. The men were slowed down by the brambles and bushes. Kate hid behind trees, continuing to gain ground.

"Hold up!" said one of the men. "I thought I

heard something behind us."

"Ain't nobody out here in the woods. They're all in the house or at the top of the hill," replied another.

The men continued up and Kate tracked them more cautiously.

"I need a break," said one of the larger men.

"We can take a break once we've killed these snipers," another said.

"I just can't do it. I'll be on up when I can." The large man took a seat on an outcropping of rocks.

Kate hated the situation this put her in. She couldn't get past the heavy man without killing him, and she couldn't kill him without alerting the other four of her presence. She peered around the side of the tree and up the mountain. Spotting a thicket of mountain laurel, which she could use for visual concealment, she dashed off in the opposite direction. She'd be hard pressed to reach the top before the four men did. With the laser-like focus of a rabbit dashing through a briar patch, she darted in and out, around brambles and over fallen logs. She gave no thought to her own comfort, scraping her palms on rough branches and skinning her knees on rocks.

Winded, Kate soon reached the crest of the hill. But she was too late. The four men were in position behind a tree with their sights set on a target. She looked beyond them to see Vicky and Rainey taking shots at the camp below, oblivious to the presence of the stealth attack about to kill them. Without hesitation, Kate screamed at the top of her lungs, "Vicky! Get down!"

The men instantly turned their attention in Kate's direction. Kate dropped two of them before they could locate her, but the other two fired. One shell ripped through the bark of the tree where she stood, sending a spray of wooden shrapnel into her face.

Kate dropped to the ground, blinded in her right eye by the debris. She opened her left eye and sprang up from her position of cover. She fired wildly at the two men, knowing that she'd never hit anything without being able to see out of her right eye unless it was by a miracle. But then, the miraculous happened. Both of her attackers fell to the ground.

She fought to clear her vision, then looked beyond the cadavers slumped against the forest floor. There stood Rainey next to Vicky who had a single crutch under one arm, each girl with her rifle in hand.

"Another one is still down the hill!" Kate called.

Instantly, her warning was interrupted by gunfire. Kate took cover and watched for the location of the heavy man who was undoubtedly the latest threat.

"I see you!" shouted a man. Then, another pounding of shells peppered the tree where she was hiding.

Kate estimated his location. She stuck her barrel out from behind the tree and unleashed a wave of bullets, providing her own cover fire long enough to get a bead on her assailant. She saw his robust form sheltering behind a fallen tree and ran headlong toward him. She maintained a steady rate of fire as she approached, then continued emptying her magazine into the fat lump behind the log, which jerked as each round pierced his torso.

She wasted no time. She changed out her magazine. "Vicky? Rainey? Are you okay?"

"We're good," called Vicky. "How about you?"

Kate examined herself but saw no injuries other than the scrapes and scratches from ascending the hill to head off the attackers. "I'm okay." She caught her breath, finished clearing her right eye of debris, then leveled her rifle to look for more hostiles at the bottom of the hill.

All was quiet below, yet Kate scoured the area, searching from one trailer to the next. "You two came up here alone?"

"No," said Rainey. "Annie and Troy are on the opposite ridgeline."

"She brought her ten-year-old son up here?"

"He was the one who insisted that we come," Vicky said. "Obviously, once I found out where you'd gone, I didn't need much convincing."

Kate inspected the single crutch. "You climbed the trail like that? How did you know I'd be here?"

"I left the other crutch at the trailhead. It's a pretty easy trail, compared to some of the places you've dragged me through.

"I looked at a map and tried to figure how you'd approach Graves' compound without being caught. This was the only way in that allowed me to get here with crutches, so I just kinda hoped this was the route you took."

Kate felt so much love for her brave young niece who'd risked all to come to her defense. "Well, thank you."

Bill's voice came over the radio, "I think we've about got 'em all. We'll need to search the camp for stragglers, but I'm not seeing any more activity."

"How is Philip?" Rainey asked.

"I'm not sure, Rainey. Does Annie have her medical equipment?"

"Yeah, it's by the trailhead."

"Good," Kate called over the radio. "Annie, we've got injured people down there. If you'll meet Rainey at the trailer closest to the cabin, I'll send her down with your medical kit."

"I'll see her there. I'm sending Troy over to you. Can you make sure he gets back to the vehicles?"

"You got it." Kate clipped the radio back on her belt. "Vicky, do you still have the map?"

"Yeah."

"Take Troy with you back to the parking lot. Get the Escalade and bring it all the way around to US-19 and follow the side road into the compound." She dangled the keys out to her niece.

"I can handle that."

"See you there." Kate hurried back down, hoping she could help Pritchard or Philip.

She reached Philip before anyone else. "You hanging in there, big guy?"

He was still conscious, but bleeding heavily. "Yeah."

"Help is on the way." Kate looked up to see Annie charging toward her location.

"Philip, you're going to be okay." Annie dropped down next to the young soldier and began cutting away the clothing around his wounds.

Rainey was not nearly so composed when she

arrived with the medical supplies. "Philip! Oh, no! Is it bad?"

He forced a smile. "Not nearly so much so, now that you're here."

Kate could see that the young man still had some fight left in him and figured that was a good sign. "I'll be back."

Kate kept her eyes sharp, keeping watch for any remaining enemy while sprinting back to the cabin. She bounded up the stairs where Amanda was giving a sip of water to Pritchard.

She sat next to him on the bed. "Annie is here. She's working on Philip, and she'll come get you fixed up next."

Mr. Pritchard patted her hand. "That'll be alright." His breathing was labored, and he took another sip of water when Amanda offered it. Mr. Pritchard opened his eyes, looking past Kate intently.

For a moment, she thought perhaps someone was standing behind her. She looked back but saw nothing. She turned her attention back to Pritchard. "Just rest your eyes. Annie will be here soon."

His face became pleasant. "She's prettier than I remember."

"Who's that?" Kate asked inquisitively.

"Mary Belle. Looks like an angel." He indicated toward the vacant wall behind Kate.

"I'm afraid I don't know Mary Belle." Kate worried that the old man was becoming delirious.

"Oh, that's alright. You'll meet her. You two'll get along like biscuits and gravy. She was my wife." He nodded as if acknowledging someone speaking to him. "Yes, dear. I'll be along directly, my sweet Belle."

A chill went up Kate's spine and she turned for another look, but still saw nothing.

"Anyhow," Pritchard continued. "My old Bible is tucked under the couch back at the trailer. I want you to give it to the boy."

Kate held the old man's hand tightly. "You mean Gavin?"

"Yes, child. That boy. Tell him he's got to take up the chore of leadin' the children of Israel. That book'll get him through. It'll get you all through. It took him a while to come around, but he's got it now.

"The Lord told a parable of two sons, their pappy told 'em both to get to the field one mornin'. One of 'em said he'd go but didn't. The other'n said he wouldn't but did. Lord said it was the second son who did the will of the father. That's how it was with your fella."

"Did Gavin tell you about his prayer to God while I was gone?"

"No, didn't have to." Pritchard motioned for Amanda to give him another drink. "But I seen it in him. He'll get the fire. Just give him a little time and keep encouraging him."

Pritchard paused as if resting for a while, then opened his weak eyes once more. "I love you and that youngin'; about as much as if you'ns was my own flesh and blood. I feel right good about leavin' you with the boy. He'll do right by you both. And he'll be the leader you need him to be."

Tears streamed down Kate's cheek. She hoped

Vicky would get there in time to say goodbye to the old man. "We love you, too, Mr. Pritchard."

He patted her hand. "The Lord bless you and keep you and make His face to shine down upon you." With that, Harold Pritchard closed his eyes and breathed his last.

CHAPTER 31

The people that walked in darkness have seen a great light: they that dwell in the land of the shadow of death, upon them hath the light shined. Thou hast multiplied the nation, and not increased the joy: they joy before thee according to the joy in harvest, and as men rejoice when they divide the spoil. For thou hast broken the yoke of his burden, and the staff of his shoulder, the rod of his oppressor, as in the day of Midian. For every battle of the warrior is with confused noise, and garments rolled in blood; but this shall be with burning and fuel of fire. For unto us a child is born, unto us a son is given: and the government shall be upon his shoulder: and his name shall be called Wonderful,

Counsellor, The mighty God, The everlasting Father, The Prince of Peace.

Isaiah 9:2-6

Kate looked out her bedroom window at the crisp even snow covering the open field between the main cabin and the smaller cabins at the Bryson Citadel. She and Gavin shared the gigantic house with Bill and Jan, Rainey and Jack, Amanda and David, and of course, Vicky.

Despite her urging that the room be given to someone else, all the others had insisted that the master bedroom be assigned to her and Gavin.

It was Christmas Day, less than two weeks since the final showdown at the Reverend's compound. Gavin sat in a rocking chair by the bedroom fireplace reading Pritchard's old, worn Bible.

Kate walked over and stood behind him. She rubbed his shoulders and looked up at the sprawling castle of a room, finished with the finest wood, yet still rustic in its feel. "You just have to read the story of Jesus' birth. You don't have to preach a sermon."

He put one hand across his chest, touching her hand. "I know, but for some reason, I just have this feeling like maybe I should say a little something. After all, God has brought us through so much."

She'd never mentioned any of the things Pritchard had said to her about Gavin, and him getting the *"fire"*, as he'd put it. But she couldn't help but wonder if the old man's final words might have been the least bit prophetic. She kissed Gavin gently on the top of his head. "If that's what you think, then do it. I'm sure Philip would appreciate anything you could say that might serve to soften Jack up."

"Oh?" Gavin looked up from the Bible.

"Yeah, he's planning to speak with him after dinner. He's going to ask for permission to marry Rainey."

Gavin chuckled and shook his head. "He is brave. Forget about running out the back door of Graves' cabin head first at the enemy, asking Jack to marry his sixteen-year-old daughter will be the true test of his grit."

"Seventeen. She just had a birthday."

"I'm sure that will make all the difference in the world." Gavin continued reading.

Kate thought back to that awful day. "I told Jack all about Philip's role at Graves' compound. Rainey might not still be here if Philip hadn't saved me. He respects the young man. If anyone has a chance at getting past him, it's Philip."

"They spent three days in the infirmary together, so he's got that going for him. If all else fails, at least he can outrun Jack."

Kate felt horrible about Jack having lost his leg. "That is not funny, Gavin."

"It wasn't supposed to be. Jack's emotions are still a little raw. His propensity to kill first and ask questions later makes this a volatile situation for your brave young soldier. Getting out of Dodge might be his only chance at living through this confrontation." Gavin turned his attention back to the book in his lap. "What about Annie and Garcia?"

"There's a spark, but I think they're trying to take it slow; for Troy's sake most likely."

Gavin shook his head. "I think Troy likes Garcia more than Annie does."

She gazed out the window at the occasional flurry floating past. "Troy wants to be a soldier, like Garcia."

"From what you told me about Troy up on that mountain top, it sounds like he already is."

Kate let her head rest on top of his. "I just hope David and Vicky don't get any ideas if everyone else starts getting married."

"It doesn't matter what ideas they get. Neither you nor Amanda would stand for it."

"True." She smiled. "They at least need to wait until they're eighteen."

"Jan and Bill haven't said anything else about moving back to Waynesville?"

"No," she replied. "I think when we first heard about Rosales' government falling apart in Asheville, they couldn't help but wonder what it would be like to go home. But after some thought, I believe they know that it's still too close to Asheville to be a viable option.

"Anyway, we've got everything we need right here: community, security, more supplies than we need."

He glanced up at her. "You're happy here?"

She smiled. "I better be."

"Why is that?"

"Women in my condition don't like to move. We need to nest."

He closed the Bible abruptly and placed it on the hearth. Gavin stood up quickly and looked her in the eyes. "Women in your condition?"

"Life goes on, Gavin. Even in the most challenging of times." She tried to hold back the smile.

His look of shock soon melted into an expression of absolute exhilaration. He pulled her close and kissed her. "I love you, Kate."

"I love you, too, Gavin." She kissed him once more. "And you'll be an excellent father."

DON'T PANIC!

Inevitably, books like this will wake folks up to the need to be prepared, or cause those of us who are already prepared to take inventory of our preparations. New preppers can find the task of getting prepared for an economic collapse, EMP, or societal breakdown to be a source of great anxiety. It shouldn't be. By following an organized plan and setting a goal of getting a little more prepared each day, you can do it.

I always try to include a few prepper tips in my novels, but they're fiction and not a comprehensive plan to get prepared. Now that you're motivated to start prepping, the last thing I want to do is leave you frustrated, not knowing what to do next. So I'd like to offer you a free PDF copy of *The Seven Step Survival Plan.*

For the new prepper, *The Seven Step Survival Plan* provides a blueprint that prioritizes the different aspects of preparedness and breaks them down into achievable goals. For seasoned preppers who often get overweight in one particular area of preparedness, *The Seven Step Survival Plan* provides basic guidelines to help keep their plan in balance, and ensures they're not missing any critical segments of a well-adjusted survival strategy.

To get your **FREE** copy of ***The Seven Step Survival Plan***, go to **PrepperRecon.com** and click the FREE PDF banner, just below the menu bar, at the top of the home page.

Thank you for reading *Cyber Armageddon,*
Book Three: Reign of the Locusts

Reviews are the best way to help get the book noticed. If you liked the book, please take a moment to leave a five-star review on Amazon and Goodreads.

I love hearing from readers! So whether it's to say you enjoyed the book, to point out a typo that we missed, or asked to be notified when new books are released, drop me a line.

prepperrecon@gmail.com

Stay tuned to **PrepperRecon.com** for the latest news about my upcoming books.

Keep Watch for my new series,

Black Swan
A Novel of America's Coming
Financial Nightmare

If you've enjoyed *Cyber Armageddon*, you'll love my end-times thriller series, *The Days of Noah*

In an off-site CIA facility outside of Langley, rookie analyst Everett Carroll discovers he's not being told the whole truth. He's instructed to disregard troubling information uncovered by his research. Everett ignores his directive and keeps digging. What he finds goes against everything he's been taught to believe. Unfortunately, his curiosity doesn't escape the attention of his superiors, and it may cost him his life.

Meanwhile, Tennessee public school teacher, Noah Parker, like many in the United States, has been asleep at the wheel. During his complacency, the founding precepts of America have been systematically destroyed by a conspiracy that dates back hundreds of years.

Cassandra Parker, Noah's wife, has diligently followed end-times prophecy and the shifting tide against freedom in America. Noah has tried to avoid the subject, but when charges are filed against him for deviating from the approved curriculum in his school, he quickly understands the seriousness of the situation. The signs can no longer be ignored, and Noah is forced to prepare for the cataclysmic period of financial and political upheaval ahead.

Watch through the eyes of Noah Parker and Everett Carroll as the world descends into chaos, a global empire takes shape, ancient writings are fulfilled, and the last days fall upon the once-great United States of America.

If you have an affinity for the prophetic don't miss my EMP survival series, *Seven Cows, Ugly and Gaunt*

In ***Book One: Behold Darkness and Sorrow***, Daniel Walker begins having prophetic dreams about the judgment coming upon America for rejecting God. Through one of his dreams, Daniel learns of an imminent threat of an EMP attack which will wipe out America's electric grid and most all computerized devices, sending the country into a technological dark age.

Living in a nation where all life-sustaining systems of support are completely dependent on electricity and computers, the odds of survival are dismal. Municipal water services, retail food distribution, police, fire, EMS and all emergency services will come to a screeching halt.

If they want to live, Daniel and his friends must focus on faith, wits, and preparation to be ready . . . before the lights go out.

You'll also enjoy my series about the
coming civil war in America,
Ava's Crucible

The deck is stacked against twenty-nine-year-old Ava. She's a fighter, but she's got trust issues and doesn't always make the best decisions. Her personal complications aren't without merit, but America is on the verge of a second civil war, and Ava must pull it together if she wants to survive.

The tentacles of the deep state have infiltrated every facet of American culture. The public education system, entertainment industry, and mainstream media have all been hijacked by a shadow government intent on fomenting a communist revolution in the United States. The antagonistic message of this agenda has poisoned the minds of America's youth who are convinced that capitalism and conservatism are responsible for all the ills of the world. Violent protest, widespread destruction, and politicians who insist on letting the disassociated vent their rage will bring America to her knees, threatening to decapitate the laws, principles, and values on which the country was founded. The revolution has been well-planned, but the socialists may have underestimated America's true patriots who refuse to give up without a fight.

ABOUT THE AUTHOR

Mark Goodwin holds a degree in accounting and monitors macroeconomic conditions to stay up-to-date with the ongoing global meltdown. He is an avid student of the Holy Bible and spends several hours every week devoted to the study of Scripture and the prophecies contained therein. The troubling trends in the moral, social, political, and financial landscapes have prompted Mark to conduct extensive research within the arena of preparedness. He weaves his knowledge of biblical prophecy, economics, politics, prepping, and survival into an action-packed tapestry of post-apocalyptic fiction. Having been a sinner saved by grace himself, the story of redemption is a prominent theme in all of Mark's writings.

"He brought me up also out of an horrible pit, out of the miry clay, and set my feet upon a rock, and established my goings." Psalm 40:2

Made in the USA
Columbia, SC
12 December 2020